HOSTILE INTENT

Revenge can be sweet – if you live to enjoy it

David Bessell

ISBN: 1500217352
ISBN-13: 978-1500217358

For Jude, my own Angel of the North.
You rescued me and I shall always be in your debt.
Thank you.

CONTENTS

ACKNOWLEDGMENTS

To Colin, without whose help and advice this would have been a shadow of what it is. You translated military into civilian and kept my feet on the ground.

CHAPTER 1

Mustafa al Said looked to the horizon and marvelled at the beautiful brutality of the Somalian desert. Barely above the equator, it was the raw power of nature incarnate. No quarter was given to any life trying to eke out an existence within its boundaries but it was here that Al-Qaeda had been forced to retreat after the West had hounded it out of its previous homes. Mustafa still believed in his cause though, as he always would, no matter what happened to them. He was reminded of a fist trying to contain grains of sand; the harder they were gripped, the more they slipped away.

He stood on a slight ridge, looking down on the latest of his training grounds a hundred yards away. It was nearly dusk. The light slipped away swiftly here, shrinking the vastness of the desert into a cloak of night and within a few minutes surrendering the fierceness of the day to a blackness and cold that could bite into the soul in desperate and sharp contrast. The extremes were a part of life to those brought up in this supposed wilderness but always a shock to those ignorant of it. To the initiated, the desert was teeming with life, able to sustain and protect, but only if you could read the signs and respected its power. Westerners, so typically arrogant, believed that it was a wasteland of little value, and for the most part had dismissed it, pitifully reflecting their view of anyone not of their world. The 'First World' believed in its own moral superiority, overtly declaring that their ways were right and they had nothing to learn from anyone else. It was this perpetual arrogance that fuelled his own hatred and inspired his men. It drove those below him now to train every day in these harsh conditions, just for the chance to respond, to hold the sword of retribution to the throat of the enemy and to show the infidel that they could dominate with their technology but they could never win.

A warm breeze started as the sun continued its journey and sank towards the horizon, running from the coast as it did almost every night, bringing with it cool air, replacing the heat of the day. Mustafa could feel tiny grains of sand pushing against him and he dragged his gaze away from his beloved soldiers and turned to the East. He was waiting; his visitor was late. Only now could he see the dust plume of three pick-up trucks as they made their way across the sandy terrain towards him. This was an important meeting. It was the final confirmation that all pieces were in place for his latest masterpiece - complicated in concept, desperate in nature, simple in execution. Since the crowning triumph of 9-11 and to a limited extent the 7-7 attacks in London, the cause had been thwarted from achieving the war on many fronts that those actions had been meant to herald. Too many times since, plans had been abandoned because human resources had been diverted to other arenas, ruining the intent and de-railing precious efforts. Without doubt, the war in Afghanistan had been a disaster for the Al-Qaeda generals. Not only had they lost their safe haven but its continued ferocity had leeched strength from the bones of the movement, taking away those fighters that may otherwise have been employed on the streets of the West to protect one of the Muslim homelands. And then there had been the ultimate calamity, the loss of Osama himself in the Pakistan raid. At that moment Mustafa, like so many others, had promised retribution. Now was the moment that Al-Qaeda's return would be announced. His men were almost ready, preparing themselves, the teams being finely tuned. His visitor would confirm that as much cover as possible had been put in place in the West. He was uniquely placed to do so and it had taken a great deal of money both to procure his services and to keep him over the many years since. It had been a dangerous gamble, they were dealing with a dangerous man, but Mustafa felt justified that the service they had gained would help him achieve the goal he longed for; the war would continue, reinvigorated.

The trucks pulled up at the bottom of the rise and stopped, their engines ticking in the evening silence. As instructed, the man walked alone to join him. As usual the coiled bearing was obvious, declaring him to be a man of violence, brought up over many years to trust no-one, to be ready for the worst. Mustafa turned back to face his fighters below as the man stood by his side. They said nothing at first. There was emptiness for fifty miles around, the only sound an occasional shout or chant from the training grounds proclaiming Allah's greatness, their own mantra that inspired the faithful to deeds of abandon in His name. Occasional small arms fire whipped across the divide from the range over to the west with the heavier boom of grenades announcing truly serious intent.

"What do you think of my brothers?" Mustafa finally asked. "They push themselves further each day because they know that God is with them." The man said nothing. "Are we ready?" he continued.

"I'm ready," said the man. "Whatever your *legions* are doing is your business." The heavy and ironic emphasis wasn't lost on the Arab.

"Explain," snapped Mustafa, the veil of calm assuredness lifting slightly at the disrespectful tone, to reveal something of the intolerant beneath.

"I have people that report to me from the National Crime Agency, MI5, MI6 and the Special Branch," the man snapped back. "And I had better warn you, there are rumours that you're putting together an operation. Once again it seems that your beloved nation of faith isn't as united as you and your people seem to believe. MI6 have gone in to overdrive. They may be centred on Pakistan at the moment but there are only a couple of places to look, and here is one of them."

"And that's what we pay you for." The ice was back in Mustafa's voice. "You belong to us. Keep them away. Sow whatever seeds you need but keep our path clear. We are almost ready."

"Almost!" the man fired back. "This should have been over weeks ago."

"There have been… complications," Mustafa stated simply. "There are inherent risks in training people with explosives."

The silence between the two of them crackled, the potential violence of both men tangible.

"Go now," ordered Mustafa, reasserting his authority. "I will speak to you tomorrow."

The man turned and strode angrily back to the trucks. Mustafa remained facing West, drinking in the scene that had always inspired him, watching the absolute dedication of his people, feeding off the religious fervour that he knew, by the time they left the camp, would make all of them happy, if not desperate to lay down their lives for their God in the coming days. He hadn't decided who would be the lucky ones yet, but he would soon. In four weeks, his plan would shatter the fabric of the British and this time the Europeans as well as he hit London, Paris and Munich simultaneously with an occasion to rival those that had so gloriously gone before. From here, the war would be re-joined.

It was dark as Chris Edwards stood looking at the house from the gravel drive. He was late home after another long and tiring day at work but often liked to savour the view before going inside. He was a career submariner in the Royal Navy, eighteen years served and waiting for the promotion that would bring him his own Command. He had joined at the age of twenty-one, having graduated from an average university with an average degree. What the course had taught him though was that his life lay as far from a commercial firm as he could get and the Royal Navy had seemed the answer. Having specialised as a warfare submariner, he had been posted to one of the RNs T-class submarines, so called because all their names started with T: *Trafalgar*, *Triumph* etc, and his first boat, *HMS Torbay*. It was this experience that would dramatically shift the path of his existence into a much more dangerous world. His first position had been as a Casing Officer, responsible for the upkeep and management of the outside of the submarine's hull, known as the casing, with a team of fourteen men under him, the Casing Party.

At dawn one cold January day, sixteen years before, Chris had been standing on the casing as the boat waited, on the surface in a holding box just off the coast of Arran in the Firth of Clyde. Ropes had been rigged and the requisite preparations made for the Special Forces rendezvous, or RV, that they were about to practice in the half light. All was quiet, unusually so for being at sea, but there was minimal swell and no flow noise caused by the submarine making way through the waves, just stillness and a light breeze. The only sound was the harsh mocking call of the sea gulls as they hovered nearby, hoping that the submarine would disturb some aquatic life and provide an easy meal. At 0700 the RV was only ten minutes away.

The first thing Chris saw was a black speck, low on the horizon, standing out against the dull grey of the wintry sky. All his senses strained and eventually, as the image grew, it was accompanied by the low drone of propeller engines. It was a Hercules transport aircraft. In it were two squads, one Special Boat Service (mainly Royal Marines), one Special Air Service (mostly Army), the two branches that together made up the 'Special Forces', that most elite of cadres. They were about to inspire the young Chris to a future that sixteen years later still thrilled and appalled him, but one that had made him the person he was.

The plane continued to draw closer and, surprisingly quickly, grew large within the last few seconds. It conducted a low pass, sweeping past the boat in a flash no more than a hundred feet away, its tailgate open and the men inside able to be clearly seen standing granite like in the blustery void of the cargo deck. It pulled away sharply and rose towards the North, towards Inchmarnock Water, starting the bank that would take it to the drop height and course. It soon disappeared around the 'Cock of Arran', the northernmost point of the island but within a few minutes became visual again, this time high and heading south towards them. Streamers were seen leaving the tail to assess wind direction and strength, then the final course adjustment for the drop. First out were two large packages, the boats, swiftly followed by twelve small specks, their initial anonymity dashed as the canopies bloomed behind them, betraying their presence to all observing. They followed the boats down into the water, hitting the surface gently with the silks collapsing above them. This was the critical moment where the men needed to get out of the rigs as quickly as possible, trying to avoid entanglement. One by one, the men appeared from beneath their temporary prisons and potential death shrouds to make their way into the boats, which had been inflated by the first on the scene. This all happened in semi-silence for Chris. Once the aircraft had completed its first low pass, the subsequent turn back had taken it almost beyond hearing. After the troops had left its tail and it cleared to the South, an eerie silence returned leaving only the scene before him, unfolding like some bizarre silent action movie but without stunt men and with no guarantee of a happy ending.

Within minutes, the men were loaded into the boats and the outboards fired up. A few minutes more and the boats were alongside and Chris's team swung into action, throwing heaving lines and jumping ladders over the side to recover the men and equipment from the blackness of the morning water. Following a frenzy of activity, all was stowed and the submarine made its preparations to dive, moving forward through the low swell, gathering enough speed to drive itself under the surface into the inky refuge of the Arran trench.

Although Chris was still relatively new to the submarine world and each dive was at once exciting and nerve jangling, he had just seen what he knew would satisfy the hunger within him. The spectacle he had just witnessed was vibrant, it was cutting edge, it was real. Even the name, Special Forces, inspired him. There was greatness latent within it and a chance to break away from the 'average' life he felt he had led so far.

It wasn't to be instantaneous. First, he had to complete the initial stages of his submarine career and qualify professionally. At every opportunity, however, he prepared himself for the massive physical and mental effort that he knew would be required to make the entry grade into the Corps. It took two years of constant dedication but he eventually earned the Royal Marine Commandos Green Beret, itself a huge challenge for most, with forty per cent of those attempting failing at one stage or another. After that, he put himself forward for selection to the Special Boat Service. He was convinced his request to be considered was only accepted for the novelty value of having a submarine officer on the course. Defying all those sceptics, another year later at the age of twenty-five, he gained the right to be 'badged' and to adopt the fabled moniker of the Special Forces. It was to be the start of seven years involved in a new world of operations, a world of danger, sometimes frustrating, always exciting, with the highest of professional highs. Eventually, however, it would culminate with being injured in action, his retirement from the Corps and a return to the submarine flotilla to pick up where he had left off.

As Chris stood on his drive he was amazed as always by the silence of the night surrounding him. Here in the heart of Essex he had found a peace and contentment that had eluded him in the Corps, and he had found it in the shape of the most beautiful girl he had ever met, a tiny northern princess called Elizabeth, who, like him, had been similarly lost. They had lived there for two years but had only been married for two months. At times like this, when he was alone, he would often reflect on his past. He had seen huge violence on the various missions to which he had been sent, tales that he could never tell, actions of which he was not proud but deep within could justify because of the cause under whose banner they had been done. A moorhen issued its harsh call loudly to his left, startling in the stillness and in its proximity and his head whipped around, his body tensing. His reactions were still good and perhaps would always be. It had saved his life on many occasions, but most specifically on his last operation, the one when a bullet had smashed his collar bone and sent him back to the submarine world. Had he not been as fast, he would almost certainly have died. As it was, he had taken out the Yardie drug trafficker, but not before the bastard had managed to loose off a couple of shots, one of which had hit. The operation had been a spectacular success, if you counted the seizure of twenty tonnes of uncut cocaine and the main distribution centre of a cartel operation decimated for a short while.

But that had been then and this was now. He walked towards the converted barn and slipped his key into the lock. He tried to be quiet as he knew his wife was asleep upstairs but the house alarm gave him away by beeping twice as the door moved ajar. It was close to midnight and he stepped through to the kitchen to fix himself a large Cruzan rum and coke, a habit he had got into following a particularly good run ashore in St Croix in the Caribbean. It was a warm night and he stepped out onto the decking at the back of the house. It was a group of two barns and a farmhouse, originally a medieval Hall House, surrounded by a moat that dated back to the thirteenth century. The moat was overlooked by the decking and it was the place Chris came to reflect and unwind. He drained the glass after a short while, too short a while for the size of the spirit, and made his way upstairs. He undressed in his wife's dressing room and wrapped in a robe, walked along the balcony to the bedroom. As he opened the door he saw the petite figure of his wife semi-curled under the bed clothes, her fine blonde hair splayed out on the pillow, her splendid form outlined by the covers. He slipped out of his robe, lifted the sheets on his side of the bed and climbed in beside her. As he did so, a small hand reached out to him, taking his in a light grip. He brought it to his mouth and kissed it tenderly before laying a kiss upon her brow. These tiny gestures were examples of what he had found. They gave him the inner peace that he needed, the final piece of the puzzle and the foundation of a happiness that he knew was his with her. His previous life had been something that would have put a

Hollywood script writer in the shade but that part of his life was gone. This was where he was now and the other part had been consigned to history, not to be repeated. Or so he thought.

The next morning was bright and clear as he drove himself to work along the M11 and M25. It could be a nightmare if you caught it at the wrong time but this was 0615, too early for much of the commuter traffic. He was working at the Royal Navy's Fleet Head Quarters Northwood in North West London as the submarine special operations planner, a post that ideally suited his previous experience as Special Forces and a post 'Perisher' second in command of a Fleet submarine, co-incidentally the same submarine that had been his first. 'Perisher' was the Submarine Command Course, the most demanding course in the Royal Navy. It involved six months of intensity and four weeks of hell as the students were taken to sea on a hunter killer nuclear submarine where they were brought to their lowest ebb, both physically and mentally, ground down a bit further and then driven to perform in the most challenging of circumstances with little or no sleep and expected to be at the top of their game. 'Teacher', as the Commander in charge of the course was known colloquially, was the man tasked with selecting the few capable of passing and on his decision not only did the professional future of the student depend but more importantly the lives of the crews of the boats they would eventually command if they got it wrong. Teacher was a big job but generally only the best were chosen to complete it.

On this morning, Chris's work load was relatively light and he was looking forward to getting into the gym. He had always maintained his fitness and was in remarkably good shape for a forty-year-old man. There was none of the middle age spread that he was seeing in his colleagues and he liked to think that he would still be able to mix it with his old friends. He would meet up with some of them occasionally, when they made it to town, and in standard Special Forces fashion they would find some out of the way pub, talk through past times and drink to remember, and to forget.

Everything was normal at the morning briefs. His last operation, an intelligence gathering effort by one of the hunter killer submarines in the Middle East, had just finished. All that remained was to finish up the paperwork, which he could do in slow time over the next two weeks, and the majority of that could be handled by his deputy. The next Op wasn't for another eight weeks and there was time to get the detailed planning for that done when it suited him. He settled down for a routine day. And then the phone rang.

"Chris, come up to my office, I need to speak to you about something." It was the RN Captain in charge of the Operations Division in Fleet Head Quarters. He was always brusque but it wasn't rudeness, just ruthless efficiency. Vastly respected and a submariner himself, Captain Absolom had a reputation as one of the best Commanding Officer's in the business but for some reason he hadn't got as far as most expected. Chris climbed the stairs from the nuclear bomb proof bunker that housed his office and made his way onto the operations floor.

"Right Chris, come with me." It was business like. He was led to a side office, away from the prying eyes and ears of the rest of the Fleet Ops team. This was unusual in itself, typically the preserve of the Nuclear Deterrent submarine planners when they had to give their briefs. As they got to the door, Chris saw the back of a familiar figure that turned as he heard them approach.

"I wondered where you had got to, Chris," said the man at the desk, a smile splitting his face immediately after a second of deadpan.

"By Christ, what the hell are you doing here?" Chris exploded with a similar smile. The two men embraced warmly indicating a friendship that can only come in the Forces from experiences where life and death come knocking at your door every few seconds and it's up to you, and fate, to decide who comes through.

"That's enough of that Edwards," grumbled the Captain. "Anyone would think I was running a dating agency. Sit down."

His name was Major Graham Armstrong, or Louis to his mates and a Royal Marine by trade. In another world, Louis and Chris had been a team. They had been part of the same troop for seven years, all the time that Chris had been 'badged'. Together they had seen action from Africa to the Middle East, South America and the Caribbean and it was on his final mission, against the drug running cartels operating from South America north to the United States that they had last shipped out together. That was the operation that had finished Chris's Special Forces career with a gunshot through the shoulder while covering his friend's withdrawal from a pokey room in a shanty town in Jamaica. Ultimately, it had been a success with a grenade lobbed through the door taking out the last of the Yardies they had been ordered to hunt down and 'persuade' that cocaine wasn't the right career choice.

"OK, pay attention. You obviously know Major Armstrong. His boss has a job on and he has asked if we can support. Apparently you have a bit of a reputation and you may be the subject matter expert they need. Listen to what Major Armstrong has to say and see what you think."

It was a typically brusque introduction but Chris's interest was immediately piqued. This had been one of his closest friends but they had dropped out of touch a couple of years before when his submarine career and Louis' Special Forces tasking had been mutually incompatible. The small matter of his beautiful new wife had also led to less time being available for old friendships, despite their depths. It was a strength of Forces life, however, that time apart meant nothing. As soon as reacquaintance was made, it was as it had always been. The question was, why was Louis here and how could Chris be involved?

"Right then," started Louis. "How much have you been keeping up with the modern world, Chris?"

"Well I know that Man United are odds on to win the league and that England had their arses kicked in the World Cup."

"Excellent, that's a good start. What do you know about Al-Qaeda's operating patterns lately?"

"I know what I see on the news and a bit more from the briefings we have here weekly. Pretty broad brush stuff, no real details."

"So you've run back to your cosy submarine world and forgotten where the action is, have you?" chided his old friend.

"Not exactly, but I've had other things on my mind, and you aren't always at the centre of the universe you know," Chris shot back.

"Sounds a bit weak to me but I'll let you off this time. OK, I'll get to it. Things have been pretty quiet on the Al-Qaeda front over the last few years outside of a few familiar areas. It seems that this whole Afghanistan thing is working and Bin Laden's timely demise has thrown them to the winds. Basically their nebulous organisation has been unable to respond to the increased security construct and resources of the free societies of the West, but worldwide they have a couple of places where they feel fairly safe. It used to be Afghanistan but we went in after them. They then moved into the tribal areas of the Pakistan border region and are still there, feeding the war. Outside of that immediate region, they have had to use failed or failing states - Yemen is becoming increasingly popular as the insurgency takes hold, but ideally for them, Somalia. With me so far?" Louis looked up and raised an eyebrow.

"I think I'm just managing to keep up. You're a marine so if you understand it, the average nursery kid should too."

"Good. They've basically had two great successes. The first was 9-11. Spectacular. It acted as the rallying cry for the Islamic nation, at least the extremists. The second was the 7-7 bombings in London. But that's all history now. Since then, there has been nothing of significance. A few small bombs here, some suicide martyrs there, but nothing big enough to rattle the cage, so to speak."

"Still with you."

"Blimey, you're brighter than you look. Now here's the crux. Afghanistan is taking all the men that would have been available to carry out terrorist activity in the West. Al-Qaeda may talk a good fight, but the majority of the Muslim population is as peaceful as the next man and just want to make a living. The young firebrands that believe in the ultimate supremacy of their religion are so outraged that the infidels are occupying one of the homelands that they flock to the banner. A huge proportion of the Taliban forces we face over there are from abroad, having travelled through Pakistan, picked up some rudimentary training at some camp or other and been taken into country via the hills. This isn't what Al-Qaeda wanted at the start and certainly not what they wanted to be spending their time doing for so many years. The master plan has them taking the offensive to the West, operating outside their own lands and pulling the Islamic nations together as a whole. At the moment, they are bogged down in a war they can't win, they can't get their point across and they are failing on almost all fronts."

"OK, I get the picture but so far I don't see what this has got to do with Fleet Ops," intoned Chris.

"Bugger me, you always were impatient but I thought age would have made you wise. Now listen. For the last few months, rumours have been coming through that the Al-Qaeda generals were turning their eyes to the West again. They need a boost quite frankly, something to inspire their men. MI6 have been looking into it and have got some fairly good intelligence to suggest that Somalia is the base. Now Somalia is pretty much a no go area for anyone overt. You can't get a delegation in there to find out what's going on without standing out like a nun at a strip club, so that's a non starter. What they have managed to find out though, or at least what they believe, is that Al-Qaeda have chosen their best operational man to make this happen, Mustafa Al Said."

Chris's eyes immediately narrowed. In his badged years, he and Louis had chased Al Said around the tribal areas of Pakistan, through the cave regions of Afghanistan and throughout the Middle East. Every time they had got close, he had got away. It was uncanny, almost prescient. They had even got to camp sites where the fires were still warm or been met by overwhelming resistance that forced them to back off, allowing his escape, as if they were tipped off. They had become specialists at infiltrating those barren areas, quite familiar with the lay of the land, the habits of the people and the ways not to be found when required.

"I can see I've got you interested now, eh shipmate?" teased Louis.

"You could say that," replied Chris. "But I still don't see what this has got to do with us at Fleet Operations."

"Well this is where you come in. We want to mount an operation and we want your input."

"How so?"

"We want to put a team in country. There are a couple of ways we would normally do that. First, we would fly them in on a commercial or military flight, get them settled in some town or other, have them meet up and get supported by the embassy or work in conjunction with the local government. In Somalia, there is no government and a load of Special Forces, even the best, would be bounced within hours. Second, we could parachute a team in. Unfortunately, that needs nation support for aircraft, landing sites etc. Nothing doing. Third, and this is most definitely where you come in, we could insert from the coast. No host nation support required, lovely and covert, no-one knows we're there. We get in, gather our intelligence or do whatever is required at the time and get out by the same method."

"And what method might that be?" asked Chris. He could see where this was going. For years, the Special Forces had been practising techniques for operating from submarines for covert insertion into a hostile coast but they had never had occasion to use it; there had always been simpler methods available. Recently there had been renewed interest with the latest class of submarine to go into production, the Astute class, designed to have a bespoke Special Forces delivery system. The hierarchy had gone a bit wet around the edges thinking about the possibilities. It wasn't ready yet, but the profile of the method had been raised and now it seemed that this was the perfect opportunity to put all the practice to some use.

"I think you've made the mental leap Edwards," piped up Captain Absolom. "What have we got in the area, how quickly could it be ready to support and what would we need to do from here?" The Captain fired his questions like an Uzi - short, staccato, direct.

"Sir, *HMS Talisman* is in the Arabian Gulf so the asset is in place, but we would need to know a lot more of the details such as how many men, where from, what endurance would be needed, staging posts, definite tasking for the submarine balanced against the tasking she already has etc."

"And that is why you are perfect for the job. The last op has just finished yes?"

"Yes Sir."

"Your deputy is around, yes?"

"Yes Sir."

"Right. You're the liaison man. Leave your deputy to get on with the stuff here. You go with Armstrong down to Poole, find out what they need, work out how we're going to do it and be our point man."

"Our point man, Sir?"

"That's right. You will go with them and be our man on the ground. It will be ideal to have you onboard with them as well, so go home and pack a bag. Get down to Poole then give me a call with the plan. Clear?"

"Yes Sir." And with that the Captain stood up and left the room. There was a silence while the enormity of the order collapsed down on Chris. It felt like the crash of a bow wave over the open bridge of a submarine in a Force ten in the Sea of Hebrides. What the hell had just happened here?

"He's pretty punchy isn't he?" opined Louis quietly.

Chris just stared ahead for a few seconds, the imminent change in his life washing over him. A myriad of emotions swept in; a surge of adrenalin – this was the part of his life that he'd so craved in his earlier years but had been forced to leave behind; a wave of fear – was he even remotely capable of performing at the level required after so many years away; confusion – what exactly would he be expected to do; go in on the ground or see them leave the side of the submarine and wish he was there with his former colleagues? Finally there was the emotional turmoil. The inner professional drive mixed and fought with a vision of his beautiful wife with tears in her eyes as he walked out of the door, her knowing that there was a fair chance he wouldn't be coming back. He wasn't sure he could put her through it. So many times in his previous life he had left, closed the door and walked away in the half-light of dawn. It was always the worst moment and had eventually left his love life a trail of possibilities never realised. It was no way to treat a partner; and now he was married to the best thing that had ever happened to him. He wondered again what the hell had just happened?

"I can tell you're having a moment, Chris," interrupted his friend. "Bit of a shock eh? Look, I tell you what, why don't you settle yourself down, I'll meet you in the mess in an hour, we can go to a pub somewhere and I'll give you the rest of the details. We can talk through your involvement then."

"Yea, alright." Chris could barely speak. He needed to collect his thoughts. Louis got up and left but Chris just sat there, all the emotions of the last few minutes a maelstrom inside him. Could he refuse if he wanted to? Did he throw himself into it, as inwardly he knew he wanted? Given the choice he would never have left the SBS. Only the injury had forced that. This could be the final chance to complete what he had left unfinished so frustratingly all those years ago. Mustafa Al Said. That bastard. He was the one responsible for at least part of the 9-11 and 7-7 attacks. To have the chance to take him down would be closure for Chris. He hadn't realised what it was, but since leaving the Corps there had been a professional emptiness as if something was unrequited. The mention of that name had made him recognise the void that had been present within the depths of his self, bringing it barrelling forward into his conscious. Would this allow him to draw a final line under his previous life? He was beginning to think that it could. But what about Elizabeth? What the hell would he say to her?

Whatever happened, he had been given an order. How far he took it, he would have time to decide after talking to Louis and going down to Poole for the initial scoping. For now it was time to snap out of it and get moving. Chris went back down into 'the hole', the bunker within which he planned his covert submarine missions, and told his deputy to crack on in his absence while he carried out his latest tasking. He shut the door on his office, wondering if he would ever be back and went to the Mess to pick up Louis. He felt he needed a drink and this sort of discussion was often better over a pint.

They drove out of the Headquarters, turning left then left again. A couple of miles down the road was a place called the *Prince William*. It wasn't exactly what you might call the most respectable of hostelries; in fact as they walked in the door, they were greeted by the welcoming site of a stripper bending over naked in front of them, leaving nothing to the imagination except where she might be putting her tips. The main benefit of this place was that they served a cracking pint of London Pride and there was a fair chance that any of the regulars had other things to occupy them rather than what Chris and Louis might be saying. Strangely, over the years, a lot of these sort of discussions had happened in places like this. Maybe it was a Forces thing.

"You all right?" asked Louis after they had moved to the most remote corner of the bar.

"I suppose so. I don't really know what to think. What exactly have you got me into here?"

"Look, this can be as big or as small as you want it to be. The Director still remembers you, you know. You and I were the best team they'd had on this bloke for years. When we were putting up the idea for this Op we were talking about submarine insertion and I just happened to mention that you were in the planning side and, you know, things sort of clicked."

"What do you mean things sort of clicked? Louis, I haven't been on an Op for eight years, and the last time I did I got shot up pretty badly. You might remember because I was saving your arse at the time."

"Yeah I realise that and I'm still grateful, and that's why I'm giving you this great opportunity to finally nail the bastard after we chased him for all those years. Think how we'll feel when we finally get to put a bullet through his head."

"You mean gather intelligence and do what is appropriate."

"Exactly that, my friend, exactly that. And don't worry about not having been deployed for a couple of years. A bit of rust removal and you'll be right back where you belong. You shouldn't have left you know. Things were never the same again."

13

"Yeah, whatever." Chris thought for a few seconds. "What do you want then? What's the Operation?"

"I'd thought you'd never ask. We pick up the sub wherever that may be and you take us to the coast off Somalia. We have enough intelligence to know that Mustafa has been training a group of men to launch a big raid in the West. We're not absolutely sure where the raid is going to be yet but it looks like it's going to be about the same as 7-7 or even bigger. We're dropped a few miles off the coast in our boats and make our way to shore. It's pretty deserted round there so we hole up for the day then move inland to the target area. The first aim is to gather intelligence, so if it's possible and we can find out names of people involved, their contacts in the West, that would be brilliant. Second, we should disrupt if we can, either ourselves if the set up is small enough or maybe using your submarine to put some Tomahawk missiles into the area. Third, if Al Said is there, we try to bring him out. If nothing else is possible, we just make notes of what we see and extract. Simple. Your boat picks us up off the coast again and we get away, back in time for tea and medals. Think about it Chris. We have the opportunity here to finally get him and given half a chance, take him out. You can't say no to that, even if you are getting fat and old.'

Chris was silent again while the possibilities played over in his mind. Louis was right of course. Every fibre of his being was driving him to say 'yes'. This was the one thing missing from his professional trophy shelf. Take down Mustafa Al Said. What a coup that would be. Several of his friends had been killed on previous Ops chasing this elusive man. Could he finally get retribution for them?

"You know I would jump at the chance normally Louis but I say again, I haven't been on an Op for eight years. I haven't fired decent weapons for about six. When were you looking to deploy?"

"One week."

"One week? Are you fucking mad?"

"Yep, and that's why I do what I do. Look, it will be a full insertion team of seven. You will be a supernumerary, just along for the ride to make it up to eight."

"Then you don't need me."

"Chris, we have seen and heard almost nothing of Mustafa since our last Op. You're still the expert… and look at it from the Director's point of view. We are about to put together an Op to find perhaps the most capable Al-Qaeda mission planner they have. The best way in is by submarine and quite frankly, although we've played around a bit in the past, I hate to admit it but none of us are as qualified as you. By lucky chance, the man who knows more about Mustafa than anyone around, who was forced out of the

Squadron against his will, is a submarine expert sitting on his arse in a shore job doing sweet FA in Northwood. Let's face it, you're made for this job. It's got your name written all over it, and in any case, the big boss has made the phone call and you've been assigned, so stop griping. Let me get you another pint and just say 'yes'. Come down to Poole, we'll bring you back up to speed on weapons and in a week you'll feel sharper than you have in eight years. You'll love it Chris. You know you will."

The problem was he was right and both Chris and Louis knew it. Another pint later and several iterations of nice London girls smiling sweetly then firing a ping pong ball across the room without the use of hands (quite accurately as it happened and rivalling the best in Bangkok) and it was time for Chris to go home to pack that bag. Whatever he thought, he had been given orders and he was wise enough to know when the hand had already been dealt. One of the best pieces of advice he had ever been given was to fight only the battles he had a chance of winning. This one, on one front at least, had already been lost. The second front was still to come when he faced his small but formidable wife. As he drove home, he composed his arguments, but each one sounded like a weak excuse for a grown man wanting to play soldier again. He decided to rely on the simple expediency of 'it's an order'. The journey passed in a blur with the Essex countryside just a kaleidoscope of green fields as he drove along the A414, staring straight ahead, unblinking.

"You're going to do what?" came the exclamation. Then came the silence. She just stared at him, disbelief written on every feature. He found that this was the worst thing, much worse than facing the Taliban. Another few seconds of oppressive silence wound its way into the room, pushing on him like a slow crushing weight as the guilt of what he was about to do swirled around him on all sides and closed in remorselessly. "Why?" The simplest of questions, the hardest of answers.

"I have to do it," he answered, the inadequacy of the statement standing in the space between them, small and fragile.

There was very little more to be said. She turned away from him and walked softly away. He could see her shoulders slump and her head fall as she did so and it was like a knife sliding through his rib cage. He followed slowly behind, trying desperately to find the words necessary and failing miserably. How could he possibly make his feelings understood? She was the world to him, his new world, but there was an old world too that was such a part of him that it couldn't be denied, even now. He had unfinished business. The thought of Al Said made him seethe inside and once again the anger rose to the surface. It constricted his gorge and he stood up straighter, the resolution giving him strength once again. He moved towards her and turned her around, seeing the tears running silently down her soft cheeks.

"I'm sorry," he said gently. "This is something that you will never understand… can never understand. It comes from a part of me that I thought was buried, that I had put behind me, but I was wrong. That man is responsible for the deaths of more people than I can remember - not only my friends but all those in New York, Washington, London and countless other places. Our people, our homes, our families. He was everything that drove my life for years and every time, God knows how, he got away to fight again. Every time I got close I missed out. Can you imagine how that feels; to be that close to evil and to have the chance to be the instrument of vengeance, just to be thwarted at the last hurdle? Elizabeth, you are my world but this will fester within me for the rest of my life if I thought that I had the chance and didn't take it. How will I feel the next time that I see pictures of a stadium up in flames or a plane fall out of the sky and know that I could have done something to help save those lives? I'm sorry, my love, but I have to do this; I have no choice."

"But why you?" she pleaded this time, the anger having ebbed away during his speech, her voice now filled with a hurt resignation. "You've been out of that world for so long. You almost died and you were younger and fitter then. What makes you think you can do it now?"

"Because it's not just a case of being the fittest, it's also about the mind, and that hasn't changed. I know everything there is to know about this man. I tracked him for years. There's no-one else that can bring my expertise to the party, Liz. What can I say?"

Again, the silence dominated. "Hold me," she said, and he closed his arms around her, pulling her to him, the diminutive figure wrapped in his embrace. She held tightly to him. "Don't you ever leave me."

"I won't. I promise."

The rest of the evening was a subdued affair. Small talk prevailed and he got together the things that he would be taking with him. He would get new kit at Poole, so the relatively small bag was just the things he'd learnt by experience that he would need in the desert. He had kept them in an old box in the wardrobe - the cut off toothbrush, his old scarf, so valuable for keeping the sun off the face and the sand from the eyes and a few other small things. Most important of all were his boots. It would have been fatal to have gone into the desert in new boots. People had tried it before and been in pieces within days, their feet ripped to shreds as the hardness tore at the skin hour after hour, the team unable to stop. He had seen men crippled - a major risk to themselves and their team. He was going to be enough of a burden as it was, he was certainly not going to make a rookie mistake like that.

And then it was time for bed. She had gone before him and when he got up there he could see once again that petite and sensual frame, this time with eyes open, looking at him intently in the shaded light. He climbed in beside her and took her hands in his, staring at her. She stared back but said nothing; there was nothing more to be said, only to be done. He put one hand to the back of her head, cupping it and brought it tenderly towards his. Her lips were soft and he placed a light kiss there, gently, holding the embrace. It was enough at first, but soon he felt the passion that she had always inspired in him start to rise up. He pulled her closer to him and pressed their bodies together, feeling her magnificent form against his. She let out a small moan as she felt the same feelings rise up in her and suddenly there was intensity between them, almost desperation. Their love-making became fuelled by lust, fear, sorrow and potential loss, knowing that it may well be the last time. The climax was immense and they clung together, not wanting to move. She started to cry as a second wave crashed through her, swamping her emotions, already at breaking point, but it was cathartic, a release, an acceptance.

After an unmeasured time he began to stroke her head again, his love for her defining the gentleness of the touch. She rested the side of her head on his chest then lifted her face, her eyes again searching, perhaps trying to truly read his. She leant forward, kissing him this time. No words were said, none were needed. They loved each other, they both knew it. This was the beginning of their lives, not the end. This time their love was calm, full, prolonged and on a deeper level than the lust that dominated the first.

Afterwards she slept. He could tell by the rhythmic breathing. He often listened to her after they had made love. He found it intensely calming that she should show so much trust in him; she had done so almost immediately after meeting and for the years that they had been together. He was her protector and it was a role that he readily adopted. It gave him a sense of completeness that he had longed for during his wild days, the days of the Corps. He would come back to her, he vowed silently to himself. This time it would be different. This time he would nail the bastard and if he got half a chance, take him out. He could feel the steel within him hardening and the familiar pre-operation focus start to pervade his being. He had forgotten how clinical he had been when deployed, how driven his personality became.

He could feel himself changing as he lay there and his mind began to tick over with what he knew, remembering the facts, running through previous encounters, the endless analysis of what had gone wrong, what had gone right. For him, there had been very little of the former and quite a lot of the latter but, despite this, Al Said had always got away. No-one had ever come up with an explanation for the extraordinary run of luck he had enjoyed. Chris had his own theories but had never been able to voice them in public. He was convinced that there was someone on the inside. Nothing else could have explained the warm ashes in the hastily abandoned camps, not once but several times. Nothing else could have explained being met with such strength of resistance when they thought that they had the element of surprise. He had mentioned the theory in passing once to a superior after one mission debrief but it had got no further, not considered worthy of further investigation, and at the time, he had been too junior to push it.

Whatever had gone before, he was now at the start of a different road. Tomorrow, he would leave early to drive down to Poole on the old route he had travelled so many times. He expected memories to flood into him as each town passed. Of course he was still nervous but now he was resolute. For the next month or so he was the old Chris Edwards: Chris the infiltrator, Chris the stalker, Chris the knife. The Chris of today was to be put away, for the immediate future at least. He closed his eyes a different man. Elizabeth had gone to sleep with her Knight Protector. When he came back, he would re-adopt the role. Until then he was prepared to kill again and his target was Mustafa Al Said.

CHAPTER 2

Chris woke early the next morning. He lay there for a few seconds, wondering if the resolve that had appeared last night was still within him. It was. He could feel its tension, that familiar emotion from so long ago; a mixture of exhilaration, excitement, fear and clarity of purpose. It had been no illusion. He looked at Elizabeth's sleeping form but didn't wake her. The time had passed for questions and he wanted no more goodbyes. The road now lay ahead.

He got up quietly, showered, dressed and was out of the house within the hour. It was just before dawn in early June and the peace of twilight was broken only by the chirp of the Chaffinch that lived in the tree outside his barn, praising the world for a new day as it always did. He paused, wanting to remember the scene, but only for a moment. He felt different, already focussed on the job in hand, still wondering what the future would bring but now keen to find out.

He gunned into life the black Mercedes SL350 that was his toy, a rare item of selfishness; three and a half litres of raw power that could kick him back into the seat if he floored it while at the same time announcing its intention with the gutsy roar that the Germans seemed to have perfected in their muscle cars. This was no time to play though. Now it was time to slip surreptitiously away into the dawn's semi-mist. He had a meeting to get to in Poole and it would take him two and a half hours to get there, if the traffic wasn't too bad.

He slipped through the country lanes and down to the M25, going clockwise and south round London across the Dartford Bridge; the north was always an horrendous snarl up of irritable and irritated drivers, defeated in their daily quest to travel a few miles of roadwork infested motorway by the inadequacies of Government planning and British seventies engineers. He was lucky though and was early enough to get through Kent before the majority of commuter traffic had built up. It was still an hour before he turned south, along the M3, heading towards the South Coast. The sun was well up but only broke through the clouds at the time he left the 'Road to Hell' as Chris Rea had so rightly called it.

He was going against the traffic now and relaxed, sticking to a constant eighty, fast enough to feel as though he was getting somewhere but slow enough not to be pulled over for speeding. His mind started to replay what he knew of Mustafa Al Said.

He knew that he had been born in North Yemen in the mid 1950s and brought up in the tribal areas near to the border with Oman. A mixture of poverty and a strict Islamic upbringing had pushed him into being caught up in the civil war that had raged in his country for an eternity, taking an anti-government stance and later blaming the West for his woes in general, perhaps with some justification. Mustafa became increasingly disillusioned with the lack of success in his own country in particular and of the state of the Arab nation in general, even more so when the British stepped in to neighbouring Oman in the early 70s to help the young Prince Qaboos overthrow his father Sultan Taimur as ruler. To him it was another example of the West pushing their own agenda, forcing their will upon the Arabs, despite the massive good Qaboos then did for his country. Two decades later and he had turned up around the fringes of Iraq for the Gulf War Part I. You could sort of see the reasoning behind his position. For a proud Muslim, he was shocked by the ruthless efficiency of the Allied attack and the helplessness of his people, even though Saddam Hussein was a recognised menace not only to the West but throughout the Arab world. Most of the other Arab nations detested the Iraqis for their arrogance and inwardly thought that they deserved to be taught a lesson. For an important number of Arab patriots however, the invasion was the greatest insult imaginable and they swore revenge. In their opinion, if their own governments were powerless to respond in a conventional sense, then it was time that individuals got together to strike where they could.

This was when Mustafa met Bin Laden. The Saudi had used his fortune and influence to gather a few to his banner and Mustafa had been one of the first. Originally lacking the education and certainly the wealth to be one of the inner circle, he was nonetheless captivated by the idea of fighting back. He was inspired by the thought of covertly slipping into the fabric of Western society and thrusting a metaphorical knife through the material, ripping it apart whenever he could. It may not have been a full frontal assault but it would be making a difference and as it turned out, he was no ordinary soldier.

Coupled with his unshakeable belief was an innate and undeveloped intelligence that belied his lack of education. He learned quickly, soaking up techniques, revising them, improving on the old ways, fast becoming an expert in what he did. He had spent time in the West, first in London, then in Germany and Europe as a whole where he had run cells that carried out hit and run attacks; small scale mostly, but learning the skills required to go back to his masters and show them how they could be so much better.

This went on for the best part of ten years and the organisation grew. What was so inspired and allowed it so much success was the fluid nature of its design. There was no infrastructure and therefore very little for the authorities to latch on to. Every cell was an individual unit. Rarely could links be traced beyond the handlers, who themselves knew little of their hierarchy; a masterstroke of obfuscation.

Then came the Gulf War Part II and this time Al-Qaeda could help. Their fame had risen throughout the world with early successes such as the 1993 World Trade Centre bombings and the 1998 American Embassy attacks in Africa. They had more volunteers than they could train and the Islamic youth of the world were being inspired by their deeds. In these actions, at last, they had found a voice, a response, a measure of pride rather than the ritualistic humiliation continually meted out by the old Imperialists. They started to channel men through Jordan and Syria, across the desert and from the north; in fact they came flooding to help. Ultimately they had been unsuccessful but they had sure as hell tried. They claimed that it was their influence that had kept up the pressure that made the British and Americans so keen to disengage.

By this time, Mustafa was higher up the ladder. He was in charge of the logistics of getting ammunition and resources to their fighters. When the focus of operations moved east into Afghanistan, he moved with it and joined Bin Laden and his second in command al-Zawahiri in the Tora Bora caves on the Pakistan border, working alongside the Taliban with the support of the Pakistani tribal chiefs and elements of the Government Secret Service. All the time, as an integral part of the Al-Qaeda operations branch and with his experience of living in the West, he had knowledge of and had taken part in the planning of all the major operations. His tally of dead and wounded had risen to the hundreds and his reputation was becoming legendary. Eventually, his master stroke had been 9-11; a plan and execution that chilled the world. Two years later, the London attacks had cemented his reputation. He was behind it all.

While this history was unfolding, the Western agencies hadn't been completely idle. As the threat had increased, so had the resources invested in gathering intelligence, both remotely and by the insertion of men on the ground, be it covert agents or when appropriate, Special Forces. There was a surprising amount of information forthcoming. Although Al-Qaeda claimed to represent the Islamic nation, the vast majority of the religions' followers had been just as appalled as everyone else by their actions. It was here that Chris had first got involved. He had been told at an early stage to make himself an expert on Mustafa and he had learnt everything he could. He had researched endlessly, working closely with other agencies such as 'GCHQ' in Cheltenham, ultimately putting together operations and deploying with his teams, supposedly for the take down; except that of the six times he had tried, he had always failed; the chicken had always flown the coop.

By the time Chris had turned onto the M27 towards Southampton, the circumstances of the various failures had played over in his mind, each a bitter recrimination and with every memory he got more and more angry. He wouldn't let it happen again, not this time. He had one more shot at this and was aware that at forty he was on borrowed time. In his heart he knew that he was slightly out of shape and definitely out of touch after returning to his submarine career, but he couldn't let the opportunity go. He passed along the outskirts of the New Forest then along the A35 before eventually turning down into Poole itself, to the west of the town. By the time he got to the gate of the familiar Royal Marines base, innocuous as the headquarters of the SBS was always going to be, he had reviewed the information then stored it at the forefront of his mind. It would act as a constant reminder of why he was there, the memories fresh again and able to drive him forward as he operated at the limits of his endurance.

He pulled up in front of the Wardroom at mid-morning, having given his friend Louis a call to tell him he had arrived. He was no longer a member of the unit and therefore 'of the cloth' so had lost his free access throughout the base. As he walked up to the ivy covered building, memories flooded back to him, as they had on his approach for the last half hour; people he had known, running circuits he had used to keep fit, old haunts. It felt odd, as if he was a stranger but an intimate one. How would he fit in with all these new boys? Would they cut him any slack?

"Hello Sir," came the quiet voice from behind the Hall Porter's desk. "Nice to see you again and welcome home." It was amazing how you could go back to a base after so many years and still see the same old faces.

Chris smiled broadly. "Hello Tony, nice to see you too. I was wondering if I would see anyone I knew."

"We don't change here, Sir. Who would look after you if we did? How's the shoulder? We were all gutted you had to leave us."

"It's fine actually. You could say I'm fighting fit again, although perhaps a little bit wider about the middle."

"You still look pretty fit, Sir. I wouldn't worry if I were you. Major Armstrong is waiting for you inside, go straight through."

"Thanks Tony, it's good to be back." Chris went through but hadn't got much further when he heard his name being called.

"Hello mate." It was Louis. "Come on then, let's get started, we've got a briefing at ten and we've got the big boss in with us, so I know it'll be hard but try and look professional. This is my arse on the line now. I've backed you, although it didn't take much I admit, so it'll look bad on me if you show yourself up."

"The Director eh? We are privileged. I would have thought the Deputy would have taken this."

"Normally yes, but he's out of the country and the Director wants to be in on this one personally."

The Director Special Forces or DSF was Major General Colin Holbrook, an Army two star, formally a Paratrooper and badged SAS man, who had gained his reputation in Northern Ireland during the troubles. He had masterminded highly covert missions throughout the Province, then went on to command the detachment that supported the first Gulf War in 91, amongst other things. He was known as being an operational machine, both physically and mentally, and was highly respected by the whole of the Corps, whether SAS or SBS.

Chris was led to one of the staff buildings, but not the one he expected. Set aside from the others was the 'special area' known as the pit because it was partly underground. It housed the planning rooms that dealt with the ultra secret missions, those that would be denied by any government. No-one who didn't need to know was allowed inside. It had a separate ops room and when running operations could be locked down entirely. Entry was strictly controlled. It was the first but not the last surprise of the day.

After getting through security he walked in and saw six people in front of him talking quietly amongst themselves. As he passed through the door, the conversation stopped and they turned. After a moment of silence, almost all of them broke into huge smiles and came across. With the exception of one slightly younger Royal Marine Captain, these were all men that he had worked with before. There were a few jokes about being a fat submariner now and ribbing about coming to do a proper job again but the greeting was cut short as the DSF was announced.

The Special Forces lacked the formality that you found in the rest of the services but even they stood to attention as the Director walked in.

"Relax gentlemen," he said in the soft Irish accent that had served him so well in his past but belied the fearsome reputation he had earned. He smiled as he saw Chris and walked over to him straight away. "Hello son.

How are you? Ready for a challenge again?" It was this gentle, paternal nature that had so endeared him to his men over the years and made him the ideal man to be in charge of a tight knit community such as the combined Corps. Chris had worked for him directly twice in the past and he had been the Assistant Director, AD, when Chris had been wounded in Jamaica that lifetime ago.

"I'm fine, Sir," replied Chris. "Just eager to find out how much I can contribute."

"I want you in there from start to finish, Chris. This has gone wrong too many times in the past and we can't afford for it to fail again. I need an expert in Al Said and you're as good as it gets. You were one of the best before and not that much will have changed. Get back in mental shape over the next few days and the rest will follow. Right, let's get on with the briefing."

The SBS Operations Officer, Major David Shaw stood up. "Sir, Gentlemen," he started. "First things first, this is very close hold. No-one outside this room knows what I am about to tell you and there is a reason for that, which I'll get to later. Over the last few months we've been getting reports of Al-Qaeda preparing for another large scale operation. Two days ago, MI6 got the lead that Somalia was the base and that the planning was being overseen personally by Mustafa Al Said, one of our long time principle targets. Further to that, in the last twenty-four hours, it seems that they have got the location of the training camp about eighteen miles in from the coast, where he is personally in charge. GCHQ has intercepted phone calls that may be him from voice recognition patterns and we are awaiting satellite imagery to confirm the reports, which should come in this morning. The bottom line is that we're fairly sure that we have the man, the intent, the location and the assets to do something about it."

Chris could feel himself being sucked deeper and deeper into the potential for this Op. He felt himself tumbling like Alice down the rabbit hole, straight back to his past, and he loved it.

"You all know Chris Edwards but some of you may be surprised to see him here," the Major continued. "Before he was injured, Chris was with us for seven years and became our expert on Al Said. We would have wanted him here anyway, if he was available, but he serves a dual purpose. The operation that Major Armstrong is leading is a covert insertion of eight men into the Somali coast. Its aim is to locate the camp, gather intelligence, interdict if circumstances allow then withdraw for extraction from the same position and by the same method, submarine."

At the mention of the word 'submarine', a collection of grins spread across the faces of the assembled men. It was schoolboy stuff but they had loved practising insertion and recovery techniques using submarines but had never achieved it for real. Now it seemed they were going to get their chance.

"Chris is currently working as the Fleet Submarine Special Operations planner and will be our link with the Navy throughout. With his previous knowledge on Al Said that makes him a pretty vital part of the chain so take care of him. Chris – what can the Navy offer us?"

He was over the moon to be making a contribution right from the start. "*HMS Talisman* is currently in the Gulf of Oman on gatekeeper duties for the Allied Forces in the Arabian Gulf. She can get to Fujairah in the United Arab Emirates within forty-eight hours and be ready to leave again twenty-four hours after that. Before she deployed she carried out a full work up and is fully certified for Special Forces operations. She has the equipment on board to support and can top up with anything else she needs in port. I have been told that if you want her, she's yours. She can get you off the coast of Somalia within seven days of sailing and put you within six miles of the coast without risking her or your integrity. After that, she can remain on station for an indefinite period and be ready at short notice to pull you out. I will act as the point of contact with the ship's crew and no-one but the Captain will know the destination until we leave port." It was a short synopsis but gratefully received.

"That's excellent Chris, better than we could have hoped. OK, that's the insertion method. You will make your way in to the shore at night then find somewhere to stow the boats, move inland and lay up during the day. We're pretty confident that we will have a grid reference for the camp before you get there, so that will be your first target. It should take you no more than two nights to reach it, if you get a move on and have an uninterrupted approach. Once there, you are to observe, see if you can get close enough to find out what their plans are, or failing that, identify the key players. The obvious target is Al Said but we have no way of knowing if he'll be there when you arrive. If he is and it seems feasible without compromising yourselves, snatch him. He is our number one target now Bin Laden has gone and we want him. More than that, the Americans want him and if we can give him to them, then we can earn massive brownie points and get more information out of him than if we brought him in ourselves.

"The second option if you can't get close enough to snatch or get any useful intelligence is to call in a Tomahawk missile strike from *HMS Talisman*. She will be well within range and can have weapons on target in minutes. This option is still being worked up because we need buy in from Fleet Headquarters, the Minister of Defence and the PM but we're pretty sure it will be approved by the time you get there.

"Throughout all this and especially once you start getting any intelligence, you will have full satellite communications back to this HQ whenever you transmit. We'll be locked down giving you support if we can and information if you request it, but it will be standard routines and one way transmissions, you to us. As backup we'll have *Talisman* off the coast listening out on VHF and ready to act as a relay if required. Report in whenever the situation allows or with a spot report if you think the situation needs it. Once you have what you need, withdraw to the extraction point and wait for the pick-up, which will be conducted at night in the same position. You'll have GPS throughout, which will allow you to find both the camp and the submarine on your return.

"It's pretty simple, gentlemen. Get in, find out what's going on, strike if we can and get out, and if you get lucky, take Said with you. Any questions on the outline plan?" There was general silence, then the young Captain that Chris didn't know spoke up.

"Sir, you mentioned that only the people in this room know about this. Why?"

"Right, I was getting to that." Major Shaw paused. "Gentlemen, we believe that there is someone in the Corps passing information to Al-Qaeda."

There was a stunned silence. Everyone had stopped breathing. Chris felt a huge surge of adrenalin. For years he had believed the same thing; it was the only explanation for the missed opportunities, the lucky escapes. Was this final vindication for his seemingly outrageous idea all those years ago? If it was, someone in the organisation had suffered his own men to die. Chris had lost friends, colleagues, people who had trusted him. The shock rippled across him like waves upon the sand as the full impact of the simple statement hung in the room.

The Major let the men take it all in. "More than that, we think we know who it is," he said quietly.

This was a double whammy. Barely recovered from the first assault, they were hit by the second.

"I'm not going to say anything more now and if we are going to get final proof, we need absolute secrecy from you all. Do not discuss any aspect of this operation with anyone. You will train by yourselves, sleep by yourselves and remain completely removed from the rest of the camp. I want you to move out from here in four days, fly out commercial to Dubai and join the submarine just before they sail in six. Chris, can Fleet support?"

"Yes Major."

"Good. Major Armstrong is leading the mission with Captain Long as the second in command. Lieutenant Commander Edwards is the third member of the deploying team but is supernumerary. You'll have another five making eight in total and your choice of weapons but keep it light. The targets are going to be lightly armed so you don't need howitzers. The finer details are up to you to work out, so I suggest you get planning.' Brief me on the finished product tomorrow at ten hundred here." He addressed the General. "Sir, do you have any comments?"

General Holbrook stood up and turned to face the men, still sitting in shocked silence. "Gentlemen," he began in his soft Irish accent. "If we had the choice we would get this man without putting you anywhere near an operation, but we don't. Given what we believe are Al Said's intentions, we have to get out there, take Said down and disrupt whatever it is that he's planning. At the same time we will be gathering the final proof we need to convict the traitor. This has been as much of a shock to me as to anyone else, perhaps more so, given who the suspect is. Your job is in Somalia, the rest of it leave to us. This is a great opportunity to do the world some good. Take it and focus on what you need to do. The rest of the plans I leave to Major Shaw. I will be in the ops room for the duration but will be with you in spirit throughout. Good luck, gentlemen."

He made his exit, leaving everyone in a brooding silence. Louis stood up and snapped them all out of it. "Right then, let's get going and get the details thrashed out. I want an outline plan on the table by sixteen hundred and ready in all respects for the briefing tomorrow morning at ten. That includes full logistics, a list of the equipment we need, the weapons to be channelled through the embassy in Dubai and the training we are going to carry out between now and Friday when we move from here. Chris, I'm going to need Captain Long with me for the rest of the day and I would normally want him for your mentor but I think Sergeant Baxter will be just as good. Are you happy with that Dodger?"

The young Marine Captain nodded. Although relatively young, 'Dodger' Long had been in the Special Boat Service for three years and was a natural. A bootneck Marine by trade, he had earned the right to be 2i/c through several operations inside Afghanistan, where he had earned the Queen's award for bravery and the Military Cross. He didn't look like the archetypal hero so often portrayed in Hollywood films, but then again, the SBS rarely were. By and large, they were understated, almost withdrawn, usually of medium height and build; the sort you would walk by in the street. That was what made them ideal for surveillance work. This was in sharp contrast to the Special Air Service, often recruited from the Paratroop regiment and traditionally known for being loud, obnoxious and with a screw loose, with the odd few exceptions of course.

"In the meantime, Sergeant Baxter, why don't you take my friend here and get out on the river, get him reacquainted with the RIB."

The Sergeant looked over and grinned. They had worked together before a couple of times in Afghanistan as well as that fateful mission in

Jamaica and knew each other well. 'Stan', as he was known - after the famous Scottish TV comedian Stanley Baxter - was about as experienced as they came, with twenty years under his belt, almost all of it in the Corps. He was about to retire and this should be his last op.

It was a feature of Forces life that almost no-one kept their given name. There was always a nickname that stuck, either by something you did or one of the standards. Typically, a short man was known as 'Stretch' and a Smith as 'Smudge'. A man who had lost half a finger would be called 'Stumpy' and someone with the surname Bell would be called 'Dinger'. It made light of things and built camaraderie so did no harm.

"How are you doing Sir? Long time no see." They had always got on well and 'Stan' had taught him a hell of a lot in those first years, stuff that had saved his life more than a few times. "Shall we do as the man says then?"

Chris made his way out and was given some suitable kit. Stan led the way down to the boat section and signed out a RIB, a Rigid Inflatable Boat, from the boat master. This was the much loved small boat that the Special Forces used for most of their water based efforts. It wasn't huge but it could hold between four and six men with limited kit at a squeeze and was fairly tough. Most importantly, for this mission at least, it could be collapsed small enough to fit into a submarine pretty easily and be hidden on a hostile shore without too much difficulty and therefore be ready when needed for the extraction.

It felt good to get onto the water again; it had been a few years but the instincts never left you. Chris had got used to being on larger vessels that would cut through waves and produce a longer, smoother movement. These small boats would ride on top of the waves and be tossed around on the surface, producing a staccato jarring that buffeted the spine continuously. Stan kept it slow and measured in the immediate area of the boat masters' view, then opened up the little outboard. It wasn't very powerful but with only two and no kit, the seventy-five HP engine was enough to get a little bit of air. After the first couple of minutes, Chris took over and loved it. This was one step closer to his previous life and the memories of many operations flooded back to him, as had been happening all morning.

"Better head back now Chris." Stan brought reality back into focus with a bang. "We don't want to keep the others waiting. You know most of them but it'll be good to get reacquainted. We'll have some lunch and then we'll do some weapon firing this afternoon, get you back into the swing of things. How long has it been since you fired a proper weapon?"

"Oh I don't know, about six years. Pretty much since I got injured I suppose," admitted Chris.

"What weapon do you fancy? The selection hasn't changed much I'm afraid."

The Special Forces were spoiled compared with the rest of the armed forces, who had to make do with the SA80 rifle and the Browning 9mm pistol. They had a much greater range of weapons available and could choose which suited them better, adapted for the missions they were about to take on.

"I was a Sig P226 9mm man myself," Chris replied. "I always liked the feel of it and I suppose it would be better to go back to something I know rather than try something new," he reasoned.

"What about support weapon?" asked Stan.

"The standard L119," answered Chris.

The Canadian made C8 Carbine, known in the UK as the L119 was the light support weapon of choice for the UK Special Forces. It was small and compact but could lay down some rapid bursts when required; easy to carry on long treks but quick to bring to bear when needed.

"OK, that shouldn't be a problem. I'll get the shoot lined up for this afternoon. What about a knife?"

"Actually, I brought my own Stan." Chris had found his old knife when routing through his stuff at home, still lightly oiled from the last time he had put it away, not thinking that he would be needing it again and certainly not in these circumstances. It was a fairly vicious looking affair, about six inches of serrated blade, grooved to allow entry into the body with minimum resistance. He had used it a number of times in anger and had earned himself a reputation as a decent knife man. Stabbing someone was never an easy thing to do. It was a particularly close and dirty method of fighting, raw and primeval; surprisingly difficult to achieve when going for the textbook rib entry, and extremely messy when going for the neck. However, the majority of his work, as with all Special Forces had been surveillance – indicators and warnings for other forces or intelligence gathering. The 'glam' work of the Iranian Embassy Siege in London back in May 1980, or the rescue of the Royal Irish Rangers from the West Side Boys in Sierra Leone in 2000 was the popular conception but not an often repeated reality. Somehow though, this time round, he hoped that he would have the chance to get 'involved' with Al Said.

They got back to the landing stage and handed back the RIB to the boat master, who looked it over suspiciously before accepting it. He had been there for years and jealously guarded his rubber charges but was happy knowing that he was supporting the 'lads', even in this limited capacity.

Lunch was great. A modest 'scran' but the rest of the team were pleased to see him again and Chris felt increasingly as if he had come home. There were four others, as well as Louis, 'Dodger' Long and 'Stanley' Baxter. The first was a Canadian communications expert called Pat Mulhoon, obviously of Irish extraction, who had always wanted to come over and be part of the Marines, emulating his grandfather in the war. The second was a west country native called Tim Cummins, known as 'Peanut' because he had lost most of his hair by the age of twenty and his head bore an uncanny resemblance to one. His was a slightly darker character, quieter than the rest and known as being vicious when the occasion required it, very quick to anger and explosive in nature but a good operator nonetheless. The third was an Essex lad called, anonymously enough, Jon Bill. He was fairly good looking and had always had the gift of the gab. He had started off as a telephone salesman and was extremely good at it, but had quickly realised that it didn't fit with his own desire for adventure, hence the Marines and then the Corps. He was, however, able to transfer this wide boy characteristic to the ladies and had remarkable success over the years, at least until he got married to a nurse, when obviously it all stopped. The last was a Geordie called Bobby Greig, the clown of the group, always quick with a quip. Bobby had had a stormy upbringing in the poorest districts of Sunderland in the North East, just south of Newcastle, so was not technically a 'Geordie'. He was brought up on a rough council estate, into petty crime by the age of twelve and on the verge on something more serious by sixteen. Somehow though, he had turned this disastrous start around and had channelled his frustration and aggression into the Marines. He joined at the age of seventeen and ultimately progressed into the Special Boat Service, finding the discipline and boundaries that he needed within its structure and ultimately the close family he had never had. He was eternally grateful for this and you could see the joy written all over his face, a reflection of how much his life had improved. Ultimately, the Special Forces had given him the best chance he was ever going to get, and he never forgot it.

Chris had worked with them all before, for varying periods, and Louis, Bobby and Peanut had been on the anti-drugs mission that had cost him his Special Forces career. The warmth of his greeting was obviously heartfelt and Chris could feel the years of absence being peeled from him. He almost started to regret having gone back into submarines, wondering if he should have given himself time to recover from his injury, but this wasn't the time for negative thinking; he was just enjoying the moment.

The others had to go back to planning immediately after lunch so Stan took Chris off to the armoury to pick up his practice weapons, the pistol and the light support weapon. As he went in through the heavy door, that peculiar but unmistakeable smell of gun oil wafted through the air and he was transported back to an earlier time.

"You're after the Sig then Sir are you?" the armourer asked.

Chris felt a tinge of excitement as the man went to the back of the racks and reappeared a few seconds later with the hand gun.

"Nice weapon that," he said as he passed it over. "I always enjoyed it."

Chris took it and felt the slightly ribbed grip drop into his hand; it had always been the weapon that he had felt most natural with. He felt as though he had never been away and he was shaking hands with an old friend.

"And I've got you down for the L119, is that right?" the armourer asked again and wandered off to the other side of the racks. Again he passed it over and looked on approvingly as Chris took hold of it. "Just sign here for the weapons Sir and we'll get you some ammunition."

Chris felt the minimal weight and compact nature of the light support weapon and couldn't wait to get into it. The sergeant signed for all the hardware and they moved out onto the firing range.

"Right then Chris, let's see how normal you've become in your old age. Let's start at ten metres with the Sig and go from there."

He set up the targets while Chris re-familiarised himself with the weapon, swapping over the clips and cocking the chamber, awkwardly at first but then with a practised ease that reflected his former proficiency. He had loaded each fifteen-round clip with ten rounds for the practice. Stan came back to the firing line and they both put on ear defenders.

Chris lined up the weapon and felt the familiar calmness as he focussed on the target. He stopped breathing when he knew he was there and squeezed the trigger. The small kick told him the weapon had discharged and he looked towards the target trying to gauge his success.

"Don't dwell on it Chris, give it another nine and we'll see what's happened then," chipped in Stan.

Chris looked towards the target and double tapped, in the way he had preferred before. Four times he wrapped out the pair, each time enjoying the snap of the weapon and the released smell of cordite; the smell he had always loved.

One bullet remained and he took a final few seconds to centre his aim, then released the bullet. This time he knew he had nailed the target. He was back in the zone.

The sergeant walked down the range and retrieved the now butchered marksman's rings. He was smiling when he got back.

"Not much wrong with that," he said. It was obvious that the first shot had gone high and left, but then there were a series of coupled shots ranging between the eighth and third concentric rings, and one single shot dead centre.

Another forty shots later, at varying distances, and the initial session was complete. Chris was thrilled with the results. He wasn't quite as rusty as he had thought he would be, but then again shooting was a skill of hand eye co-ordination and once you had it, you had it; it was just muscle memory after that.

Next it was on to the L119. They moved onto another range for this, one with a greater choice of targets and field of fire. The first burst surprised him slightly, even though he had fired this weapon many times before. However it wasn't long until he was pinning the target down with the short volleys he had been taught were the best way of preserving his ammunition but still giving the volume required to either suppress the enemy or stop them dead, depending on what was required.

An hour and a half later, they walked off the range and returned the weapons, Chris feeling about as happy as he had in years. He had passed the first test and he knew the word would get around that he was still in the game. It was important that the others around him knew he could take care of himself and that they could depend on him to cover their backs as well.

By the time they got back to the planning room, it was almost four and the details of the operation had been pretty much finalised.

"Ah, Davey Crockett returns," offered Louis as they walked into the room. "How did it go? Did you murder a small tree's worth of paper?"

"He was actually pretty good, for a has-been." Stan got in quick to settle the doubts that would have been playing on everyone's mind. "Objectively speaking, about twice as good as you I would say."

Louis grinned and turned back to the table. "Well while you two have been having a bit of fun, we've been doing some proper work and the plan is pretty much there. What we need from you is the details of the sub. Given that we fly out on Friday, when does the *Talisman* get into Fujairah and when do we meet it? Also I suppose I should ask if there is anything else that we should know about you weird submariners?"

"The only thing you need to know about us weird submariners is that we are going to risk life and limb to get you to where you need to go, will act as your lifeline while you are in area and save your arse when it's time to get you out. I'll make a phone call in a couple of minutes and the orders will be given to get the boat into Fujairah on Thursday, in two days time, and she will wait there for us to embark four days after that. The rest is up to you."

"Good stuff Chris, I always had faith you know." Louis grinned back. "Right then, people, I want you to get onto the parts of the plan that you are responsible for and start making it happen. I want to go into the brief tomorrow at ten not with just a plan but with markers down for achieving all the support we need. Over to you."

The good thing about the Special Forces was that they had their own supply chain and support assets. Because of the nature of their business, no-one else could be involved and therefore they skipped the vast majority of the bureaucracy associated with normal operations. It was quite possible to set up an operation and within a few hours to have all the moving parts in place. In this case, Chris was pretty sure that the RIBs and most of the heavy, bulky items required for the mission would be on a flight from Brize Norton within the next few hours. Their weapons would probably move the same way or via special channels through the embassy to bypass normal customs. Certainly, by the time they got to Dubai in a few days, the pieces would be in place.

Chris took the chance to get into a back office and to phone his Captain on a secure line.

"What's the story?" Captain Absalom was typically direct. "Are we on?"

"Yes Sir, we need to get the boat into Fujairah so that she is ready to leave in six days."

"Excellent." You could tell that the Captain was an operations man. He couldn't stand the banality of endless exercises and anything that promoted the usefulness of his submarines in the face of massive government cutbacks was a huge bonus for him. The thought of achieving such a coup at such a politically sensitive time was going to be grabbed with both hands.

But then, uncharacteristically, his voice softened slightly. "And how are you, Chris? Are you OK? I realise I blindsided you on this."

Chris was slightly taken aback by the change in character and wasn't too sure how to respond. He decided to be honest, as the Captain was well known for being able to spot bullshit from twenty paces.

"Actually I'm fine Sir. I didn't know how I would be initially but after I started to get into it, I felt as if I were coming home. I've worked with most of the boys before so I've sort of slotted straight back in."

"Well don't get too comfortable." The gruffness was straight back. "I want you here on completion with your report tied up. I've got a job for you and you're not going anywhere else, so don't get any funny ideas."

"No problem Sir, just doing as ordered." Chris realised the psychological support box had been ticked and was equally business like in return.

"Report in when you can but I'll keep tabs on you from the signals sent in from *Talisman* and the reports from the Poole operations room. Consider *Talisman* alongside as planned and good luck. Sounds like a holiday to me at the governments expense, so if you don't come back with some extreme form of Diarrhoea and Vomiting, I'll believe that you've been round the pool in Mogadishu sunning yourself at the Hilton instead of out in the field. I'm sure that's what all you Special Forces boys do anyway, then get all the money and the glory!"

"Roger that Sir," and before he knew it the Captain had rung off. So there it was, he was on his own, back where it had all started so long ago. Actually he was glad to have official sanction to leave his last job behind for the next few weeks. It gave him licence to concentrate exclusively on what lay ahead.

The next few days passed pretty quickly for Chris. He got down onto the range a few more times and got back his proficiency with both the weapons. He also had the 'pleasure' of being taken off to the Royal Marines Training Centre at Lympstone for a day with Sergeant Baxter. He may have thought that he'd kept himself in shape but suddenly he realised what a huge effort it was to maintain the fitness levels required of just a normal Marine, let alone someone in the Special Forces. The aching started on the journey back and only got worse as the night went on. The next morning he was racked with pain as his muscles protested the extreme mistreatment of the day before, a stiffness that only reluctantly gave way as the day progressed.

It was also good just to be part of the scene again. Even just wandering around the camp helped to re-tune his mental attitude. The small detachment had been told to keep themselves separate but it didn't stop Chris from seeing a few people from the past, some he had worked with, others he had worked for. Walking back to the mess one evening on the last day of training across the periphery of the parade ground he saw a junior rank salute a man who returned the salute with the wrong arm, his left. This could only be Colonel Robin Taylor Royal Marines, another legend in the Corps and now Deputy Director of Special Forces and in charge of the Special Boat Service at Poole. He had lost the lower part of his right arm when shrapnel from a grenade had almost severed it when on operations in Afghanistan a couple of years ago. Always one to lead from the front, his reputation and ability had been so high the Corps had kept him on and even promoted him to his current position, a massive achievement. Chris watched him go with nothing but admiration.

The last night before everyone left was traditionally spent in a local pub, not pissing up, just a quiet couple of pints and a meal where the men were able to adjust themselves mentally to what lay ahead.

"So are you ready Chris?" asked Louis as they took a swig of the Wadworth's 6X in front of them. "I guess the last few days must have been a bit of a shock to you. By all accounts, Stan has told me that with the exception of your time on the Lympstone assault course being truly reflective of the fat bastard you've become, you've done ok. How do you feel?"

"Well, if you mean do I feel ready enough to save your sorry arse for the umpteenth time then I guess the answer is yes."

"And when it happens I will be eternally grateful I'm sure."

Chris looked around the table at the rest of the boys. There was a quiet calmness about them that always amazed him. They were about to go out into a very hostile environment, conduct a mission that was probably as dangerous as any going on in the world right now, where if it went wrong a large number of them might be killed, and they were sitting in a country pub sipping a pint as if it was a normal evening out with friends. They were too professional to be seriously drinking, so the evening carried on with quiet conversations between any combination of the eight of them. Chris took the time to get to know the Marine Captain and 2i/c, 'Dodger' Long, and found that he liked him too. He was obviously a highly intelligent and thoughtful man and you could see he had an innate confidence that would reflect in the way he commanded his troop. His calm mien said that he knew that the decisions he made could ultimately cost people their lives, but at the same time he was confident enough of his own abilities to make the right choice and to deliver the right outcome. Chris could see him going a long way, both in the Corps and in the wider Royal Marines.

A couple of hours later and it was time to head back. The next day was Saturday and they were flying out on three separate flights from Heathrow and Gatwick but all ultimately ending up in Dubai, two via Amsterdam. It was common practice and actually common sense that if you were trying to insert a team of eight into a country, for whatever reason, you didn't do it with a block booking on the same aircraft. Although by physical appearance they were all types that were meant to be able to pass casual inspection, eight single men trying to pass airport security at once would have been pushing it just a little.

Louis drove Chris back the few miles to base in his Mazda MX5.

"They haven't changed have they?" Louis stated after a couple of minutes of quiet. "And they all like you, you know. They're all glad you're back, at least for the time being. It reminds me of old times, some of which should be forgotten, but a lot of which were some of the best years of my life, my friend."

"To be honest, mate, I'm over the moon to be back," replied Chris. "The submarine thing is OK, but my heart has always been here. Nothing gets the blood flowing like jumping out of an aircraft at night into a hostile area or watching the outside of a drug lord's camp in the middle of the jungle. It just doesn't come close. And the more I'm reminded of what we used to do and the times we've been here before, the more I want to get to grips with Mustafa. What about what the General said at the brief though. What the hell is going on there? Have you got any idea who the bastard might be?"

"All I know is I'm as stunned as the rest of the boys," replied Louis. "I knew nothing about this, Chris, but it does sort of remind me of what you used to say way back, when we were trying to nail Said before though, doesn't it? I get the feeling that to have the sort of influence that the General was implying, he's got to be fairly senior but God alone knows who. It's not exactly a cast of thousands, is it?"

Chris could feel the anger rising up in him again, this time for a different reason. The joy of returning to the Corps, at least on this temporary loan, had pushed thoughts of Mustafa Said and the other bombshell about the traitor from the front of his mind. Now though, the memory of the many frustrations over the years acted as a fan to the flames of the retribution he intended to dish out over the next couple of weeks. He could feel the focus coming back to him, as it had the evening before he had come down here, when he lay in bed at home with his wife next to him, possibly for the last time.

"Whoever it is Louis, I hope I'm going to be part of taking him down; that would be enough for me. First things first though, let's get out there and nail that arsehole in Somalia. He can't hide forever. This time we're going to bring home the prize."

That night, Chris lay in bed lost in a myriad of thoughts, but with only one purpose in mind. He had made the final torturous phone call to Elizabeth, then had got himself ready, both mentally and materially. His kit had already been shipped with the other stuff so that if he did get stopped through customs in Dubai, it would be the sort of gear any normal holiday maker would have. In a couple of days, he would be on board *HMS Talisman* and on his way into theatre. He couldn't wait.

The next morning was another grey day, perhaps fitting for the low key departure they intended to make. For the first time, Chris could feel a sense of tension among the boys. They were relatively quiet; still they could be forgiven for that. They were all as focussed as Chris, the time for small talk, such as they ever made, now gone. All their movements spoke of efficiency and practicality. There wasn't even a send-off from Major Shaw, just three groups of men getting into three non-descript cars with their bags, heading off out of the gate. Nothing suggested the danger they would be facing in just a few days time. But that was all well and good.

At the top of the M3 at the M25, one of the cars turned right to make its way to Gatwick, the other two to Heathrow. They parked in separate car parks and made their own way into different terminals; one the new British Airways Terminal 5, the other to Terminal 3 and Gulf Air. Chris had drawn the lucky straw and walked into the new BA complex which somehow, despite British engineering efficiency and the initial teething problems on first opening, they had finally got right. He sat in a bar on the other side of security with a glass of tonic water, looking out at the end of the runway and the queue of planes waiting to make their getaway. He had no idea where the people on board were bound for and what their individual futures would hold. At this point he could only try to imagine his own.

He moved through to the departure gate when the flight was called and passed Louis on the way to his seat. They didn't look at each other, they were now individuals and on a job. As the plane taxied out, he felt no more emotion, no second thoughts. This was business. The engines started to roar and he felt his spine being pushed into the back of his seat. He knew where he was going to land. Where he would eventually end up was anyone's guess.

CHAPTER 3

For Chris it was as if time stood still during the six hour flight. The economy cabin, filled with noisy families and anxious businessmen, was basic and relatively cramped. In any case, he was too preoccupied to watch anything on the entertainment system and he sat there, oblivious to those around him, with a plethora of thoughts running through his head. With the time difference, they would arrive in the evening so there wasn't going to be much time to do anything other than grab a bite to eat and get their heads down, and in any case they were in four different hotels so meeting up wasn't an option or desired for operational security reasons.

As the plane circled for the final approach, Chris could see the lights of the city below him as they banked. The Arab states always amazed him from the air because of the contrast of landscape, the absolute blackness of the desert and then the amazing light show that was the modern metropolis below. It was the same with all the big Arab cities, especially in the oil rich Gulf States, where it seemed the rulers wanted to demonstrate their wealth by building the most imaginative and architecturally impressive buildings they could. Ironically, these modern wonders would be surrounded by the most basic of out buildings and further out still you would get into the rudimentary houses used by the locals. The stark contrast acted as a mirror to the society itself, on one side extreme wealth, designer labels and custom built Mercedes and on the other, those untouched by the golden wand of oil inspired prosperity.

They cruised in for a gentle landing and the Boeing 777 touched down smoothly before taxiing to the stand. Chris could feel the expectation rising in him with each passing moment, the adrenalin starting to build again, slowly but surely. They filed off the aircraft into the air conditioning of the terminal and Chris was struck at how much had changed in the years since he had last been there. The building he now entered was as opulent as any Mall you would see and provided exactly the impression for new arrivals that the rulers would want. The marble of the floor and walls was highlighted by glitzy lighting throughout and the shops screamed affluence, with Rolex, Cartier, Louis Vuitton and the others represented in full measure. The whole package was meant to say, this is Dubai, wealth and wonder abound.

The first test was passport control. These border points always made Chris feel nervous, even when the visit was purely recreational. As irrational as it seemed, he always felt as if there may be some doubt about getting into the country. This time when approaching the small booth knowing that he was going through under semi-false pretences, it was doubly so. He had to play it straight. When asked why he was there he had to say simply business and/or pleasure and make it sound real. As always when lying, the best thing was to say nothing at all or when forced to, say as little as possible. The more you embellished with details, the higher the chances that something would trip you up. The elaborate lies always brought you down.

As it was, his turn came fairly quickly and he moved up to the window to hand his passport through. It was his second passport, the one kept for operations and it had minimal border stamps, the sort that might be used by a tourist, not a professional traveller. All Special Forces had them, just one more way to blend into the background. The Arab behind the plastic looked at the document then paused, looking up at Chris without saying anything. With great effort, Chris managed to look straight back at him and continue breathing.

"What is your purpose here?" the man asked in heavily accented English, holding his gaze.

"I'm here to do a little investing," replied Chris. "I'm looking for property and possibly an engagement ring."

He kept it to that and waited for the response. He got nothing, just a continued look for a few seconds then the passport was scanned. He couldn't read what had come up on the screen as his Arabic was minimal but it all seemed to be taking just that little bit too long, certainly longer than the last few people before him. He was starting to get a bad feeling about this. Surely they couldn't have been rumbled so early in the mission. In any case, Dubai was a neutral country and even if he had been flagged as UK Forces, the Allies were coming in and out of the country all the time for various reasons. Suddenly, the man seemed to shout at the supervisor at the back of the hall and Chris's adrenalin flared momentarily, but in one fluid motion the Officer flipped open the passport at a blank page, stamped it, handed it back and beckoned to the next person in the queue. Chris took it and mumbled thank you, "*Shukran*", one of the few Arabic words he knew. As he moved away, the supervisor came across and there followed what seemed like a heated conversation where the clerk gestured at his screen. Chris kept his pace steady and walked on towards baggage reclaim and customs. Surely it wouldn't be like this all the way.

It only took a couple of minutes for the bag to come through and he waited patiently, trying to look around nonchalantly for Louis. Their eyes met across the carousel but they passed no sign of recognition, just a pause of a few seconds. Chris was out of practice and this was a lesson for him. Don't read more into the situation than was there. Fight only what you see. If called into action react hard and fast but otherwise keep your cool. As yet, there was nothing to worry about. Somehow he wondered how long that would last.

They took separate cabs to the same hotel, the Al Habtoor on Jumeirah Beach. It was ten in the evening by now and you would have thought that rush hour might have ended, but not here in Dubai. The trip from the airport was only eighteen miles but while the city had expanded at an exponential rate, the transport system had not. Rush hour here started at about three in the afternoon and would continue until about two in the morning. The new metro system would make a significant improvement when finally completed but for now, travellers just had to endure the stop start traffic. They crawled along the Sheikh Zahad Road that passed by the Old Quarter, then through the more modern city markets and out into the hotel belt at Jumairah. Here you found the Mall of the Emirates, one of the more splendid in the Gulf, complete with full length indoor ski slope, truly a marvel of the Middle East.

Chris passed the Al Burj, the sail shaped seven star hotel that was true opulence, complete with gold taps and butlers to every suite. Shortly after he pulled up outside his own, not bad but not up to the Al Burj standard, although there was an old white Rolls Royce parked outside for some reason, he guessed to give it an air of class. He walked in through the central lobby between the two towers of the hotel and into the blessed cool of the air conditioning. Even in June and in the late evening, the humidity and temperature were reaching uncomfortable levels. Louis was already checking in and Chris waited behind him until welcomed forward by another member of staff. As Louis turned away he mumbled something about the downstairs bar in half an hour. Chris completed his registration and crossed the marble floor to the lifts following the porter that had taken his small case. There were marble floors in all these hotels; oil had been a true gift from God to these otherwise resource-sparse nations. He was whisked noiselessly through fourteen floors in seconds and with a soft hiss, the lift doors opened onto a plush corridor, his man leading the way to his room a short distance down and on the right. After needlessly showing him that the curtains opened and closed and that the fridge light did indeed go on and off when you opened the door, Chris gave in and slipped him the tip he so obviously wanted before grabbing a quick shower, then down to the lobby again to find the bar Louis had mentioned.

They were the only two of the eight-man team staying in this hotel, so it was fairly safe to be seen together. Stairs led Chris down to a subterranean level, past a well equipped but empty gym and into a dim bar called ironically, *The Underground*, with London's finest tube signs emblazoned on every wall. He spotted Louis in a fairly secluded corner booth, one that would allow a degree of privacy, away from the groups of Japanese kids playing pool. He grabbed himself a beer and made his way across.

"What do you think so far you fat old bastard?" Louis chirped enthusiastically.

"I'm quite enjoying the adrenalin rushes," Chris replied. "I'd forgotten what it feels like to be in the field but it's what I joined for all those years ago and fundamentally it hasn't changed. I'm loving it."

"Glad to hear it; and this is just the start. Wait until the bullets start flying and we'll see the adrenalin really start to flow. At that point you just hope it's not brown. As long as you don't get too excited and do anything stupid, that'll be fine."

"Have you heard from the others?" Chris asked.

"No and I won't until the morning. I've arranged to meet one of each pair at various points around the Emirates Mall, just to make sure they're all OK, then about midday we'll pick up Bobby and Pat at their hotel and carry on to Fujairah. It should take us about three hours if my reckoning is right. Dodger will bring the others in a second 4x4 about the same time, so we should arrive together. Sound about right to you? I'm relying on the boat being ready for us."

"No problem," assured Chris. "She got in on Thursday and will be ready to leave the day after tomorrow on Monday. We've got rooms booked for us in the crew hotel for tomorrow night and we sail at ten the following morning."

"In that case, I suggest we get our heads down and you can come with me to the Mall tomorrow. I wouldn't want you stewing by yourself in the room and inventing something with that vivid imagination of yours. The car is being delivered early so I'll meet you out of the front of the hotel at eight."

They finished their beers and headed off to their respective rooms, Chris first with Louis a couple of minutes later. So far he thought it had all gone pretty well. The men were in country, the sub was waiting for them in port and the supply chain had delivered their kit the day before. All they had to do was get across the peninsula and they were away on the second leg of their mission.

Chris got into the lift and pressed fourteen. With an almost imperceptible slowing announcing his arrival, the doors opened. As he looked down the corridor, a solitary Arab in traditional dress turned away from a door and walked towards him. Chris stepped out but something seemed wrong and he felt another ounce of adrenalin surge into his blood stream. The man walked purposefully and as they closed each other, Chris could feel his muscles tensing. What was it? What had set him off? The man seemed to be staring at him, or was it more that he was deliberately ignoring him? Chris's internal alarm bells were deafening. He couldn't see the man's right hand, which seemed to be held behind him slightly, as if carrying something close to his body. Why would he be doing that? He clenched his own just in case it was needed in a hurry but he had nothing else to defend himself with if attacked. They got within ten feet, then five and then their eyes locked together. Just as Chris thought he was about to explode into action in response, they passed and he was clear, the immediate tension flooding out of him as if a relief valve had been lifted. He walked on for a couple of paces before looking over his shoulder. The Arab had continued but this time his right hand was in front of his body and his left was reaching for the lift button. What was in that hand? Chris replayed the scene on getting out of the lift. Was he going mad and this whole thing just a figment of his over tired and stressed imagination or had there been something? And then he had it, the room the man had been turning away from was his, he was almost sure. He spun around to see the lift doors closing and again he looked at the man, this time getting a glimpse of the right hand. There was nothing in it, but was that a faint smile on the man's face? What the hell was going on?

He reached his door and looked at it closely, trying to see if there were any marks that suggested it had been tampered with. There were none but he decided to go very carefully in any case. He pushed the card into the slot and when he heard the lock click he pushed. It opened slowly but nothing else happened, thank God. Moving very slowly, he stepped inside and stood there, breathing, smelling the atmosphere. Was there anything different? Could he pick up the faint smell of a musky cologne that hadn't been there before, or was it just the smell of the room freshener? He flicked on the light and all seemed normal. He inched forward, straining to hear anything different. A quick scan and everything seemed to be where he had left it. He moved towards the bathroom and pushed on the partly closed door. It moved slightly but seemed to stop before fully opening. He froze and wondered what to do. Another slight push and again there was a slight give, but not enough. He edged closer to see if there was room between the door and the frame to see through; there wasn't. In case there was someone concealed behind the door he decided to try the direct approach and gave himself a count of three then barged hard with his shoulder, aiming to use the door as a weapon. This time the door gave and he found himself propelled forward, throwing the door aside as he turned, only to find the towel from his earlier shower on the floor between the door and the bath, preventing its full movement.

This was ridiculous. He straightened up and turned on the light fully, illuminating a perfectly normal bathroom, with his toiletries where he had left them and a slight sheen of water still on the floor. He went back into the main room and looked around, this time feeling foolish. Again it was a perfectly normal scene. His bag lay over by the dresser where he had left it and his sliding wardrobe was slightly ajar where he had hung up his clothes for the morning. In short, there was nothing to suggest that anyone had been there at all. He wondered if he had imagined the whole thing and replayed the mental picture from getting out of the lift. Where had the man been? Had it been his room? Could he swear that the man had looked at him that way or given the last few minutes was it more likely that his imagination was playing tricks and that he had made everything up?

He sat down heavily on the side of the bed and blew out a long breath. He had to get a grip of himself. At this rate, he was going to find it hard enough to make it to Fujairah, let alone get to the end of the mission. He was beginning to think that he had made a big mistake by believing that he still had the mental reserves to make it with the players again. Was he just fooling himself as a result of some sort of middle aged crisis and by doing so getting himself into an operation that he was totally unsuited and unready for, making him a liability to the other members of the team? Chris decided to say nothing of this to Louis. It was up to him to sort out his own demons, regain the cold dispassionate resolve that he had always prided himself on. Nothing was going to stop him from being involved in the take down of Mustafa Al Said, especially not himself.

He decided not to waste any more time on this indulgence and got ready for bed. He brushed his teeth and took one last long look in the mirror.

"Are you ready?" he asked himself aloud after he had stared deep into his own eyes.

When his reflection said nothing in return, his head dropped and he looked at the floor; and there it was. In the slight dampness left after his shower only a couple of hours earlier was a footprint. It wasn't his. It was smaller than his own with a pattern on the sole of the shoe that didn't match the light Timberland trainers that he was wearing.

Fucking Hell.

He put his clothes back on and put in a call to Louis' mobile.

"What's up Tonto?" Louis said sleepily. "Is it morning already?"

"Mate, get over here, we need to talk."

"Chris, I've missed you but if this is some plan to get me alone in a hotel room with you, I have to say you're a lovely man but you're just not my type."

"Louis, stop clowning around and get over here. This is important."

"All right all right. Keep your negligee on, I'll be there in ten."

Chris sat on the bed and thought about it all. There was a knock on the door in five minutes and Louis was there.

"What's happened?"

"We've been busted."

"What do you mean?"

Chris explained what had happened while Louis sat in silence, considering the options.

"That's not good news Chris," he said finally. "But fundamentally nothing has changed. We're just tourists spending a night in a hotel on our way to Fujairah with some friends. We have nothing in our luggage to suggest anything different and we have a perfect right to be here. We'll carry on with the plan but tomorrow as soon as we get to the sub we'll talk to the Captain and use his secure equipment to tell Head Quarters what's happened."

"I'm actually quite relieved," commented Chris. "I thought my mind was going into overdrive after so long away."

"Seems to me that your instincts are just where they used to be," replied Louis. "Trust them, my friend. You always used to and it kept us both alive on more than one occasion." Louis stepped outside then as a parting shot grinned and said over his shoulder, "If I were you I would double lock the door though, just in case," then walked swiftly down the hall.

Chris shut the door and did as Louis had suggested. He looked around and considered his defensive options. He had no weapons but there was a pen that could always be used to stab and the spare pillow for a shield. He lay down and tried to close his eyes but he was too pumped up to sleep immediately. Eventually he enjoyed the half sleep that accompanied any mission, if you were lucky.

Before he knew it, his alarm was going off and he got out of bed. He should have been groggy but the adrenalin still seemed to be in the bloodstream and his mind felt sharper than ever. Clearly, as he absorbed each incident he was dropping back into this old self, getting mentally harder. The events of the night before no longer worried him and he looked forward to what the day would bring. In a couple of hours they would be into the desert where he had spent so much time and a few hours after that he would be back onboard a submarine. There were people seemingly alerted against them, that much was obvious, but who they were or what they wanted only excited him now. It was the promise of impending action that had always driven him and he could feel that now looming large.

He showered and dressed, ready to meet Louis and after a light breakfast he went down to the front desk for eight. At ten past a long wheelbase Mitsubishi Pajero pulled up outside, that familiar face looking in from the driver's seat. He went outside and jumped in as Louis pulled out of the crescent drive and into the morning traffic. It was already relatively busy with mostly city commuters, Arab style, supplemented by the open backed lorries carrying the blue robed building workers that were engaged on the next monumental edifice. They were on the coast road instead of the highway for the first mile but it wasn't too bad and they reached the Mall within about twenty minutes.

They parked up and walked through the impressive front entrance onto the ground floor of the two story building, cocooned by the sandy marble that was such a hallmark of the higher end of Dubai life. The arbitrary guard on the automatic doors made the pretence of paying some sort of interest, as they always did, but they entered unmolested, straight into a central ground floor café space. They had three people to meet, initially on the first floor and they climbed the ornate stairs immediately in front of them, turning left at the top to walk the thirty yards to the De Beers outlet. It was relatively early and the mall was quiet but still you could find the wealthy parading the walkways; the women in their traditional costumes hiding designer clothes underneath and the men, if there were any, sporting designer sunglasses and immaculate robes. They reeked of expensive perfume and their entourage often consisted of a trail of children and servants, usually several paces behind.

As they approached the outlet they could see the Royal Marine Captain and second in command 'Dodger' Long sitting on a bench a little way ahead. He saw them and got up, sauntering over to the impressive display of diamonds. They passed him initially and rounded the corner of the shop stopping at the next window. Dodger followed moments later and came close enough that they could talk in lowered voices.

"How ready are you?" Louis asked, getting straight to the point. "Everything quiet last night?"

"Yes fine," replied Dodger. "We're ready to go."

"OK. We think we may have some local interest so I want you to pick up your passengers and we'll get on the road as soon as possible; I'll give you the details later. About five miles out of town there's a Gulf petrol station on the right, we'll meet up there. Once we're out of the city, I want us all to stay together. Got it?"

"Got it." And with that, Dodger peeled off and headed towards a separate exit.

"One down two to go," muttered Louis.

This time they turned back on themselves and retraced their steps. They walked to the other end of the Mall, towards the wonder that was the full size indoor real snow ski slope, complete with viewing gallery. They expected to see Stan Baxter and sure enough, his familiar frame was leaning against the railings, watching the early morning skiers make their descents.

Chris stopped early and went to look at the cinema off to one side, feigning interest first in the film listings, then grabbing a position at the far end of the ski viewing rail out of earshot of the others. He scanned the few people that were milling around while Louis and Stan got close enough to talk and saw nothing but a younger generation of Arab, absorbed in the spectacle in front of them and being entertained while their mothers spent a fortune. Thirty seconds later, Stan moved slowly off to the far end of the mall and Chris joined Louis as they both headed towards the next RV, this time back on the ground floor.

Sunderland Bobby was sitting at a coffee shop outside the Rolex concern, drinking a bottle of water and gazing longingly into the window. They sat down at the table next to him.

"I want a gold one," the slightly lovesick man pined, still not taking his eyes off the display.

Louis smiled. "Maybe if you're good, Daddy will get you one for Christmas. For the time being get your arse in gear and be ready to be picked up in forty minutes; we're leaving early. Everything OK with you and Peanut?"

"Sort of boss but I'm not sure. I think I may have been tailed this morning and both of us have been feeling uncomfortable, as if something isn't quite right. Nothing we can put our finger on, just a gut feeling."

"Well you're in good company. Chris here got the same feeling yesterday and his privacy was invaded, so to speak, last night and not in a good way. I'll explain on the trip."

"Roger that," Bobby replied and made to go.

"Just be cool Bobby," Louis finished. "There's nothing to be worried about yet. If anyone had wanted to have a go at us, they would have done so by now."

"Not a problem skipper, it's not me man, it's that fanny Peanut. I could swear he's a girl in drag. I've long suspected he was hiding a lovely pair underneath those baggy shirts of his. One day I'll have a rummage around and see there's any truth in the rumour but he's bigger than me so I'll have to choose me time, maybe get him pissed first. See you in forty."

They stayed at the table for a minute or two longer, ordering a couple of bottles of water to go and watched the passersby. There was nothing out of the ordinary and they moved on as soon as their drinks arrived, finding their Pajero where they had left it. A cursory check seemed to show nothing had been tampered with and they drove back to the hotel to grab their gear. A quick turn around and Chris was back down in the lobby, waiting for his friend, who turned up moments later. They paid their bills and as Chris turned to his left towards the revolving door, he froze. There, getting out of a black Mercedes on the forecourt was the man from the corridor, this time with a second man following and another in the front alongside the driver.

"Louis, that's him."

Louis turned and looked at the man leading through the entrance. They were only a few yards away and it was too late to avoid them so they stayed where they were. As the Arab came through, he glanced to his left and saw them standing there and with a slight double take, he'd given himself away. Both the newcomers carried on to the gift shop at the back of the entrance atrium, staring ahead once again but it was too late. He knew that he had been made and that was sloppiness on his part. Whatever he was doing or whoever he was working for, it was pretty obvious he was meant to be trailing, not engaging.

There were no alternative options; Louis and Chris had to carry on. They picked up their bags and made their way outside, passing behind the black Mercedes to their 4x4. As they loaded up, they could see the two men inside the hotel approaching the front of the entrance and Louis started the engine.

"Bollocks to this," Louis said. "Let's lose them in the traffic," and he accelerated fairly hard towards the exit and the increasingly busy main road. A quick check in the rear view saw the two men running hurriedly to their own car and it surged into motion behind them. Luckily the inadequacies of the Dubai road system worked perfectly for the Brits. By the time they had got off the roundabout, there were already half a dozen cars between them and their pursuers and before long, a couple of shifts of lanes and some shielding by a handily placed lorry allowed them to watch the pursuers sail past, weaving aggressively in and out of the traffic in an effort to catch up. By taking the next turning off the main road they were clear to get to the RV with Bobby and Peanut.

"Well I guess that sort of confirms it then," Chris said matter-of-factly. "I wonder who the fuck they are."

"God knows," replied Louis. "What I'm interested in is how they knew we were here. It looks like we may have to watch our step on this one Chris. I reckon that bastard back home, whoever he is, is up to his tricks again. I don't know about you but I've got a couple of scores to settle now."

By the time they pulled up outside the hotel, they were twenty minutes late and Bobby and Peanut were waiting in the lobby looking anxious.

"We were starting to wonder what had happened to you," Peanut chipped in as they got straight into the vehicle. "Any snags?"

"The company that Chris had last night turned up again, this time with a few friends," replied Louis. "They decided to try and come along for the party."

"So what exactly did happen last night?" asked Bobby.

Louis pulled out in to the traffic and continued to head north along the Sheikh Zahad Road while Chris gave them the low down on the previous evening. After he had finished and had brought them up to date with the morning's event, the two of them sat in silence.

"What's going on Boss?" Peanut asked. "Are we in the shit here or what?"

"To tell you the truth, Peanut, I'd like to know exactly the same thing. It seems pretty obvious that we've been compromised; by whom or to what extent I don't know. It could just be the Dubai security services keeping tabs on us. It could be something else entirely. Without having a chat with those men or unless something else happens, we're not going to find out either way. At the moment, we need to get to the submarine where we can make some secure transmissions and decide what the best plan is. My gut feeling is that we crack on and just accept the risk. I would prefer to keep the element of surprise and we may still have it, but we don't know what our situation is exactly and until we do, this thing is too important to let go. We've still got one bastard to nail unless I'm told otherwise."

They continued north and passed the Old Quarter to their right, the sprawling centre and traditional sandstone buildings a reminder of the ancient trading nature of the city. Soon though, it was back to the newly built office blocks and out towards the airport. This time, however, they drove past and turned east heading out into the desert. It was amazing how quickly the glitz of the city ended.

Their route was to take them along the east-west Dhaid highway across the Emirate to the port of Fujairah, on the east coast and to the south of the Straits of Hormuz. Despite being primarily a commercial shipping port, the town had become a well used asset for some of the coalition's maritime forces as it contained some support infrastructure for surface warships, but more specifically for submarines. This meant warships could avoid having to transit the potentially vulnerable waterway to the north that was constantly held at risk by the Iranian naval forces but more importantly, keep unfettered access to the Gulf of Oman, the strategic approach to the area.

Before too long, the multi-storied buildings on the outskirts of the city were starting to peter out, to be replaced by strings of low storey merchant shops in the typical Arab manner, each one selling everything from soft drinks to bags of rice to washing up liquid and easy chairs. Occasionally you would get the odd building trying to be more grand, offering rich carpets or 'artefacts' of various sorts, but generally it was the small traders that dominated, giving the tourist the feeling that you were finally seeing the genuine nation, not the façade of massive wealth that Dubai city tended to suggest.

Five miles after the city proper had stopped they sighted the service station where they were meeting the rest. Sure enough, as they pulled in, they saw the other Pajero towards the back of the lot, all four men inside. After a quick acknowledgement they pulled straight back out onto the road and were away. There seemed to be safety in numbers and Chris started to relax. There was no sign of being pursued, indeed there was very little traffic at all, but this was now approaching lunch time and as the song said, only mad dogs went out in the middle of the day here, or tourists.

They all fell into an easy silence as the scenery started to change. Everyone knew that the Arabian Peninsula was fairly inhospitable but the terrain here brought it home with a smack. As you looked away from the road you could see several different landscapes stretching away towards the horizon. First there was the scrub land; flat, hard, dusty and bare, and with the exception of a few withered looking thorny bushes, sandy brown in colour, the sort of colour you would expect from a desert panorama. Next however, and seemingly out of nowhere, rose staggering mini mountains, jagged and steep as if the ground had been ripped apart and the rock thrown up into violent peaks. Most strange was the colour, not the same as the scrub, but a mixture of purple and black, angry, as if the ground had bled in protest at being ravished so badly. This was nature demonstrating its power and declaring its dominance, reminding man that he may build his shiny cities, but the world belonged to another. It served as a signpost to anyone about to venture out into the desert that they should beware, they were there on sufferance and were stepping into a world that could claim them at any point.

Two more hours of the dramatic scenery and they had come out of the mountainous regions heading towards the outskirts of Fujairah. It was early afternoon and not only was the traffic increasing but they were starting to see more people. They gained the outskirts of the town easily enough then made their way directly to the commercial port, where the submarine was berthed. The Emirate had always been supportive of the UN coalition and had been especially accommodating here, given the circumstances. It was fairly hard for the government to play both sides of the political coin, trying to appear supportive of international efforts to bring peace to the region but at the same time having to show their fellow Arabs that they weren't whipping boys for the West.

They had done well and the submarine was about as secure here as it was ever going to be. Although it was a commercial port, the authorities had constructed a barrier of shipping containers that shrouded the hull from view; there was no way that anyone could attack it from the landward side of the facility. You also had to pass through several different layers of security to get onto the site and even then drive a distance across open ground to the edge of the barrier. Forced to get out of your vehicles, you were checked by armed police to ensure you were on an access list before you got to walk anywhere near the boat.

As they pulled up and opened the doors, they were suddenly hit by that wall of heat so common in the Middle east as you leave the false cool of air conditioning and enter the furnace of reality. They walked towards the guards and Louis led the way. By some miracle, their names were actually on the access list and they were let through after walking through a metal detector and with a cursory pat down from the attendant. Chris now took the lead. The situation was changing subtly; this was moving into his world and he immediately felt a slight release of tension as he stepped onto familiar ground.

By the time they had got onto the gangway Chris could see the Commanding Officer climbing up through the Main Access Hatch to meet him. Commander Mike Saggers had joined the Royal Navy with Chris and had made it through the ranks ahead of him, primarily due to the time Chris had spent away in the Special Boat Service. They had been junior officers together on his first submarine, *HMS Torbay*, the same class as *Talisman*. The CO reached the casing, turned to the gangway and as he caught sight of his old friend, a large smile spread across his face. Chris returned it with equal warmth and moved to meet him.

"You old bugger," Mike said in his trademark manner, a voice that carried with it an implication that a bit of conspiratorial humour was lurking just beneath the surface. "I nearly popped a pile when I got the signal. What the fuck is this all about? You're not going through some sort of mid-life crisis are you because if you are, go and buy a Porsche or something, playing with sharp sticks can get you hurt."

Chris smiled back at his long time friend. "This has got nothing to do with me and everything to do with that old goat Captain Absolom. The first thing I knew was when I was called into his office six days ago and was told that I was deploying."

"So is this your band of merry men?"

Chris turned and introduced the team starting with Louis. "This is Major 'Louis' Armstrong the Officer Commanding the mission and an old friend."

"Afternoon Captain," offered Louis. "I think we've met before actually, round at Chris's place a few years ago."

"I think you may be right there," replied Mike, extending his hand in a warm greeting. "Face looks familiar anyway. Well let's not stand around here for too long or we'll melt onto the casing, get down below out of the heat and you can tell me what all this kerfuffle is about."

He turned and headed back to the Hatch. With a speed that always amazed non-submariners, he disappeared down the vertical ladder in a second or two and was gone. Chris followed him at the same speed and that left the Royal Marines to make their way gingerly through the narrow space.

As Chris reached the bottom he looked around at the familiar picture and wondered how long it would be before he was the one in charge of such a machine. It was a truly special feat of engineering; almost a billion pounds worth of technology as complicated as the Space Shuttle, powered by a nuclear reactor and with up to one hundred and thirty crew members. Every time he had stood on the bridge, it had thrilled him. Every time he had sailed from port, he would look at the sea in front of him and wonder what journeys lay ahead. Every time he came back, as he sat at home in his favourite armchair for the first time, he smiled at what he had experienced. He was, in truth, overdue for promotion and was ready for it several times over.

The submarine itself, despite outward appearances, was cramped on the inside. The CO's cabin was just at the bottom of the Main Access Hatch off the main passageway that led forward to the Control Room and aft through the reactor airlock to the engineering spaces. Mike was waiting at the small door.

"Chris, why don't you and Louis take a pew in here with me and my boys will take care of the rest of your gang. That way we can have a bit of privacy. We've set aside the torpedo compartment for you with all the kit that arrived yesterday and we've put up some bunks. There's not enough room in here for everyone so the others may as well make themselves at home down below."

Chris and Louis filed off and the remaining members of the team were taken down another set of stairs, this time not quite as steep, on to 'two deck' where the living quarters were. Once they were in the cabin, the Captain shut the curtain behind them and sat down at his desk. There was just enough space for one to live, with the bed folding back to make a seat during the day. With three, it was definitely 'cosy'.

"What gives then Chris?" Mike was typically direct; it seemed to be a trait of the higher ranking submariners. There wasn't much point in hanging around, just get the facts, analyse them and make a decision.

Chris started from the beginning with an outline of the last six days, leaving out the potential traitor aspect; had it only been that long? When it got to the last twenty-four hours, Mike sat back and put his hands behind his head pursing his lips. After a few seconds he asked, "Does anyone back home know about what's happened overnight?"

"Not yet," replied Louis. "If it's all right with you, I'd like to phone HQ telling them where we are and what's happened. We'll see after that but I'm going to recommend that we crack on with the plan as it stands. How are we set for sailing?"

"All good so far. When the kit started arriving I told my lot that we were doing a bit of in theatre Special Forces training with you guys, so they're expecting you and looking forward to it. You shouldn't get too many questions and you're all capable of keeping your own counsel until tomorrow I'm sure. I'll tell them after we've sailed what's really going on."

It was a fact that whenever the Special Forces were onboard submarines, they kept themselves to themselves, not out of any distrust for the crew, just that they were usually focussed on the job in hand and they would nearly always be a tight knit group. Being who they were generally gained them an automatic measure of respect anyway, so it was seldom an issue.

Chris and Louis finished the conversation and joined the rest of the team. After they had put their kit away in the 'Bomb Shop', next to the torpedoes, they got the guys a tour around the boat to familiarise them with the layout. Chris and Louis went to the Communications Office and after clearing the area put in a secure phone call back to HQ. They were under strict instructions to report only to select individuals and the story they had to tell needed to go straight to the top, to the Director.

"Sir, it's Major Armstrong."

"Louis how's it going?" replied General Holbrook.

"Everything is going OK, Sir, but someone knows we are here."

"How's that, Major?"

Louis told the Director the latest, from arrival in Dubai to their trip across. He ended by summarising. "All that's really happened is that someone has taken an interest in our rooms and our movements. We don't know who or why at the moment. It may only be Dubai security, we just don't know. Bottom line is that we're here now and we're good to go. We can see how the land lies when we get to Somalia, which could be entirely benign."

There was a pause at the end of the line and then the Director spoke in a measured way.

"I'm sorry to hear all that Louis but you're right. We don't know what the true situation is so we have to go on. We'll make enquiries from here and if we hear anything after you've sailed tomorrow, we'll let you know. I have to say I'm disappointed that we should have been compromised so early and it raises some questions this end. Where are you staying tonight?"

"We've got some accommodation in the crew hotel in town. We should be able to lie low there for the evening and then we're off at about ten tomorrow."

"I have to say I'm not over the moon about you being ashore in another hotel; it's a risk we don't really have to take." There was another short pause. "All right. Stay with the crew though and stay alert. There's obviously something going on and I want you all on that boat tomorrow. Keep in touch as and when you feel appropriate. Anything else?"

"No Sir, that's it," replied Louis and the Director rang off.

Chris and Louis turned to each other.

"We're still on," said Louis. "Just keep our heads down and get out to sea."

"Excellent. Let's get out of here," started Chris. "I need a decent shower before we get going. You can never really get clean once you're at sea on one of these things."

It had only been a couple of hours since the boys had been onboard, but already the temperature outside had lowered significantly, as it seemed to do here. There was a point, around four o'clock in June, where it eased off to bearable and the evidence of life increased accordingly. Once in the Pajeros they drove to the hotel that had been booked for them and checked in with the minimal baggage needed for the night. As they pulled into the Holiday Inn with its familiar green and white signage, nothing seemed out of the ordinary. What they didn't see was the young goatherd sitting on the rough rise on the opposite side of the road get up off the ground and stare intently at them as they pulled in, or see him turn quickly as they were going in through the door and scuttle away at a run.

They made plans to eat in that night, unlike the rest of the crew who were planning on celebrating their last night in typical Matelot fashion by getting rat arsed, regardless of any direction they were given. After long showers, Chris and Louis ordered from the room menu and made small talk. There would be plenty of time to go over the plans on the voyage, when they were all together. The rules of the job meant that you couldn't make personal calls and Chris's thoughts turned to Elizabeth. It was early afternoon at home and she would be wondering where he was, what he was doing. He tried not to think of it. There was enough going on for him without being distracted by that sort of thing; it was a luxury he couldn't afford. Tonight they would get a good night's sleep, get down to the boat early and run through the drills that they would need when they were dropped off and brought back on the submarine before and after the mission. Sleep came at about eleven.

The explosion slammed them awake, the walls shuddering as the force of the event caved in the sides of the hotel what seemed like feet away. The both of them threw themselves to the floor in a typically instant reaction then took stock.

"What the fuck was that?" exclaimed Chris.

"I've got a fair idea," said Louis from the other side of the room.

They grabbed the clothes they had been dressed in the night before and went out of the room into the corridor that was filling up with dust and shocked looking people, wide eyed, scared and half asleep. By the sound of it, the explosion had come from the next room along the corridor, heading towards the back of the hotel.

They knew the occupants weren't one of their team but a quick look round the now broken shell of the door told them the unfortunate truth; the two matelos inside wouldn't be joining them later that day. Their bodies lay grotesquely positioned by the blast, covered in blood and dust as the glass from the window had torn through the bed sheets and lacerated their bodies. There was nothing more to be done for them so thoughts turned to mustering the rest of Louis' team. While they did so a few other walking wounded started to stagger along the passageway and the sight of blood and visible injuries goaded them into action.

"Right boys," announced Louis. "We're all here but get in there and see if you can help."

It was as if they had been let off the leash and all bar Louis and Chris sprinted into the thick of it to see if there was anything they could do. It was obvious that they had been the target; it was the least they could do to assuage the guilt.

"I need to find out what's going on," Louis continued. "Are you coming Chris?"

They moved out into the corridor and made their way through the people towards the lobby. As they did, they could hear the wail of sirens coming their way as the emergency services caught up with the event. They started to see some pretty scared and partially bloodied sailors standing in stunned silence, waiting for guidance and help, but for the moment there was none, understandable given the small time elapsed since the incident. By the time they got to the lobby, the police had made it there too and they were met by a crowd of people, a mixture of crew and civilians shouting or just making every effort to get out of the building. They did, however, see the Captain of the submarine on the periphery.

"I'm sorry Captain, I think you've lost two of your crew. They were in the room next to ours and we were obviously the target," said Louis. "Given what's happened now and in the past the worst thing we can do now is to hang around waiting to get slotted again."

Mike Saggers looked devastated and it was a few seconds before he spoke. "I'm going to make sure there are people ready to take care of my men here but it's obviously too risky to be alongside in this port. I want everyone on board and I'm sailing as soon as the ship's company can be brought back. The reactor is flashed up and we're set to go so get your men together and wait for transport. My men will deal with the details but for now we need to get the fuck out of here."

Within the hour the transport had arrived and the crew were shepherded out past the evacuated hotel guests and crowds of local police. The visitors looked terrible and had been shocked into silence as the night's event hit home. Remarkably, it seemed that there were few serious casualties among them. With the exception of the two dead, the crew were relatively unscathed, certainly able to be treated onboard with the limited facilities available and with the exception of the damage to the building, it would be a lasting mental issue, not a physical one.

The coaches were similarly quiet as they drove the fifteen minutes to the dock, the men groggy and on a downer after the massive spike of adrenalin and the news of the deaths. Somehow the Captain had got the tug support they needed and by half five they were ready to go, the light and stillness of dawn providing an extraordinarily peaceful backdrop to the departure, belying the recent chaos. The Captain took it particularly carefully, given the obviously still shocked condition of his men, but before long they had cleared the harbour wall and were out into the flat calm of the Gulf of Oman.

Louis had gathered the men together in the Weapons Compartment to keep them out of the way. "It looks as if our suspicions are confirmed boys. We've been busted and this can only be Al-Qaeda. Bottom line is that we've got away and we're safe. I'll get in touch with HQ but for now settle down as much as you can. We'll start running through the plan starting tomorrow."

He took Chris and Dodger aside. "I think we should start talking to the Captain and working out exactly what to do next. I'm half thinking we should abort."

"Not a chance," replied Chris immediately. "Once we get to Somalia, the game changes again. They had us from the moment we got into Dubai and tracked us through. Somalia will be different. They won't know where we are coming from and we will be driving the moves there."

Louis paused. "I hope you're right Chris. I suppose we have a way to go before we can justify backing out. We'll put that to the Captain and HQ when we get in touch."

At that point the ship's tannoy system came over the air. "Fall out from Harbour Stations, second watch, watch diving. Major Armstrong and Lt Cdr Edwards are requested in the Captain's cabin."

"I guess they're playing our tune," Chris said, without a trace of humour.

"Lead the way, my friend," added Louis. "This is your patch."

The two men made their way through the submarine to the Captain's cabin. The whole place was eerily quiet as the ship's company continued to be in a state of shock. The messes seemed to be full but no-one was talking.

They moved up to one deck and looked into the Control Room. There was the usual bustling efficiency as the men prepared to dive the submarine for the first time, but they were going about their business in near silence. There was no doubt that their arrival had made an impact; a number of fearful sidelong glances confirmed that. Chris and Louis turned away and headed aft, pausing outside the curtain, which was swept back by the CO.

"I think I had better know what the fuck is going on Chris, don't you?"

CHAPTER 4

Two days before the bombing in Fujairah Mustafa had got off a plane at Heathrow and shuddered. How he hated this country: the weather, cold and uninspiring even on this early summer's day, but most of all how he hated the people. They swarmed around like an army of ants, secure in their beautifully materialistic surroundings, paid for by the exploitation of the rest of the world during a bygone era. They didn't realise how lucky they were and how much they owed.

The day before, he had heard from his contact in the UK; the Somali camp had been discovered and a team was being put together to track Mustafa down. He jumped straight onto the first flight to the UK. The end of training was close but he needed another two uninterrupted weeks with his men before they would be ready to infiltrate the heart of Britain, France and Germany. A dramatic simultaneous strike would put them back onto the world stage, breaking out of the quagmire that Afghanistan had become. If there was a threat to that glorious goal he needed to hear the facts first hand so he could work out what had to be done. Nothing worked as well as a face to face meeting.

He was wearing a very smart suit, playing the wealthy Arab businessman. The British always respected the appearance of wealth; it played to their misplaced sense of the class system, where worth was measured by the clothes you wore and the car you drove. He was quite safe; he had a variety of passports issued from Saudi Arabia, plus a couple from the UAE. Even given his notoriety he could move from port to port without fear of recognition. He switched on his phone and waited for it to register with the local network. His Al-Qaeda driver was waiting for him and once through the terminal and in the back of the Range Rover he rang his contact.

"Hello," came the familiar voice he had talked to in the desert only a few days before.

"We need to meet. I'm on the way down now. I suggest my hotel in two hours. You can explain yourself there."

"What the fuck do you think you are doing?" came back the immediate reply. "You're risking everything. Don't you understand the danger you are putting us both in? Christ, if they have the slightest inkling about me then we're both dead."

"Watch your mouth, traitor. You belong to me, never forget that. I hold your life in my hands. I want to know everything you've got and then I can take appropriate steps. Bring details of who, how many and where... I'll take it from there. I'm on a flight out tomorrow so don't disappoint. Borrowdales, outside Southampton, two hours, that's an order."

He cut the conversation short. The Englishman needed to understand where he was in the pecking order. He might be almost at the top of his tree here, but he still worked for Mustafa and it was time to deliver a reminder.

He sat back and watched the M3 pass him by, thinking deeply. He needed to act fast and eliminate the Special Forces before they could jeopardise all his work. Apparently they had left the base that morning and were flying out to the Middle East. He didn't know the details yet, but he was sure he could arrange something in any of the countries there. His organisation had support both within and outside all the governments.

A short time later he pulled up outside the luxurious Borrowdales, a very private and beautiful hotel set in the New Forest. An hour after that there was a knock at the door and the Englishman entered looking angry.

"This is suicide, you fool," he snarled. Mustafa's bodyguard started towards him from the other side of the room.

"Stop, both of you," ordered Mustafa in a barked tone that immediately assumed the high ground. "Enough of this. I am getting tired of your attitude. You have almost outlived your usefulness. Just pray that after our business is completed I don't decide to remove you from the picture completely. Now tell me, what is going on? I need to know everything."

Mustafa gestured to a chair opposite him and the man in front of him sat down. As always at these meetings, Mustafa couldn't resist his view straying to the man's right hand, which he had placed upon the arm of the seat. It always amazed him how technology could produce such a life like replica of a limb.

Colonel Robin Taylor, Royal Marines, Director of the Special Boat Service and number two behind General Holbrook was silent for a moment, considering the options. He decided that they were few and paused as he looked at that abomination of a man Mustafa. Why and how had he ever got himself mixed up in all this? It had started so long ago he had difficulty remembering. For twenty years though he had been feeding information as and when he had it, in return for a sizeable increase in the bank account he kept in Switzerland. As his career had blossomed, so had the quality of the information he passed. Now he was the Director at Poole and privy to everything, with the highest access and the ability to tap into sources in every intelligence agency in the land without question, without referral. He was perfect for them. In the past he had saved Mustafa or his people countless times in Afghanistan, Pakistan and Iraq, calling in the position of Special Forces strike teams just in time to allow escape, or the preparation of a strong enough defence to overwhelm the approaching men. A couple of times he had been on those teams himself. A couple of times people had been killed from the information that he had given away. But that was life… or in this case death. They all played a dangerous game and should be prepared to take the consequences; it was every man for himself in the end and he was looking after number one.

He had a very bad feeling about this though. Something was different here. He had been kept out of the loop on this operation and he didn't know why. OK, he had spent the last couple of days supposedly on leave but in reality out in Somalia meeting with Mustafa and this whole thing had moved very quickly, but he couldn't help thinking that it may have been more than co-incidence. Even on his return he had been told nothing officially.

"Well?" pushed Mustafa.

Taylor had managed to control himself. "We have put together a team over the last few days to react to some intelligence about your training camp. We know the position, the terrain and who's there, including you. The men they have selected are just about the best we've got, and one other, you'll be interested to hear. Lieutenant Commander Chris Edwards, remember him?"

"Of course I remember him," Mustafa shot back. "He was your so-called expert on me. But where have they dragged him back from and why? Isn't he out of the game now?"

"Because he's still the expert on you, and from what I hear, he hasn't lost his touch. If I hadn't given you the heads up on numerous occasions, he would have easily had you in the past, so don't underestimate him."

Mustafa looked thoughtful. "Where are they now?"

"They left the camp this morning and got on their way today. I think they were on the morning flights to Dubai. The plan is to stay one night there, go to Fujairah tomorrow and sail the day after that to be taken into area."

"What do you mean 'you think'?" Mustafa repeated slowly.

Colonel Taylor hesitated; he had given too much away and weakened his position already. He decided to be honest, or at least as honest as was necessary.

"This operation is being kept on very close hold. Even I am being kept away. The Director himself and the Ops Officer at HQ are the only people in on the planning. No-one else has access." What he didn't say was that this was extremely unusual - he had never heard of it before and that was what made him so nervous.

"So how do you know about it at all then?"

If there was one thing that Taylor could be sure of though, it was that Mustafa wasn't stupid. This was why every lie had to be kept as simple as possible; the inconsistencies could be spotted by someone skilled immediately. Did the Colonel give everything away now, or could he hang on to this last trump card? He had pretty much backed himself into a corner and after a few seconds, decided that he would have to come clean.

"Because I, and in effect you, have someone on the team."

Mustafa paused then smiled broadly. "Once again my friend, you have proved your worth," he said through that sickening, nauseating grin of his. "And who exactly is your man?"

Again, Taylor hesitated. He was being kept on the back foot and didn't like it, forced into giving away too much of his advantage.

"I think I would like to keep that to myself for now," he said.

"No matter, Colonel. He's your man, just as long as he keeps you in the loop that will be fine. What else do you know? How are they coming after me?"

"All I know at the moment is that they'll be inserted into the coast in the next eight to ten days. They'll make their way across the scrub and watch the camp, then either send back information, interrupt what's going on or if they can, snatch you. If I were you, I would get the hell out."

"But you're not me are you, Colonel. Let me decide what I do from here. Your job is to keep the information coming to me. Is there anything else I need to know?"

"My man will have a transmitting device on him, but it's small. He won't be able to give constant positions, only sporadic messages when he can, but he will send me updates that I'll forward on to you. They'll be slightly late but it is the best I can do. It would be too dangerous for him to have bigger, more capable equipment that he couldn't explain away. This way he can stay covert. I'll leave you a copy of a map with a coded grid overlaid on top of it. The positional reports I get from him I will forward to you in accordance with those codes."

"Excellent. Colonel. My mood has improved already. Have you any other surprises?"

"No, that's it. I hope it was worth the risk."

"Life is risk, my friend. I am his faithful servant, Allah will protect me. Can you say the same of your God? Now go. I have some phone calls to make."

The Colonel put the map on the table in front of Mustafa then stood up. As he did so the guard took a half step towards him. Taylor stopped him with a piercing look that rooted him to the floor, symptomatic of a powerful man in a position of authority, even though he was the underdog here. Taylor looked once more at Mustafa, feeling the cancer of his own betrayal churn his stomach, then turned and strode to the door. There was no space for regrets. He had chosen this path many years ago and had profited from it. For good or for ill, this was the hand he was playing.

As soon as the door shut, Mustafa grabbed his own phone. By his calculation, the Special Forces would be landing in Dubai in the next couple of hours and were therefore ahead of him. He needed to get hold of his men in Dubai and trail them from the moment they arrived, preferably straight from the airport. When he knew where they were he would work out exactly what he was going to do.

If he understood this correctly, they were staying in the centre of the city tonight, then heading out over the peninsula tomorrow. The city was too crowded for a strike, too risky and he wouldn't want to upset the Dubai government by hasty actions that would alienate the friends Al-Qaeda had there. The desert was tempting but too difficult to get a lock on the target and at such short notice the manpower required would be hard to muster.

Fujairah, that was the place. He would have enough time to call in adequate forces and generate some sort of a plan. And if he remembered rightly it was a smallish town, which meant the security wouldn't be anywhere near as tight as the city, certainly outside of the port. He may even be able to find locals to help; the area there hadn't been totally corrupted by the trappings of western life and it was always easier to get support in the hinterlands, especially with a bit of money.

A succession of calls later and the arrangements were made. He had a team on the case and they would track them down in the hotels to start with, then go from there. He sat back in the chair by the desk and looked out of his room window to the wooded area beyond. He needed the peace to take stock of his position. The enemy had deployed their forces, he had countered with his. As had always been the lot with generals, he could now only stop and wait for events to unfold while considering potential outcomes and counter moves. One thing was for sure, this was a critical time. He was only a few days away from being ready and he was angry that something had given him away. His priority while this phase played out was to get back to Somalia and make sure his troops were taking the final steps they needed. First though, he had a couple of bases to cover here in Europe, then a flying visit to his sponsor who was currently in the Caribbean. Later tonight he would meet with the British co-ordinator, tomorrow he would travel early to Paris by train and do the same there, then a short flight to Munich to complete the triumvirate. His heart surged with pride. This was going to be the greatest gift he could give the Arab nation. Once again they would be taking the fight to the enemy, striking hard and with devastating effect, not only in the flesh but through the media; the legacy promising to live far longer than the act. By the time he got on his flight to the Caribbean he expected to hear from his men in Fujairah. He had to disrupt and if possible kill the British team to give himself the time required to finish his job. This was crucial, this was war, a holy war that he relished. Allah would provide.

He left the hotel the next morning feeling considerably better than the night before. The man arranging the mission in the UK had visited him and it seemed that although the teams in Somalia needed another two weeks, *insha Allah*, all the arrangements here were in place.

The plan was a simple one but would be devastating. The heart of the West was its consumerism. Every week of the year you could go to any of the huge shopping centres throughout Europe and find crowds of drone like people, mostly women accompanied by weak, emasculated men at their beck and call, ready to sign the card and carry the bags. The security at these places was non-existent. At some of the entrances you might find a token uniformed man who would be unable to stop more than a young shop lifter from diving out of the doors. It was a wide open target and symptomatic of the arrogance of the 'First World' that they thought that they were immune. Mustafa's people lived in fear of American bombs, dying by the hundreds while these perpetrators went about their lives remote, unworried and untouched. It made him sick.

It was time to take the fight to these places of domestic tranquillity, to strike at the heart of their society, to make them afraid to engage with even the most basic facets of their lives. Mustafa's men were going to replicate the glorious Mumbai attacks that had been so simple in design, so easy to execute but so powerful in result. At the appointed hour, a team of men would walk into the middle of Lakeside shopping centre outside London, the square of Notre Dame in Paris and the central Bahnhof in Munich, opening fire with automatic rifles and grenades. With each target they would be able to gain easy access through multiple entrances and with each man of a four man team working a different angle, they could herd the gullible before them, slaughtering as they went. The victims wouldn't know where to run; there would be no escape. With a fifth man waiting in a car, they could cause maximum effect and be away inside ten minutes, far too fast for the security services to react. They would also leave delayed fuse grenades to catch the survivors as they thought their nightmare was over. If by any chance the glorious died in the attack, they would immediately become martyrs. As happened with 9/11 and 7/7, the entire Muslim world would rejoice, would realise that they, and therefore Mustafa, had struck a massive blow at the heart of the enemy, which would do wonders for their pride. So simple but so effective. He couldn't wait.

Early the next morning Mustafa set off for Ashford in Kent, to catch the Eurostar to Paris. This was so easy. For the sake of convenience it was now the easiest thing in the world to move around Europe. Didn't they realise how vulnerable this made them? All the border guards would do was a cursory check when they got into France and then allow him free access to scores of countries. It was pathetic.

He boarded the train and within a few minutes was speeding through the 'green and pleasant lands' of the Kent countryside. The fields flashed past and he reflected for a moment on what he was about to do. He would be shaking this peaceful setting to the core. On the outside, nothing would change. On the inside, everything would.

Before long he was in the tunnel. Now this would be a target, he mused. Get a bomb into a car in here and explode it in the middle of the journey and you would succeed beyond your wildest dreams. It would be a suicide mission of course but there were plenty of volunteers. He filed it away for his next project.

As expected the border proved to be no issue and a couple of hours later he was pulling into the Gare du Nord in Paris. He came out of the front of the station and was met again by one of his local team. There was no intention of taking his time, this was business and besides he had a long trip ahead of him. He was driven down to the Seine, past the Eiffel Tower and along to a Sicilian restaurant that overlooked Notre Dame. How ironic that he should be meeting his man at one of the centres of European religion and certainly an iconic place for the French, at the heart of their city. A strike at a French religious centre would send such a powerful message. Religion still had far more sway in France than the UK, something to do with the strictness of the Catholic faith he suspected, so much more powerful a force than the commercialised UK, who worshipped more at the altar of money.

It would be slightly more difficult here as the French were more security minded and it would be unlikely that his men would be able to get into the Cathedral itself, but that was immaterial. The square, even today, was packed with blissfully unaware targets, devout people coming to immerse themselves in the wonder of Notre Dame and tourists taking in the architecture. All they would have to do would be to approach from the three sides in front of the cathedral towers, shooting as they went. It would be a massacre. Their exit would be more difficult as the streets were narrow and likely to get blocked. He would have to be careful who he chose for this mission; they would have to be the more devout, those that wouldn't balk at almost certain death at the hands of French armed police.

His French contact approached the table he had chosen on the pavement, slightly more exposed but with a view of the target area and little chance of being overheard. His bodyguard had taken the table next to him so his privacy was virtually assured. The conversation was brief but again satisfying. All was in place, the weapons, the vehicles, the contacts. All he had to do was to send in the teams.

The next stage was Munich. This time he took an early evening flight that got him in at seven. He was booked into the Konigshof hotel for a night, where he would meet with the German organiser. Mustafa felt slightly irritated after the meeting as this was the only one of the three that wasn't completely ready, despite the German reputation for efficiency. The final delivery of weapons was still to arrive, but he was assured they would be in place within the next few days.

All in all, it had been a very successful trip so far. He was satisfied that each of the targets would provide maximum impact and that his plans as they stood would reap the rewards he wanted. He had one more stop to make on the final leg of his journey but this was the most important. The next morning he would be taking a shuttle to London then boarding a flight to St Lucia. Waiting for him there was the backer. Al-Qaeda itself was a figure head organisation and had relatively limited funds per se. A mission like this took a lot of money and as always, they relied upon a small number of wealthy individuals that, although usually embroiled in the international business scene, were loyal to Allah's cause. Mahmood Al Sarahi was one of them. He had made a fortune in Saudi with contracts in the oil industry and moved on to become a truly international player. He wasn't the richest man in the Middle East but his wealth was counted in the billions. At present he was sitting in his motor cruiser the 'Divine Inspiration' in Marigot Bay on the west coast of St Lucia. It would be Mustafa's last meeting with him before the operation.

Mustafa's phone rang at midnight. This was wrong. While he was on his trips all calls, unless initiated by him were to be kept to an absolute minimum. In the moments following the first ring of the phone his mind was awake and he was functioning at full speed, imagining possibilities, going through options, making plans, as only a military trained man could do. By the time the phone had rung for the second time, he was ready to make decisions. He picked it up.

"Yes?"

"They've gone."

The voice was that of his right hand man, Omar, and the man he trusted more than any other, but even so Mustafa was incensed by the news. "What do you mean they've gone?" he asked with a voice full of ice.

"Our efforts have been unsuccessful and they have left the way they intended. We have been unlucky," said the voice unemotionally.

"Unlucky!" Mustafa tried extremely hard not to shout down the phone. The voice at the other end was silent. He knew him for what he was, an extremely effective and professional man. If there had been an error, it would not have been his; it would have been in the execution, not the planning. There were a few seconds of silence before Mustafa spoke again, this time his voice back under control.

"That is not the news I would have wanted. You can give me the details when I get back. I should be with you in two days."

He ended the call and lay there thinking. What to do? His first gambit had failed but it had always been a risky option, limited in scope and prepared in a few short hours. He knew as a military planner that the secret was in the detail and having as much knowledge as possible about the task ahead. Any operation that was conducted on the hoof was always fraught with danger and liable to error. The next option was going to be Somalia, when the team arrived in country. In some ways, this was preferred. He would be able to choose the time and method of interception, using the considerable assets that he had at his disposal there, and, coupled with the man on the inside, he should be able to plan much more effectively. Yes, he could still achieve what he wanted, albeit slightly closer to home than he had intended. The next question was whether he mentioned any of this to Mahmood. He would not be pleased and may get cold feet about being involved in an operation that may have been compromised, thus rendering him vulnerable by association.

Mustafa took a decision. This was just another part of the military operation, the details of which should remain with him as the military commander. Mahmood was the money and while he wanted to know the plan, the targets and the potential effects i.e. the potential glory, it was best that he be kept divorced from the grittier side of the job. The last thing Mustafa needed was an amateur interfering, even if he did need his cash.

He always flew first class; it was a perk of the job, especially given the man he was going to meet. Unfortunately there were no Arabic airlines that flew from Europe to St Lucia and he was forced to take British Airways. How ironic, he thought, as they smiled and pampered him during the flight. He smiled back and made the right noises, laughing on the inside. If only they knew what was about to happen to them, to their world, with him the architect.

The plane touched down at Henowarra airport on the south of the island after some eight and a half hours in the air. It was a ramshackle affair with low buildings and minimal infrastructure and as he moved through to the laughably titled passport control he decided he liked the place. The people might be misguided in terms of religion but they had an inoffensive attitude that said that they were happy doing what they wanted and weren't concerned about forcing their opinions or way of life upon anyone else. The border officer made some pretence of inspecting his passport knowing full well that she was going to wave him through.

As he moved through the outside doors a man made his way directly towards him and smiled.

"Come with me please," he said, motioning to a large black Mercedes at the kerbside. The car looked out of place next to the Toyota minibuses that were being lined up to take the holiday makers to their destinations. Many of them would be disappointed he thought. He had been to the island once before to visit his patron and had expected the legendary Caribbean jewel. What he had seen was a massive volcanic landscape with grey volcanic beaches and tropical rain forests. In fact, the only beach on the island that fulfilled the 'idyll' criteria belonged to a hotel that had brought the white sand from Trinidad to keep the reputation alive.

The road from the airport to Marigot Bay was extreme, winding its way round the mountainous peaks and although the island was under twenty miles long, the trip took an hour due to the constant switch bends. When he got there however, he had to admit, it deserved its reputation as the most beautiful bay in the Caribbean. High sided and lushly covered with tropical rain forest type vegetation, it was quite simply beautiful. It was a natural harbour and was protected from all storms by both its location on the west side and the precipitous nature of the slopes, which rose several hundred feet straight up. He was driven to the end of the marina jetty and as he looked around, he could see why the wealthy would line their multi million pound yachts up side by side in this stunning bay. Walking past their sterns he could read the names of registration; Nassau Bahamas, Hamilton Bermuda, Austin Texas, Douglas Isle of Man, the last a particularly impressive ocean going yacht of the highest class. And it wasn't just the yachts. As he looked around at the villas ranged around the slopes, he could see that some serious money had landed in the area. A bright yellow, turn of the century house caught his eye at the head of the inlet, taking prime position, looking out to the bay exit and the sunset: magnificent.

The last boat he came to was, however, a cut above the rest. A motor cruiser of blue hull and white superstructure, it shone out as supreme. This was his destination, the 'Divine Inspiration'. He was ushered onboard, the second time he had been there, but he still found it imposing and he felt less in control than he normally did, obviously the impression the owner was trying to create and not one that Mustafa was used to. The anteroom he was left in was something you wouldn't have believed could be on a boat, unless of course you had the resources to accomplish anything you wanted. He was surrounded by mahogany and highly polished woods, leather seating, crystal and deep carpets. It was more like being in a luxury hotel. But he wasn't left long to consider his position; a few moments later the door opened and Mahmood entered, smiling broadly.

"Mustafa, my friend," he said warmly, extending his hand and offering him a seat, "You are most welcome. I am eager for news of our project but I am ahead of myself. First you will be shown to your cabin, then we shall dine onboard and talk of the glory of Allah and to our small contribution to his greatness. Please, did you have a pleasant flight?"

Mustafa hated this sort of small talk. He had come from very humble beginnings and although he now liked the trappings of wealth that association brought him, he was at heart a soldier, more at home with his men in the desert, taking charge and living an unpretentious, austere life. Polite small talk used by the truly wealthy to try and make those less fortunate than themselves feel at ease was anathema to him. However this was a game that he had to play, for the sake of the cause and out of respect for the man that was doing so much for him. He smiled back and chose his words carefully.

"Mahmood, it is good to see you again also. Thank you for welcoming me so graciously, your hospitality is once again overwhelming."

Mahmood inclined his head and said, "The taking honours the giver. Please, settle in and I will see you back here for dinner at nine."

At that, the attendant who had been hovering in the corner led Mustafa away to a luxurious cabin and left him to it. He showered, changed, and with thirty minutes left until dinner, checked his emails. Nothing extraordinary had come through to any of his accounts and, satisfied that his plans were still on track, he was ready when there was a soft knock at the door and the same steward invited him back to the anteroom.

The conversation pre and during dinner mentioned nothing of the operation. Once again it was the small talk of the rich, but engagingly so; it was obvious that Mahmood was skilled in the arts required from a man of his position and wealth. It wasn't until the dishes had been cleared away and the final steward had left that he turned and was more direct.

"What of our plans?" It was the first time that his face had carried a serious demeanour.

"We are on the verge of something great, *insha Allah*," Mustafa replied. "Our preparations are almost complete and we are moments away from setting the final date. I have seen our men in London, Paris and Munich over the last forty-eight hours and can tell you that with the exception of a minor delay in Germany, all the assets are in place. I myself will be going back to Somalia tomorrow via London and will carry out the final training for our men. My friend, it is time for us to strike back. Your name will be written large in the heavens as a true servant of Allah."

Mahmood smiled, the serious demeanour broken as quickly as it had arrived. "Good, good my friend, but why is Germany late? Should it not all be ready on the ground?"

"It is a matter of small consequence," Mustafa replied. "There was a delay in getting the German weapons through the Turkish borders. We have had to be careful but they are on the way now and should be in the safe house outside of Munich within the next two days. All is going to plan. When I get back to the camp, I will decide on the final details of the attack and train our people for their specific missions. They are good men, each and every one of them willing to set their lives down for our cause. At the moment, I have set Saturday in three weeks as the glorious date. That gives us more than enough time to sharpen the sword."

"Excellent news. It is wonderful that our efforts are about to be rewarded. Is your man in the UK still providing you with everything you need?"

This was the moment of truth. Mustafa had to be very careful here. This man was no fool either. If he let slip his concerns or that there was a team ranged against him, it could put him in a seriously uncomfortable position. By the same token, if later on it emerged that he had known about the Special Forces team and Mahmood found out that he had been lied to, the trust between them would be broken and future investment would be put at risk.

"Our man has been invaluable," he said after only a moment's pause. "I saw him only the day before yesterday and he continues to feed me the information I need to see off the opposing forces. Perhaps understandably, with an operation of this size, there have been rumours. There is a general feeling that there will be some sort of attack in the next few months but they don't know what, where or when. As far as we are concerned, they cannot cover everything and our plans remain unaffected."

Mustafa stopped there. He had told half the current story, which he thought was quite enough. This would tell Mahmood that there were forces ranged against him but that he had it under control. If any action became necessary further down the line, he could say that he had got the information from the Colonel and acted upon it.

"And what about the explosion in Fujairah last night? Was that anything to do with us?"

This was just what Mustafa hadn't wanted but exactly what he should have expected. It was these spectacular leaps of faith relating two seemingly random events that made the difference between the truly gifted, and usually therefore the rich, and the rest of mankind. What did he say now? He felt cornered. With this man he couldn't risk it. When asked a direct question, he had to give a direct answer.

"You know that the allied Special Forces are engaged throughout the Middle East, my friend. We keep tabs on them and with the information that we get from Colonel Taylor, we are able to intercept or avoid most of them before they become difficult for us. This particular team was dispatched to join a submarine in Fujairah, where they were expected to board earlier on today. Once they had left, we wouldn't have known where they were so we decided not to take the chance. I ordered a strike last night. The bomb was ours."

"And was it successful Mustafa?"

"No," he replied simply. "They were unaffected by the blast. They got onboard the submarine immediately and left as soon as they were able. We don't know where they are now."

"But what about the Colonel? Can't he tell you what their tasking is?"

Once again he had asked the question that Mustafa least wanted to answer. If he told him that his source was being kept out of the loop then he was showing a weakness, and with this man's intellect, it would lead to the inevitable question of 'why?' But this conversation had gone too far already. It was probably time to stop giving half answers and let him know the trump card.

"This is the one mission that he has been unable to tell me about," he said, now prepared for the inevitable follow up from this very astute man.

"And why is that?"

"For some reason he has been kept out of the direct loop. He has told me that they are being deployed to the Somali coast on a search and reconnaissance mission, but little else."

"And doesn't that alarm you?" Mahmood asked quietly, a note of intensity slipping into his voice.

"Sir." it was time to be ultimately respectful, he was now on weak ground. "He may not be in the loop himself but he has a wonderful advantage. He has a man on the Special Forces team. He will get his information first hand and forward it on to us. Once again, he has proved his worth."

Mahmood sat back and considered for a few seconds, looking directly at Mustafa, his piercing and astute eyes delving into his very soul, testing the truth of his words, assessing the risk he now faced.

Moments later he sat forward again. "You are the general, my friend," he said. "Deploy your forces as you see fit. I leave it entirely in your hands."

This was music to Mustafa's ears. He had trodden the minefield and chosen a path to the other side. The rest of the evening passed with him going over the plans in a lot more detail and talking about the efforts of the teams in each of the different countries. When the amount of travelling and changing of time zones he had undertaken finally caught up, his host realised that it was time to bring the meeting to a close.

"Enough my friend, you must be exhausted. I must let you rest. I gather you are on the flight tomorrow night. I will let you sleep now and rest here during the day tomorrow. You will need your strength for the fight ahead. I unfortunately will not be here. I have to fly up to New York early but I have left instructions for you to be given every hospitality in my absence. Good luck Mustafa. It is a great thing that we do. Allah will be proud. Go with my blessings and bring the fight to the enemy for all our sakes."

"Mahmood, your patronage honours me and our cause. News of our success will be heard throughout the world."

With a slight smile and nod of the head, Mahmood left the room and Mustafa was escorted back to his cabin. He slept soundly and awoke late the next morning. After readying himself, he was taken to the breakfast table laid out on the quarterdeck of this magnificent motor cruiser. The peace of the bay was disturbed only by the songs of the many tropical birds that flitted from tree to bush, immediately opposite the quayside. He looked around him and took in again the lushness. He might come back here after it was all over. He would need a break after the intensity of the last few months, somewhere to switch off and to lose himself for some extended time. If the yacht were still there he may even be able to persuade his sponsor to allow him to use it. If not, there was a lovely hotel on the shore where he could take stock of his success.

He was getting ahead of things and, admonishing himself for the indulgence he had allowed to creep into his reverie, he focussed back on reality. As the tranquil setting supported contemplation, he considered the weeks ahead. His next move was to get back to Somalia as quickly as possible. His flight left St Lucia tonight and he would arrive in London the following morning. A further flight to Europe and then direct to Somalia, the extra leg to confuse the trail. He couldn't afford to take any chances at this late stage so he would make sure he used different passports for each leg. Once back in the training camps he would check on progress, get an update from his number two and allocate team members to each mission. The final two weeks would be intensive, repetitive and mission specific. There could be no margin for error. Each of the men would need to know exactly what was required of them, down to the smallest detail. The desert would shortly contain basic area layout mock ups and they would go through different defensive scenarios with his own men playing the parts of both attackers and security forces. Every foreseeable permutation would be considered and rehearsed.

This was why he had been so successful in the past. His military planning was equal to the best in the West. He understood his forces strengths and weaknesses and he understood the enemy. This last component was crucial. It allowed him to know where they could be hit hardest and most effectively. In two weeks he would deploy his teams ready to strike, giving them a few days to become familiar with the target area so that nothing would come as a surprise. Once they were deployed, he would base himself in Bahrain, receiving intelligence updates from the team leaders on a previously unused line; virtually untraceable if you were careful with the language you used and didn't give the computers the chance to home in on you. Just in case it all went wrong and he was compromised, he would be in friendly territory and also at the hub of a global airline network that he could use to get anywhere in the world within a few hours. As far as he was concerned, he always had a backup plan, a way out. For his men it wasn't so important. If they were killed it would be a glorious martyrdom, if captured they could give little away; they knew few details.

No, the plan was sound. The one annoyance was that someone, somewhere had let the details out that something was about to happen. There was no way he would be able to find out who it was. It was entirely possible that the combined might of the Western security services had managed to piece together enough scraps of information to lead them to the Somali camps and to his involvement. The assets at their disposal were truly awe inspiring. Their ability to use satellites, interception techniques, computer tracking, email interception and many other more covert and technologically advanced methods would defy common belief, not to mention the simplest method of agent insertion and double agent working. It was something his own organisation could never hope to match and was their greatest weakness.

However, after due consideration, he was still confident. They may be coming for him, but it would be on his ground. In Somalia he could range forces against the intruders openly and bring massive firepower to bear at will. And they still had to find him when they got there. He felt comfortable. There were risks but the odds were still significantly in his favour. He took a long drink of his fruit juice cocktail and looked around. Yes, this would be a great place to come when it was all over.

The car took him to the airport at seven. There was no such thing as a first class lounge but there was a separate area for 'special passengers'. He got onboard and settled down to the overnight flight, using the time to try and switch off, but he found it more difficult than it seemed. The last period before an operation was exhausting for him. His mind was a kaleidoscope of possibilities and eventualities. He couldn't help but go over and over the plan, looking for inconsistencies and potential flaws. Only when he could think of no more possible alternatives did he stop reviewing; and then his mind turned to his foe. What strength were they deploying against him? What were their skills? That Edwards man had dogged him for years previously but had recently fallen off the radar, apparently after some sort of injury. Many times Edwards had got close in the past. Many times the traitor Taylor had saved him at the last minute by feeding him the information he needed to stay ahead, sometimes just half a pace but ahead nonetheless. Now Edwards had appeared again out of nowhere. What was it that drove this man and would this be the final confrontation? It was probably time to do something about him. When it was all finished he would have to take care of him. And the Colonel too. If they were keeping Taylor out of the loop then he was compromised and that was a risk he couldn't afford. It was time to move on to the next generation. He would find out who the Colonel's other man was and invite him to take his place.

He was annoyed that the Fujairah hit had been so ineffectual. All it had succeeded in doing was alerting the Special Forces they were being tracked and their mission was compromised. But that made little real difference. Mustafa was enough of a general to realise that the pieces were committed to the board. It was time to play the game and see how the battle would turn out. The key, however, was intelligence, and he was missing a few pieces of vital information he needed. Once the submarine had left the port he had no idea where it was, where it was going to drop the men on the Somali coast or when. That knowledge was vital in order to deploy his forces optimally. Eventually he fell asleep asking himself that question. Where exactly were they?

CHAPTER 5

"Mike, there's a bit more going on than you know."

Chris sat opposite *HMS Talisman*'s Captain, Mike Saggers, with Louis next to him. In the background, the noises of the submarine making preparations to dive were relayed over the Captain's communication box by the side of his bunk.

"I fucking gathered that," Mike replied.

Chris was unable to say anything about the potential informant back home but he owed it to his long time friend to tell him something.

"We think we were compromised back in Dubai. How badly and who by we don't know but we were getting a bad feeling about things. A couple of us thought we were being followed and my hotel room was checked over. We thought it was most likely routine checks by Dubai security. Nothing had actually happened except for a bit of surveillance and we thought it would stay that way. It looks like we were proved wrong."

"No shit Sherlock. You could have told me this before, Chris. I realise you have to keep things close to your chest and I'm sure there are lots of things about this whole fucking thing that I still don't know, and by the way I wouldn't want to, but we're talking about the safety of my fucking ship's company here. If I'd thought they were in danger I would have kept them onboard last night or even sailed early and now two of them are dead."

"I appreciate that, Mike, and I'm sorry but we had nothing concrete to go on in Dubai and we can't react to half arsed, highly speculative guesswork. Before last night we had no idea they would try something kinetic in this country. As far as we were concerned, they were just keeping tabs on us. I'm really sorry that what should have been limited to us has involved you and your men; that wasn't the intention, but this is big Mike. Without going into details, this mission is more risky than normal but from the highest levels we've been told it's a risk worth taking. The prize is the take down of Al-Qaeda's highest military planner and in both the short and long term the saving of potentially hundreds of lives. Mike, any risk for us personally is worth that gain." Chris paused momentarily. "I know that we lost two of your men but actually we were lucky back there at the hotel. It was as shocking for us as it was for you and your ship's company but actually, it could have been a lot worse."

For a while there was silence. It was obvious that Mike was considering what had been said, seeing it from the other side and not just as *HMS Talisman*'s Commanding Officer, responsible for nearly a billion pounds worth of submarine and the lives of one hundred and thirty men.

"I'm sorry Chris," the Captain replied eventually. "I know we're in a uniformed service but the number of times we face direct action are pretty few. We operate off a coast somewhere and no-one knows we're there, or we lob Tomahawk missiles off somewhere into the interior but it's rare that the reality of close action is brought home to us. Last night was something different, something shocking. We're not used to it. I appreciate that what you are going into is far worse and you're right, we should thank God most of us survived but try telling that to the wives and families of the two men who died. Look, I've got to make sure that all the preparations for diving are going ahead and there are reports I have to take. Why don't you do what you need to do and I'll see you later. We'll be diving in about two hours when we reach deeper water and have cleared territorial limits. Louis, your boys are welcome to come up into the Control Room and witness it if you like."

For the first time Louis spoke up. He had let Chris get on with it; the Captain was his old friend and he knew how to relate to him. He had said what had needed to be said without help.

"Thanks for that Sir," he said. "I'm sure there will be a couple of takers."

"Good, oh and I think we can dispense with the Sir, at least in private. You're an old friend of Chris, so you're a friend of mine."

They left the small cabin and went back down to the 'bomb shop' and the rest of the lads.

"Everything OK boss?" piped up Bobby in his typically irreverent way. "Only if we're going to have to swim back I won't pack away me budgie smugglers just yet."

"No, we're all right so far," Louis replied. "The Captain is pretty shaken up but he's coming round. The crew might take a little bit longer so tread carefully with them. We'll be diving in a few hours and you've been invited up to witness it in the Control Room if anyone wants."

The others went about the business of settling into life onboard. It was going to be a long seven day trip out to the Somali coast and there was plenty of time for preparation, rehearsing and plan refinement. Some chatted in groups of two or three, others got accustomed to the space they were in, which didn't take long given its size, and Chris got used to being on a submarine again. It had been two years since he had been on board but as soon as he recognised the smell, that combination of hydraulic oil and human existence that was so instantly recognisable, it all came back. He had spent a couple of months living down here in the Weapons Compartment when he was a trainee, so many years before. That experience and the years of service in between meant that he knew every inch of the submarine.

In order to qualify as a submariner, to earn your 'Dolphins', you had to undertake what was known as your 'Part Three'. This Holy Grail was an intensive training regime where you went to sea on your first submarine and studied the minutiae of each of the myriad of systems throughout the entire length of the boat, and how it all fitted together. It was an immense task that took up to three months of twelve to fourteen hour days doing nothing else. You were given no let up by your shipmates and if you started spending too much time in the Mess, it was made perfectly clear that until you qualified, you weren't welcome. At the end of it all there was an interrogation in front of a triumvirate of experienced men, usually the Head of Departments and the Captain, which could take anything up to eight hours. Your entire knowledge was laid bare and explored, which proved how much you still needed to learn in addition to what you had already achieved. Only if you reached the very high standard required would you 'qualify' and be given respite. At that point, however, you were welcomed by the rest of the crew incredibly warmly, with those who had been most dismissive usually the most effusively friendly. Next the Captain awarded you the badge of honour, a gold broach of two arched dolphins meeting at a Royal crown in the centre worn on dress uniform. It was traditionally presented in a large glass of rum and caught in your teeth as you downed the liquid in a single gulp. This ancient ritual signalled your transition was complete and your entry into the brotherhood assured. It was a club membership hard gained, always treasured and never lost.

Just under two hours later a man appeared at the top of the hatch leading to their compartment.

"Captain said to tell you that we'll be diving in five minutes, if you want to see it."

There was something about the first dive out of port that was special. It wasn't an expectation of failure, it was the pleasure of seeing a crew at the top of their game, the normal jocular disposition put aside for a completely professional performance. The transition from the surface to the dived condition was about moving from one established state to another. There was always risk and until that risk was despatched, the crew wouldn't relax.

Chris, Louis and two others made their way to the back end of the Control Room where they could see what was going on but wouldn't get in the way. The Captain was in his chair and he nodded to them as they arrived but said nothing; his concentration was centred on ensuring that every system report was correct, that the men were concentrating on what they were doing and that the surface tactical picture was properly compiled, so that when they were underwater and effectively blind, they knew what was around.

The mere presence of a Captain in the Control Room was usually enough to ensure that the extra concentration needed was achieved. It was rare, but not unheard of, for a Commanding Officer to properly bawl someone out, probably more so in the previous generation of Officers, where tyrannical behaviour was commonplace and accepted. This had been replaced, gradually, by much more professional behaviour, with the old proponents either promoted out of harm's way or out of the service completely. Mike Saggers was new school and it was clear that his men worked for him in order not to let him down, not because they feared him.

The final technical reports came in and the Captain acknowledged them one by one. He took his microphone and spoke to the Diving Officer of the Watch on top of the submarine's fin.

"Officer of the Watch, Captain, I have the submarine, clear the bridge, come below, shut and clip the upper lid."

The order was repeated back and the evolution began. The somewhat laborious and mechanical process of shutting down the bridge ensured that nothing was left in the area that would rattle when the submarine dived. Subs relied on their ability to operate undetected on operations because they made virtually no noise. It would be their worst nightmare to have a spare bolt or clip banging about and producing a transient noise that could be detected and identified as only being from a man made machine. Such instances would mean surfacing to put right the defect, hugely increasing the risk of detection and therefore of prosecution.

A few minutes later the Officer of the Watch appeared in the Control Room to make his report. "Bridge secure, Captain."

"Very good," was the simple acknowledgement.

One last check and then Mike gave his last instruction.

"XO, dive the submarine."

The second in command or Executive Officer repeated the order and turned to face Ship Control. "Open three and four Main Vents," he stated.

The valves at the top of the two after Main Ballast tanks were opened first and the stern dropped away as the air within them escaped. This gave the propeller some water to bite on and when he was happy he opened vents numbers one and two at the forward end and the boat started to level out, but now deeper overall. He increased engine revolutions and started to drive the boat deep.

The 'look' was being kept by an officer on the main 'Search' periscope, with the Captain on the second, 'Attack' periscope. As the boat went deeper it took on a steeper angle and the level of the top of these masts got closer to the surface of the sea. First the Search, then the Attack dipped below the waterline. As each one did it was lowered. The Captain returned to his seat to ensure that all was still in good order. It was. All the systems were responding and the 'Sound Room', the sonar operators who listened through the huge array of sonar sets around the outside of the hull, reported that they could hear the air clearing out of the Ballast Tanks. At forty metres keel depth, the dive was reversed and the boat brought back to Periscope Depth, or PD.

It had been a textbook dive. The bodily weight of the boat had been right, allowing control of depth without having to fight the boat's natural instinct to go deeper or rise too shallow, and all systems were operating well.

"All positions carry out post diving checks and report to Ship Control," came the final order.

In a matter of moments, the reports came back, symptomatic of the professionalism and attentiveness of the crew – all correct.

You could see the Captain ease back. Where he had been alert and poised to take any emergency actions required, he now took on a more relaxed posture.

"Officer of the Watch, you have the submarine. Tell me when all long post diving checks are complete, catch a good trim, then we'll get going."

He turned to Chris and Louis. "One half of the equation complete." Chris smiled and Louis looked puzzled.

"Am I missing something?" he asked.

"It's the oldest submarine rule," replied Chris. "As long as the number of surfaces equals the number of dives, you've won. As soon as the former doesn't equal the latter, you're in the shit."

Louis didn't know whether to smile or not. It was a fact that submarines operated in one of the most unforgiving and potentially dangerous environments known to man. A submarine was a hugely complicated piece of machinery with a myriad of things that could go wrong. The way that the men seemed to deal with the inherent danger was with irreverent humour, almost black. There was almost no situation, however tense, that wouldn't inspire some sort of comment, often out of the box and usually very funny. Others who were new to the game would start off by feeling tense, worrying about the possibilities, thinking about the immense pressure exerted by the sea around them when operating at two hundred metres below the surface or more. Before long however, the complete disinterest from the rest of the crew would make them feel at ease. In a few short months, they would have joined the rest and be taking it in their stride.

With the initial excitement over, Chris and Louis made their way back to the bomb shop. Although they had the right to use the Wardroom as any other commissioned Officer, the Special Forces had a habit of staying together when deployed. Rank and rate were only nominally adhered to in the unit. Given the operations undertaken, it was crucial that you knew your fellow team members as brothers, not as subordinates or superiors. Chris, Louis and Dodger would take their meals with the other Officers but would stay with their men for the rest of the time.

And so the long transit began. It would take seven days of high speed running through the Indian Ocean to get off the coast of Somalia from Fujairah. Given the non-stop action from the moment Chris had been called into Captain Absolom's office at Fleet Head Quarters to the point of leaving Fujairah, it would be welcome respite. Chris soon heard the pipe 'the submarine is going to two hundred metres' over the ships tannoy, an indication that all post diving checks had been completed and that the Captain was happy he could increase speed, get deeper in order to gain cooler water (it helped with the efficiency of the propulsion systems), and to increase to cruising speed.

The beauty of submarines was that changes of speed or course when submerged were almost imperceptible. Very occasionally at higher speeds and more severe rates of turn you might feel a slight heel but generally you could be doing anything, with those onboard being none the wiser. The exception was changes in depth, where people's innate sense of balance through the constant pull of gravity would tell you that you were inclined. This was exactly what Chris and the boys now felt as the submarine dipped its nose forward and sniffed its way into the deep, away from the light of the outside world. He watched the faces around him. They had all looked up when the main broadcast pipe was made and he was interested in their reaction as the angle came on. No-one said anything but eyes turned to the depth gauge at the front of the compartment, which had started to descend, silently; forty, fifty, sixty metres, the numbers kept moving, ninety, one hundred, one hundred and ten, not an eye left the read out, one hundred and sixty, one hundred and seventy, one hundred and eighty.

"Bang," screamed Bobby at the top of his voice. Each one of the highly trained Marines jumped a mile, some hitting heads, some with looks of complete panic on their tense faces until they realised that the grinning idiot in the corner from where the noise had come was laughing his head off.

"You fucking arsehole, Bobby! What a twat," came the first cry, after which they all joined in. "Does your village know you're missing?" added Peanut. "Because somewhere they're a fucking idiot down."

"Away man, cheer up, I couldn't stand the pained looks on your bonny little faces any longer," came the giggled reply.

"The submarine is at two hundred metres," was the follow up pipe. "All compartments check for leaks and report to Ship Control."

"I don't know about the compartment, but I reckon there are a few leaks in some of these underpants down here," carried on Bobby. "Shall I report that?"

And this was how they bonded. For the ship's company, there were watch keeping positions to go to, places and jobs to occupy their minds. The routine was to spend six hours on watch then six hours off, in which they would relax or grab some sleep, repeated the whole time they were at sea, sometimes for months on end. For Chris and his team mates it was different. They would talk among themselves, eat, sleep, clean their weapons and go over in exhaustive detail every facet of the plans.

And so it was for the next couple of days. Once the initial rush of planning was over, most of the time was spent reading or sleeping in the bunks that were secured next to the Spearfish torpedoes and Tomahawk Land Attack Missiles; strange bedfellows but something that you got used to fairly quickly. They were generally left alone apart from the members of the ship's company that worked in the 'bomb shop', who would turn up periodically to check the weapons or systems and to do their rounds.

Occasionally Chris would wander around saying hello to some of the crew he had known before, all of whom were generally glad to see him, despite what had happened in Fujairah. He would have chats with his old friend Mike, always being careful to keep his counsel over the full details of the mission background, but talking through the ground plans with him. It was mid-afternoon, two days out from Fujairah after one of these sessions as he had taken the final step down into the 'bomb shop' when there was a bang from above and forward of the hatch, then the unmistakeable sound of high pressure oil being sprayed into the Forward Escape Compartment.

Within seconds his worse fears were confirmed as he heard the clatter of boot shod feet and the scream, "Hydraulic burst, hydraulic burst, hydraulic burst in the Forward Dome."

At that point Chris's submariner's instincts took over and he instinctively grabbed the nearest broadcast handset, flipping the transmit switch and repeating the cry. He knew his warning had been received when he heard the General Alarm klaxon broadcast, bringing the submarine to its highest state of emergency manning.

"Emergency stations, emergency stations, hydraulic burst, hydraulic burst, hydraulic burst in the Forward Dome, man all ship's systems in hand."

The response was immediate: within seconds, he could hear the clatter of many feet rushing out of the crew sleeping quarters underneath the forward dome, each man getting to his allotted emergency station as quickly as possible, each one properly dressed and ready for action as required within a minute of having been deep asleep.

As befitted the emergency, he could feel the submarine take on a bow up angle to regain a safe depth as the two hundred metre transit did not give many options if they had to quickly reach the surface to survive. He looked around at his fellows, the majority of whom had been in the compartment and asleep or relaxing and saw immediately that he had to take charge.

"Stan, break open that locker and get an Emergency Breathing Mask out for each of the men, just in case this turns into a fire and we need fresh air. Any second now we'll be inundated with the compartment watch keepers so when you've got your mask, get to the end of the space and keep out of the way. For God's sake, don't touch anything. These systems are mostly hydraulic down here so be very careful."

Being given an order was just what the boys needed. It gave them something to concentrate their minds and react to; it was something the military man could understand, even if it was to do nothing.

Sure enough, while he was still speaking, the watch keepers turned up, began their closing up checks and reported to Damage Control Head Quarters, now being set up in the Wardroom. This was a tried and tested routine, practiced many times while the boat was preparing for their deployment East of Suez. The Service knew the implications of any sort of catastrophic failure onboard a dived submarine and trained relentlessly to be able to take the correct actions immediately.

Chris could hear the next of those prescribed actions happening above him as he heard the shouts, "Make way, attack BA coming through." This was a two-man team nominated from the people on watch that would be the first on any emergency scene. Hydraulic bursts produced a fine mist of hydraulic oil that would saturate the atmosphere of a compartment within seconds, rendering breathing impossible and producing a huge fire risk. Ship Control would already have crashed all the hydraulic plants to reduce the system pressure at the burst site, but the mist would remain. The attack BA, short for Breathing Apparatus, would be the first into the compartment and would carry with them a dry powder fire extinguisher. The absolute priority was to beat down the hydraulic mist with the powder before the atomised oil came into contact with anything hot such as machinery, generating a flash fire as a result.

Chris held his breath; this was the crucial time. If they were successful, the chances were that the situation could be recovered and there would be only minor consequences. If they were too late, there was nothing that scared submariners more than the thought of a fire at sea. It caused untold amounts of damage to the ship's mechanical systems, electrics and worse still, atmosphere, something so crucial to their existence.

Chris could hear a hush descend upon the submarine while the crucial moments slipped by. The enormous activity of the previous two minutes suddenly became still. After what seemed like an age, but can only have been another ninety seconds, there was another pipe, this time from Damage Control Head Quarters.

"Do you hear there, DCHQ speaking, the hydraulic mist has been beaten down by the attack BA. There is no risk of fire, I repeat, there is no risk of fire."

"By Christ," Bobby was the first to speak. "You Navy lads know how to put on a good party but do you think you could choose your timing a bit better next time, it's playing havoc with me beauty sleep. And by the way, Peanut, you can take that horrendous looking breathing mask off now, it makes you look like a freak." You could see the men in the compartment relax as the tension was broken, especially Peanut, who had been looking particularly scared and had never put the mask on.

The situation was by no means over, but it could have been so much worse. There followed a couple of hours where the clean-up operation got fully going, the burst site was investigated and a repair effected to the system valve that had given way, during which Chris stayed completely out of the way. He was an experienced submariner, not far from promotion but he knew that this boat had its own fully trained specialists and the last thing they needed was another 'expert' trying to help.

Two hours later, Chris made his way up to the Control Room.

"Hello shipmate," chirped the Captain, who was still sitting in his seat, looking vaguely pleased with himself. "I couldn't have put on a better training drill if I'd tried. Thanks for all your help."

Chris smiled back at him. "I thought I would contribute to the best of my ability and stayed at the back of the bomb shop, keeping those rascally Marines under control. I couldn't resist hearing my voice one more time over the tannoy, however, so chipped in there at the start."

"Yes I thought I heard your dulcet tones," Mike chuckled back. "And very nice they were too. Well done, you must be very proud."

"How's it looking?" Chris asked.

"Not actually as bad as it could have been," Mike replied. "There's been no real damage, nothing that hasn't already been repaired and it's sharpened the crew up as well. I have to say I was pretty happy with the way they performed, all in all, so it gives me and them confidence that they can handle things when it gets tough. It's all good Chris."

Being as they were in the Control Room, Chris could see the smiles on the faces of the watch keepers as they faced their panels and knew that the last remarks were meant to be overheard; another reason why Mike was such a good Captain. The news that he thought it had gone well would filter through the crew within minutes and be discussed in the unofficial post incident debriefs going on in all the messes at that time. That would relax and inspire them if, God forbid, it ever happened again.

"How long do you think it'll be before we get going again?"

"We'll test the leak site and engage warp drive shortly, Mr Spock," replied Mike, still obviously high after the event. "Don't worry, it won't affect your delivery into theatre; we can still get there as planned. Your date with destiny is still on."

With that, Chris went back down below and life for a few more days got back to normal. As time passed, however, and as the submarine got inevitably closer to the insertion site, tensions started to increase and minds started to be more focussed.

The morning of the day before arrival, the CO made an unexpected appearance in the weapons compartment.

"How's it going then, lads?" he asked in his easy manner. "Everything ready is it?"

He was met with a few half smiles of agreement but not much more; the boys were all getting a bit more serious.

"Louis," started the Captain. "We're getting pretty much into area and I thought it would be a good idea to go through a dummy run for getting you guys off. My team have done this before but it was a while ago so I think for everyone's sake, while we are in quiet water, we should give it a go. That way, you'll know where all your equipment is under the casing and we'll know how we are going to integrate you into the ship's team. OK?"

It wasn't really a question in all fairness but everyone could see the merits in it.

"No problem, Sir. Is it going to be just a dry brief or are we going feet wet?" Louis acknowledged.

"There's nothing around and the Indian Ocean is flat calm here, so I'll surface tonight and we can go through the motions on the roof, stopping short of inflating the boats and putting you in the water."

"Got it, Sir."

The Captain left and the boys got back into their preparation routine. These men were the best in the world, the ultimate professionals in their field; nothing could touch them and their minds were now fully engaged. It wasn't a brooding silence of fear, it was a concentration that promoted excellence of outcome and each man respected the next.

Later that afternoon they got a brief from the Casing Party, the members of the ship's company that would be part of the drill, about where all the kit was stowed and what would be expected of them. Not long after that, it was time for the run through.

"All Special Forces are requested to muster in the Junior Rates Mess," was the pipe. With all the men and kit assembled, Chris and Louis made their way to the Control Room and waited patiently. The submarine had already come up to safe depth and the Captain was making sure that everything was completely ready. When he was fully satisfied, he gave the order.

"Officer of the Watch, bring the submarine to Periscope Depth." After such a long time deep, and because of the inherent danger of the transition above safe depth to the surface, this was always a tense time for the submarine crew, and especially in light of what they were about to do.

The submarine came slowly shallower but arrived at PD within a couple of minutes and without incident. They were still two hundred miles off the coast but the Indian Ocean at this latitude was often glassy smooth and so it was tonight. The Captain sat in his chair and looked on, checking the tactical picture as the Officer of the Watch raised the Search Periscope to take the first look.

"One sweep," he said after the first rotation. "Two sweeps, nothing close, lower Search. Sir we have no contacts visual, no contacts any sensor."

"Very good, establish the look," ordered the Captain.

The periscope was raised again and a lower order watch officer took the look, keeping a constant eye out for contacts that may have been missed on the other sensors. The Captain called the Casing Officer to him and once he had established that his men were ready, gave the order.

"Standby to Surface."

The well drilled Ship Control team went into action and made the preparations. When all the reports were ready, they reported back to the Captain as much.

"Very Good," he acknowledged again. "Surface."

Again the team went into automatic and within seconds the Marines could feel the boat shudder as thousands of litres of high pressure air were forced into the Main Ballast Tanks, giving the submarine the buoyancy it needed to sit on the surface once again. After he was confident that he was sufficiently high in the water that opening the tower hatch wouldn't put the submarine in danger, the next direct order was given.

"Officer of the watch, Captain. On the surface open up."

At this, the young officer nominated leapt into the tower. The whole evolution was being timed so that they had a baseline to compare against the following night when they were doing it for real, which also encouraged everyone to operate at the height of efficiency.

"Casing Party stand by," Mike followed up next.

The eight crew members got into their final positions below the main access hatch and readied themselves for action. They knew their role was crucial and were just as keen to get it right, to prove they were up to the job. When the Captain had heard the Officer of the Watch from the bridge report that the casing was clear, meaning it was above the water line, the CO gave the order:

"Open the Main Access Hatch, Casing Party to the Casing."

This was the part Chris and his team had been waiting for, their time had come. The Casing Officer cracked open the hatch and bounded onto the casing, closely followed by his team. They began the immediate task of retrieving the Special Forces equipment from a bay underneath the after casing and arranging it on the deck. The Marines were close on their heels and, with the exception of inflating their boats, arranged all their equipment in the positions they would need the following night. When ready, they gave the thumbs up to the watching team and the Casing Party got below again. The entire operation had taken twelve minutes, at which point the submarine would dive, with the Marine's boats moving away from the side to their objective.

Drill over, it was time to stow all their equipment again and get below. The Casing Party came back up and it was all away inside another ten minutes, with the Marines getting more used to the layout of the deck and what was expected of them. As soon as they were clear and below, the Captain gave the orders to dive and the boat was very quickly back down at safe depth, clear of the surface. As soon as Mike was happy, he appeared down in the bomb shop again with the Casing Officer.

"Well what do you think?" he asked.

"That was absolutely fine," replied Louis. "It seems to be just as the lads remember so I reckon it should be OK tomorrow."

"As far as I'm concerned, we're on," Mike continued. "We should be able to improve on the timings as well. Remember, though, we'll be diving again as soon as we shut the Main Access Hatch and you're over the side, so I'd get as far away as quickly as you can. Apart from that, I think we know our drills."

"What about recovery when we get back to you?" asked Chris. He knew the answer but wanted it explained to the rest just to be sure.

"That's even easier. You guys get alongside, the casing party slings your equipment back on board, you go straight down the hatch and we stow it away under the casing. The whole thing should take just a few minutes. Anyway, let's see where we are at the time for the fine tuning and play it by ear. Any more questions? Right, I suggest you get some sleep while you can." The Captain looked around at the men. "If I don't get to say it tomorrow lads, good luck. I'll see you all back here whenever you call for me. Chris and Louis, you've got one last chance to talk to your boss at about ten tomorrow morning. I'll come up to periscope depth again and you can get your final instructions before I make a covert approach to the coast."

"Sounds good to me," Louis replied and the Captain left.

"Let's do what he says guys," reiterated Louis. "This will be the last night's sleep we get for about the next seven days, so let's make it a good one. I know the boys are laying on some midnight food if you want some, just do what you need to."

Each man did something slightly different. The night before an operation was nearly always the same. In a way, this had been different from the norm. They had had a long time during the previous week onboard to think about what lay ahead. Luckily, Louis had ultimate faith that they wouldn't get fazed by thinking too much, that they would approach the mission with the same, clear, concise mindset that they had on so many previous occasions. They were his men, he knew them and he trusted them with his life.

The next morning Chris and Louis went up to the communications office. It was time to get the latest instructions from back home before the submarine went covert for the final approach to the coast. They had received a few signalled updates on minor pieces of the plan and the reaction to the bombing in Fujairah, but on the whole, nothing had changed. There had been more sketchy information on the position of the camps, GCHQ had a line on some of the transmissions from there, but intelligence on the prime target, Mustafa, had dried up. For a few days it was if he had disappeared from the area, which was mildly annoying, then eventually plain frustrating to all concerned. Chris had thought back to all the other times he had been so close, primarily in Afghanistan, and wondered bitterly if history was going to repeat itself once again. Surely not this time, he thought. They were all heartened though when word came through that Mustafa had once again been located in area, just the day before, and that the game was still afoot.

They had already come to periscope depth and by the time Louis and Chris got into the comms shack, the men were making the final connections to the Special Forces Head Quarters in Poole. Before long they were speaking directly to the General.

"Major Armstrong, I gather you are now lying off the coast and about to make the final approach." It wasn't a question, it was a statement, as was so often the case when speaking to General Holbrook. "As far as the mission is concerned, you have everything you need and we have no further updates. Al Said is back in area and as far as we can make out, he is carrying on where he left off. He remains the primary target for extraction if possible. If not, then you know what to do. You know what's at stake here, Louis. They're planning something big. Stop it if you can. What have you got for me?"

"Actually, Sir, we're good to go. We practiced the insertion last night, which was all fine, and we've been fine tuning the plan for the last seven days. The lads just want to get on with the job. All our equipment is working well, so the next time we'll be in touch it'll be feet dry when we've made a position about twelve miles in from the insertion point. We should be there before first light after the drop and after laying up during daylight, we'll be in contact at around eight pm the next evening, before moving further inland."

"That's fine Louis, I'll speak to you then," the General came back. "You have mission command. The decisions are up to you. I won't try to second guess my man on the ground, but just know that you will have my full support for whatever you do. Pass my best wishes on to the rest of the boys and good luck Louis. There's a lot riding on this as you know. Oh and keep that tame submariner out of trouble will you. Capt Absolom will be extremely annoyed if anything happens to him."

"Got it, Sir."

And with a few more short words, the conversation was over and the link broken.

The rest of the afternoon passed slowly for the team but eventually sunset arrived and the appointed hour was close. The submarine had made its covert approach at depth and was sitting just short of the insertion point. At T minus thirty minutes to go, they were sitting in the bomb shop, doing their last checks as the submarine was brought to action stations with a main broadcast pipe. They heard the clatter of boots as once again, all compartments were manned, ready for any eventuality. At T minus twenty, they moved into position, just below the Control Room. Chris and Louis went up to check on progress.

"You set boys?" the Captain asked for the last time as they stuck their heads in. He was already in his chair, ensuring that everything in the surface picture was right for the operation. He had tactical control at this point and if he thought conditions weren't right, he would abort. It was a tense time.

"How does it look?" asked Chris.

"All good so far," he replied. "There's nothing around so we're on." He got out of his chair and took Chris to the back of the Control Room where they could have a quiet chat. "Be careful, Chris," he started, looking serious for once. "You know you're not that young anymore don't you, and all this playing around with these lads is liable to give you ideas above your station. I don't want to have to tell Elizabeth any bad news."

Chris smiled. "Don't worry, Mike. I know what I'm doing. I'm good at this, remember. And anyway, what makes you think I can't do it? I'm not as old as you, you know."

"And that's what worries me, you're only three months younger and you should know better."

"Shipmate, I'll see you in a few days."

"God willing my friend, God willing."

The Captain went back to his chair and checked one more time.

"Officer of the Watch, Captain, anything visual or on the picture?"

"No Sir."

"Right, standby to surface."

The boat shuddered as the drill was carried out and high pressure air was once again forced into the Ballast Tanks. Before they knew it, they were being called up and forward, with the casing party leading the way into the moonlight.

Chris was the last to climb the ladder and as his head gained the fresh warm night air, he thought he could smell the coast. He looked off to one side and could see the black outline of the shore against the horizon, devoid of any lights and hopefully of any life.

He looked ahead and could see the boats already being inflated on the deck with the compressed air cylinders that had been packed with them. As soon as they were ready, they were slung over the side on ropes and ladders were deployed for the Special Forces to get down into them. Half the teams were now embarked, with the rest making sure that their equipment was evenly distributed between each of them before they themselves got in.

Chris was the last one down and as he descended and his view became limited to the submarine's hull, a foot in front of him, his thoughts became similarly introspective. Any doubts threatening to intrude, however, were blown away as a surge of resolve rose within him. This next phase was the hard part, and although he had been out of operations for a long time, it was what he had always adored and had been so good at. He could feel the cold dispassion that had been such a mark of his professional life before, returning in a steady flow of clarity and confidence.

His feet continued down the ladder and he felt the bottom of the boat beneath them. There was a silence between the team and the submarine crew, who even now were re-stowing their kit and making preparations to dive. Without a word, the Marines started the outboards and pushed themselves away. The small boats slipped into the darkness and in moments the submarine had become barely visible, a patch of ink in the blackness of the night. The sound of the main vents being opened told them that they would soon be by themselves and they headed towards the shore.

They had four miles to make landfall and it would take them about an hour. As the boats glided across the silky smooth waters of the Indian Ocean and the coast of East Africa started to loom large, Chris prayed that this mission would be the one. The pre-operation adrenalin that he remembered so well was already coursing through his veins and he could feel his natural instincts become heightened. He felt confident about what lay ahead, but only God knew what was actually between him and his goal. He stared ahead into the darkness. He was back. He was ready. Bring it on.

CHAPTER 6

The drone of the outboards continued at a low but constant level for the next thirty minutes; they were kept below maximum power to minimise the sound travelling over the flat and noiseless ocean in the still of night. They had no idea what lay ahead of them. This would be one of their most vulnerable moments; as with the submarine, it was the transition between operating environments that brought such risk. They were moving from the relative safety of the boat to the unknown of the shore. They could be engaged when still off the beach, ambushed as they got out of the boats or there could be nothing. And hand in hand with the unknown came adrenalin.

They could see little as they approached apart from the silhouette of the shore and the indistinct outline of scrubby sand dunes. Still three hundred yards out, they cut the engines and drifted to a stop, the gentle slapping of the waves against the hulls the only thing that gave indication of their presence. It was time to get the paddles out; if there were a reception committee, they wanted to get as close as possible without giving away their exact location.

As noiselessly as they could, they started to approach. The site they had chosen was flat and wide, with a low sand dune twenty-five yards back from the water's edge. Every sense was focussed on the shoreline, trying to gain any indication of something out of the ordinary. All of them had either weapons out and to hand or within grabbing distance; this was a time to be as prepared as possible.

Chris was in a boat with Louis, Bobby and Peanut and was one of those on the bows. He was excited at how he had slipped back into this. He could feel the adrenalin flowing, heightening his senses and bringing that cold, calculating feeling of potential violence back into sharp focus. He had faced many situations like this, where the expectation of action was the driving force. It was a thrill he loved.

The boats closed the shore and paused again, this time no more than fifty yards out. They were fairly confident they would be invisible at this range, given the light conditions and their low profile. Their position allowed them a panoramic view of their objective and after seeing nothing to raise their suspicions they started forward again. Chris's eyes continually scanned the beach and eventually he felt a silent lurch as the keel grated over soft sand and they came to a halt.

The first two from each boat jumped forward and took up positions either side of the bow, the other two shipping their oars and readying their weapons an instant behind them. For a moment they remained frozen in position in case they would have to conduct an immediate fighting retreat with the boats, back to the relative safety of the water. They were greeted by a deafening silence, thank God, and a few seconds later, at a whispered command from Louis over the throat mikes they wore, the two front pairs sprinted forward, making the sand dunes in seconds, the other four still guarding the boats. This was all conducted with the minimum of noise, with everyone taking their cue from Louis, each of them knowing exactly what the next stage should be and pausing only when told to and for as long as directed.

They were in luck. Behind the beach, only some one hundred and fifty yards from the shore were a set of low bushes. It was under these that they would bury the boats, the plants providing some sort of landmark for their return. The scouts retraced their steps and with two men each side, they carried each hull forward. After removing all their equipment and covering the engines in the black waterproof bags that would protect them when buried, they covered them over, the whole operation taking no more than twenty minutes; the pits didn't need to be deep, they just had to pass a cursory inspection.

"Right boys," started Louis, breaking the silence for the first time. "It doesn't look like we've been compromised so far but let's not assume. The next objective is a position twelve miles inland. It's almost midnight and we have to cover the distance in the next four hours, which will be tough going if we're going to find a safe place to hole up for the day as well. If for whatever reason we get separated, Dodger and I both have the co-ordinates and we have GPS. Any questions?"

There were none. They had all gone over the plan constantly during the voyage and they set off, not at a break neck speed, as it was folly to wear men out at a pace that would drain them of their energy too quickly, but at a speed that Louis knew from experience they could keep up for a prolonged time and if required, for many days. It wasn't fast, but it was fast enough.

The hinterland was ideal for hiking, a mixture of scrub and hard baked, flat sand, easy on the feet and for the first ninety minutes nothing interrupted their trek. They had been dropped approximately one hundred miles north of Mogadishu, the capital city. This was pretty deserted territory and although the vast majority of the Somali population lived within about ten miles of the coast, there was still little sign of life, just the odd settlement here or there, sometimes permanent, but a lot of the time nomadic. It was one of these temporary settlements, they supposed, that brought the group to a halt.

They had walked in silence again; there was no point in trying to make a covert transit then inadvertently giving your position away through the spoken word. As they reached a low rise in the hard sand, Jon on point froze and put up a clenched fist. They all stopped in their tracks and assumed covering positions that would allow all round defence against an ambush, as much as eight men could. At this point they were carrying packs that weighed approximately one hundred and forty pounds, two thirds of their average body weight. It was certainly enough to throw them off balance easily, but was necessary if they were to carry what was needed to give them the best chance of survival over the coming week. Louis and the second in command Dodger took theirs off quietly and inched forward.

In front of them was a small collection of roughly erected tarpaulins, spread around a shallow depression in the landscape, deep enough to have hidden the camp from view. They could see the outline of a couple of Toyota pick-up trucks, the vehicles of choice for the African desert, and a few bodies stretched out around the glowing embers of a central fire. Louis checked his watch; it was half past one. Again, the two inched forward and then stopped. They stayed that way for five minutes, within thirty metres of the nearest truck, making sure that their arrival had gone unnoticed. When Louis was satisfied that there was nothing more to see, they withdrew as slowly as they had come, back over the ridge and to the waiting men.

They picked up their packs and moved off to the south a couple of hundred yards before Louis called a halt again, this time gesturing Dodger and the rest to him.

"We've got a small camp back there," he explained to the others. "Dodger, what did you see?"

Dodger was silent for a couple of seconds before replying and Chris could see his mind replaying the scene. "There were two pick-ups, one on either side of the camp," he started. "As far as I could see, there were eight men on the ground, I couldn't see under the far truck. There were four tarpaulins with a man under each and another four men ranged around the fire in the open, covered by blankets."

"Weapons?" asked Louis.

Again, there was a slight pause. "Kalashnikovs by each of the men," Dodger replied.

"And that, my friend," Louis' bitterness was plain, "is the issue. I think that was a reception committee. It could be just the local militia but my guess is they knew we were coming. We knew they had us through Dubai and Fujairah but the last thing they saw was us sailing off into the pale blue yonder on one of Her Majesty's finest. At that point, we could have been going anywhere. Now we get to a couple of miles from our drop off point and we find a group of locals, heavily armed and looking like they're waiting for the nod. We're going to have to be on top form here boys because somewhere along the line, some fucker's playing us for fools. It's obvious that we're expected and I would suggest that our friends back there aren't the only team in the hunt. The objective remains the same but the rules of the game have changed slightly. We must assume that anywhere we go will be compromised. Everyone understand?"

He knew that there would be no comment. This was a crack team. They took new information onboard, analysed it and generally came to the same conclusion.

"What do you think, Chris?" he continued, when no-one said anything.

Chris had been in the centre of the group during the hike and had been happy to be back in the saddle but also a little frustrated at not being in charge; he had got used to making the decisions and liked it that way. At the same time, he was aware that he was out of practice and the hierarchy here was as it should be. He was just pleased to be there.

"Sounds like we've got to shift around and clear the area then watch our backs," he contributed.

"I agree," continued Louis. "We carry on west for about another two and a half hours before holing up. We've still got to get inland by sunrise to hold to the planned timings. Let's move."

The packs were donned and they set off, this time skirting to the south of the camp by a good four hundred yards. Luckily the ground stayed the same for the next hour and they continued to make good time, seeing nothing more. An hour before they were planning to find cover for the day, they started to notice a change however; the ground became rockier and there was the odd lump of sandstone, no more than a few boulders at first, then becoming more prevalent, signs that the surroundings were changing, even if only slightly.

By half three, they were starting to have to pick their way around some fairly major rocks and at four, as they came upon the largest group yet, Louis once again called a halt to the march.

"Fan out and find a place to hole up lads. This is as far as I want to go today," and they paired off, Louis with Chris. Within a couple of minutes, Bobby came back.

"I've found somewhere that looks all right," he said in his best Geordie accent. "But it's nowt like the Ritz so don't get yer hopes up," and he led the rest towards what seemed to be the slightest of hollows in the wall of a nearby rock feature, one of six in roughly the same place.

He was right, to call it a cave would have been an extreme exaggeration, but it did offer defence through one hundred and eighty degrees to the east, which would also shelter them from the prevailing winds. It would give them a reasonable chance to rest for at least a few hours with shade in the morning. They would have to see about the afternoon.

The watch rota was set and the men got themselves as protected as possible. They had camouflaged webbing that would offer some anonymity but in reality they were still horribly exposed. This was nothing new, however, and was the chance they took. Chris was exhausted. He was just about coping with the physical aspect but add in the extended day and the mental tension and he was being hit pretty hard. He remembered how many other times he had done something similar, but was still amazed at how sapping it really was, especially now that he was those few years older.

After boiling a kettle and eating their morning rations, high on calories, low on weight, Chris tried to settle into his nominated patch. He lay down, trying to get as comfortable as possible, using what bits of clothing he had to make it softer. He failed. God he'd got soft, he thought, angry that he had let himself go. From every angle jagged pieces of rock seemed to be trying to pierce his flesh as if the land itself was rejecting him as alien. Regardless, he was physically drained enough that it didn't matter. He was asleep within minutes in the light of the early dawn but in that half world between one state and the other he could hear the occasional movement from his colleagues, the odd murmuring, the sound of a boot kicking a loose rock. Apart from those man made noises however, it was the semi-silence of the desert that he remembered so well.

It was very rare anywhere that there was complete silence. As Chris closed his eyes his mind focussed on the audible and started to pick up what had slipped below the visual, the dominant sense. He could hear the sound of the light wind blowing around them, setting up a brushing noise as it crossed the desert, a noise that was the sound of millions of sand crystals rubbing against each other to produce a background hiss. He could hear the odd scuttle of some desert creature or other, probably a lizard, as it came back to its daytime patch to find it taken by a herd of ungainly interlopers. Above all, he could feel the change in temperature stealing through the atmosphere. The night had been very cool, verging on cold later on and perfect walking conditions. As the dawn came on, however, and the sun crept above the horizon, the chill was rapidly put aside by the fire of the day's heat.

Behind his closed eyes, Chris could feel the air becoming warmer, even in the shade of the overhang. As his mind wandered, he wondered what the next twenty-four hours would bring. When he awoke for his watch, some six hours later, they would be only a few hours walk away from their goal. Would there be kinetic action? Would they be able to get any information? Would Mustafa, their prime target, Chris's own ultimate prize and the whole reason that he was on this mission be there? Only time would tell. As he lay there it seemed strange that they should be so close and yet not closing on the objective. Fundamentally he knew that they couldn't move during the day, not in open scrubland. They needed the cover of the night to make their approach. However risky it seemed to stay, it was infinitely more risky to go. He slept on that thought.

Chris was shaken awake after what felt like only a few hours, but not to keep his watch. He felt a hand on his shoulder and opened his eyes. Instead of being greeted with a cup of tea, as was customary, he saw a finger being placed to Peanut's lips, urging Chris to be quiet.

"We've got company," he whispered, and motioned Chris to follow. The others had spread themselves around the outcrops, the far left flank taken by Bobby, the far right by Pat Mulhoon. Louis and Dodger had climbed above him, on top of the rock Chris had been sheltering behind, their faces looking to the east intently, their weapons by their sides and their posture one of tense readiness. Peanut took Chris's pack to stow with the rest on the far side of the rocks, then signed for him to climb up to Louis, which he did as quietly as he could after picking up his own weapon. Peanut took up his position on the ground and to the right of the centre outcrop, the opposite side to Jon.

When Chris reached the top, he could see immediately the fragility of their situation, something that had been hidden by the night. The six rocky mounds that surrounded where they had chosen to rest were equally spaced along the two longer sides of a north south oriented rectangle. There were gaps between each rock that provided access to the central area. The whole arrangement provided a naturally defensive position but it was the major feature to this part of the landscape with the next landmark a good couple of miles to the south so far as Chris could see. It would be an obvious honey pot for anyone stationing themselves in the area and therefore not ideal for a group wanting to remain discrete, covert and anonymous.

A quick look at his watch showed that it was eleven thirty and he had slept for about five hours. The sun was now high and the heat of the day becoming extreme, even this early in the summer. As he stole a glance to the east over the top of the rock and in the same direction as the others, he could see the plume of dust caused by vehicles as they crossed the scrub. It was the same direction they had come from and it didn't take a huge amount of intuition to suspect that these two trucks were the same they had passed the night before - their reception committee.

Chris had no idea how the local men had realised they had been by-passed. If it was the same group, and they had been waiting for them, why had they suddenly moved to head for the team's current position? This smacked of all the other times that Chris had been close to Mustafa and had been thwarted at the last, either by the lack of a target or by being met by vastly overpowering forces prepared for their approach. It was as if the opposition knew every move they made and countered it, even when that knowledge seemed impossible. Not this fucking time, he swore to himself, not again, and he could feel his jaw clench.

The trucks got closer. They had been about three miles away when he first got to the top, now they were barely two, coming closer but not at a race, at a slow pace, slow enough to allow decisions to be made.

Louis conferred with Dodger then called the others to him and issued his instructions. "It looks like it may kick off here, boys. Wait until they get right on top of us. If it's the same bunch as last night, we know that there are eight of them and they're lightly armed. Someone has tipped them off so we have to assume they're in touch with back up forces. That means we have to get away if possible. If they stop outside the rectangle, great, we watch and let them get on with it. If they look as if they're coming into the centre here, we fall back to the other side of the second row of rocks. If it looks like they are coming further or spot us, we're going to have to take them out. Dodger's team, take the right hand truck, mine will take the left. If they dismount, allocate targets among yourselves, one man each. If it does go that far, I want it to be clean and clinical with minimum rounds down. The last thing we want is to bring more of them in when we're so close to our objective. If at all possible, I want us to leave everything alone and get out of here uncompromised. Got it?"

With single words of acknowledgement, they took up their positions and waited for the trucks. As Louis, Dodger and Chris regained the top of the rock, Chris could see the figures of the men, now only some half a mile away. He made his weapon ready and waited. A couple of hundred yards out, the lead truck stopped, facing directly at them, the second following suit, some forty yards behind and a little to the right. Chris could see the men in the lead vehicle staring ahead but could hear nothing else from this range, no talking, no movement. Then doors opened and the two men inside the lead cab got out. They paused, leaving the doors wide, and stared at the rocks in front of them. Was this natural caution or had they seen something to make them suspicious? Chris could only guess and wait. The Marines had been extremely careful not to leave any sign of their presence and this team wouldn't make elementary mistakes like that.

It seemed that their position passed initial scrutiny because the front man, presumably the leader, turned and walked back into his cab, gesturing for the others to follow. The trucks moved slowly forward again and made for the gap in the rocks immediately to Chris's left. At a sign from Louis, the Marines melted away from their current spots and ran back the fifty yards to the reserve positions on the far side of the second line of mounds. Within seconds of reaching their fallback positions, the lead pick-up edged into the middle area, the other following some ten seconds behind, one fanning left, the other fanning right. Here, maybe only thirty yards away, they came to a halt and the men disembarked.

Chris checked his watch again: midday.

The natives said nothing but scanned the area, obviously looking for recent signs of use. The 'leader' said a couple of words in what Chris thought was the local dialect and motioned for three of his men to take up positions on the first layer of rocks, looking east. If Chris had been in any doubt, this confirmed that they had been the targets and this was a group that had been set to wait upon their arrival. Another man was detailed off and a pack was retrieved from the back of the first truck, from which he produced a stove before starting to boil up some water.

If the unfolding scene wasn't bad enough, the leader then started walking towards the Marines' position, scanning the area as he did so, but before the militiaman had got even five yards closer, he was called back by the driver of the first truck. He turned and spoke briefly into a radio set in the cab, then went about supervising the others.

This was becoming far too domestic for Louis. It was obvious that this group was setting up camp but also that the Marines had yet to be compromised, at least for the moment, and it was time for his team to withdraw. He signalled to those on his left and right to come back to the centre rock. When they had noiselessly got behind him, he pointed to the packs that were resting at the bottom of the mound and indicated directly out from behind him, showing two fingers to mean two hundred yards. The others knew immediately what he meant and four of them took their own pack onto their backs and picked up one other. While this was happening, the three on the top of the rock stared intently at the Somalis in front of them, watching for any sign that they had given away their presence. There was none; all their attention was to the east and setting up for lunch. Louis gave the nod and the four moved away, out into the desert. Chris could only pray they made no noise.

Step by step, Chris watched Peanut, Pat, Bobby and Stan take the packs to safety. It was surprising just how good their desert camouflage actually was; if they hadn't have been moving, Chris doubted if he would have seen them at all. When they reached the rough position ordered, they had obviously found a slight dip in the landscape because when they stopped and lay flat, they disappeared. Now it was time for the others to follow and Louis indicated that Chris should move first. He slipped off the top of the rock and climbed down to the ground below. There he met up with Jon and the two of them started to move out into the desert. He looked back every few yards while choosing each footfall as carefully as possible; he wasn't going to be the one to give away their presence. Before he had gone forty yards he looked back and saw Louis frantically signalling for them to stop. Chris and Jon dropped to the ground and froze. It wasn't a moment too soon because at the same instant, the Somali leader came around the corner of the centre rock, the same one that Louis and Dodger were on top of. He must have caught a movement because he stopped in his tracks and his attention snapped out towards the hinterland, staring towards them, his hand reaching for the Kalashnikov at his side. Both Chris and Jon stopped breathing. They were only yards away from him and all Chris could hope was that their camouflage was as good as the others. Now the enemy's attention had been gained, the slightest sign could be disastrous, not only for them but most probably the mission and potentially the rest of the men.

The local stood there for what seemed like an eternity, staring towards their position. Chris could see the other two perched on top of the rock, Dodger with his knife drawn, ready to jump into action if required. The moments turned into a full minute, an agonising sixty seconds of unendurable mental torture.

Without altering the focus of his gaze, the militiaman called out a few words in the guttural tones of the local language. He was answered from behind and a couple of moments later another two men appeared. This was not what Louis had wanted and the situation was fast becoming beyond control. It was obvious that the leader hadn't seen the men, but he had seen enough to want to investigate further. After a brief conversation and with now the three of them staring into the scrub, he gave a final jerk of the head and the two newcomers started to move outwards, away from the rocks, slightly apart and weapons levelled.

There wasn't much distance to cover and Chris knew that the time for action was on them. He looked to Jon and motioned that he would take the man on the right. Jon nodded and fractionally altered his aim. A look towards Louis and Dodger, still on top of the rock saw that they too appreciated the inevitability of the situation. He watched as Louis held up a hand and could see him count down on the fingers from five to one. As the last digit fell, he saw past the aiming point on his rifle and saw the figure of Dodger drop from the top of the rock onto the man below. At the same time, both Jon and Chris squeezed their triggers and the two approaching men, now only a scant twenty yards away, were thrown backwards as a single bullet smashed into each of them. From that range, the shot was devastating and Chris saw his man's head spin to one side as the bullet took half the skull away. In his peripheral vision he saw Jon's man thrown back as a round tore his throat out and his body deflated on the spot.

As the noise of the discharges shattered the fabric of the desert morning, movement exploded around Chris. The four men that had been another one hundred and fifty yards distant and therefore unable to help came charging back; there were still five more men to deal with and now it was damage limitation. Their presence was announced, they needed to regain the tactical advantage and fast.

Chris and Jon rose from their positions and surged forward themselves, hoping to gain cover from the rocks ahead. Chris could hear shouts from the centre of the formation and looked at Louis, who was still on top of the centre outcrop. For the moment he alone was protecting the rest of his team and he started laying down fire towards the remainder of the militia. Dodger was involved in knife work with the leader and as Chris approached he watched as he almost took the leader's head off with a sweeping cut to the throat. As each artery was severed a vast spray of rich coloured blood shot to the front of the body as the heart continued to try and supply the brain. Dodger kept pulling back on the head though and the knife cut deep. In a moment, the red jet subsided. He let the man drop and without a second thought or pause he rejoined Louis in his elevated position. Chris reached the base of the central rock shortly behind him and as he looked left and right, he saw the rest of the team reach the extremities of the rectangle; the counter-attack was set.

All the militia fire from within was being directed towards the two on top of the rock, pinning them down. They were obviously unaware of the supporting forces waiting to engage. At a order from Louis, two Marines from either far end broke cover and opened fire at their nearest targets. The bullets from the semi automatics shot forward and there were audible thuds as the torsos of two of the remaining five were smashed, the convulsions brought on by the impact making the bodies look like rubber puppets, not flesh and bone. Louis had changed his delivery from general suppressing fire to more aimed shots and was able to rip the stomach from one more unfortunate, seeing the look of incredulity on the man's face as pain lanced into his abdomen and his intestines appeared in front of him. The two remaining didn't know where to turn and the seeds of their destruction were sown. As soon as their focus had shifted elsewhere, Chris and Jon moved out of cover in the centre and opened fire. Again, Chris saw his man only a couple of yards away take a full belt of fire from his weapon and watched as a line of bullet holes exploded across his chest from low left to high right, ending up in the neck. Each new mark produced an initial spot of blood on the shirt until, like Dodger's man, the neck shot produced a huge spray of fluid. It was swift, clinical and merciless. The enemy were caught in an inescapable crossfire and were cut down in seconds.

As the last body dropped, the Marines automatically silenced their weapons. There was a pause where no-one spoke or moved and then Louis climbed down from his position and, with Dodger at his side, he inspected the fallen, covered by the team around him. Each body in turn proved the success of the engagement. When he had finished, he called his men to him and they all walked forward, unscathed.

"Jon, Peanut, go and check those vehicles," he started, and the two went quickly as ordered. "Bobby, Stan, Pat, bring the three bodies from outside back into the middle, we need to contain this mess as much as possible."

Chris could tell from Louis' face and attitude he was not impressed. It may have been a clinical disposal of the enemy, but the risk had been high that at least one of his troop could have been hit or that the action would have given away their position, either through the sheer noise or by at least one of the militia getting away or radioing for support. If that had happened the mission would have been over before it had begun, achieving nothing. To Chris though, given the outcome, they still had a chance.

Soon the report came back that the vehicles were undamaged and the group was back together. "What about that radio?" Louis asked, grimly.

"Only one of the trucks has a VHF set," replied Jon. "And it made a couple of static squawks but I switched it off."

Louis considered the options then turned to face the others.

"Don't count this as a success," he stated. "This was about as bad as I could have predicted. We've been forced into an action that could have jeopardised everything. We did everything we could to avoid it but this tells me we continue to be sold down the river. It would seem that not only did they know to expect us here on this coast after we left Fujairah, but they knew the day we landed and the rough direction we were taking. What pisses me off the most is that the day after we passed those men during the night, they knew it and came after us, almost straight to our position. That tells me that they have an almost real time link into our networks. Any thoughts?"

Chris mulled over what Louis had said for a few seconds, drinking in the dreadful import of the words. "We were told before we left that they were keeping the details of this operation within the strictest of circles. They had a suspect and he was being shut out. Well, either they've got the wrong man, or he has some other link into this that we don't know about. Whatever we end up doing, we need to tell Head Quarters about this, and probably with a direct link into the Director. My gut feeling, however, is we're only a few miles or so from the training camp, which we can reach in a couple of hours, especially as we've got the trucks now. They still don't know exactly where we are or they would have sent more people and not come straight into the rocks, and that's a massive bonus. I think we have to go on with the rest of the plan as is," he finished.

Louis paused while he took in everything Chris had said then turned to his second in command. "What do you think Dodger?"

"We've got to call it in but I agree with Chris. We have to go on," he almost whispered in urgent and angry tones. "What fucks me off is that some bastard in our own fucking camp is trying to get me killed. Whoever it is, I'll be having words with him when I get back."

The scowl on his face said it all and it was obvious that most of the lads felt the same by the general murmurs of assent.

"OK then," continued Louis, decision made. "Pat, you've got the radio, get a link into Head Quarters. We're about six miles from the position we have for the training camp, which is our primary objective. We'll talk timings after I've spoken to the General."

After a brief conversation where the report of the latest near catastrophe was relayed to General Holbrook, Louis called them over one final time.

"The decision's in. We've got to get away from here but it would be suicide to move any closer to the objective during the day. There's another outcrop to the south so we'll take the trucks and bodies down there and hole up. With a little bit of luck we'll stay anonymous but even if they do send someone to hook up with this lot, all they'll find is an empty area. If we leave a bit of their kit and cover any blood stains they may even assume they've just moved on. Whatever happens, we wait until sunset and then move west in accordance with the current plan."

Half an hour later the recent battle zone had been scrubbed and almost all signs of the encounter removed. The bodies were placed in the back of the trucks and they mounted up for the short trip south. They had seen no other movement or indication that anyone else was approaching so they set off at as slow a pace as possible to minimise the amount of dust they sent up into the still air.

Only a few minutes later they got to the next group of rocks. Although it wasn't quite as large as the last, it was big enough to give some protection and they set themselves in to wait.

The heat was extreme. This was the middle of the day in sub-Saharan Africa and there was little forgiveness in the burn of the sun's rays. Even now in June as time moved to two, then to three, Chris could feel himself cooking in his uniform, exposed as he was in the afternoon sun while resting against the side of the rocks. Shade or not, it was a hellish place to be and they saw little sign of life. Every once in a while Chris stole a look at the small pile of Somali bodies off to one side, wondering who they had been and what had driven them to this end. It had been a sharp reminder of his old life.

He was now sweltering and losing copious amounts of water from his bruised body. All of them ensured they kept themselves as hydrated as possible by taking regular swigs from their bottles but this was a light mission; they had brought only as much as they thought they would need in order to cut down on pack weight.

The time continued to pass with nothing but the movement of the sun to observe. Then at about four thirty, and suddenly, which had always surprised Chris about the desert, the savage heat went out of the day. It was as if someone had turned down the thermostat and they knew that the worst was over. By five they could shut their eyes and by sunset most had managed to get an hour's sleep, or as much sleep as you can ever get after slaughtering eight people.

The going down of the sun brought about an inversely proportional increase in the group's awareness. They knew that the next phase was upon them. There was a thirty-minute twilight period where they allowed dark to truly fall then Louis gave the order for them to move out.

The two teams climbed into the trucks, with Louis and Dodger taking one each and Chris getting in with Louis. Jon and Peanut were the nominated drivers and they moved out, heading to the west, following the direction given to them by the GPS that would take them directly towards the training camp.

They made their way carefully as it was relatively dark with little moon to help light their way and the noise of the engines had to be kept to a minimum, especially this close to the enemy. Sound in the desert, like the sudden reduction in heat, was a strange beast; it could travel for distances much further than you would expect.

The ground eventually changed again and became loose packed sand with the occasional small drift, giving some indication that the nature of the area was different. The further they got inland, the more they could expect larger drifts and eventually a limited number of smaller dunes as the scrub gave way to the desiccation of the interior and the boundary of the true desert.

After the first hour they had covered two thirds of the distance, about four miles, with progress tentative over the rough terrain and hampered as they were by frequent stops to check for signs of life, pursuit or discovery. Once again it had become a solitary journey with no-one and nothing to see but themselves. They were aware, however, that they were getting within touching distance of the first *planned* engagement of the operation and alertness increased with every minute. It didn't take them long to cover the remainder of the distance and Louis stopped them a mile short of the GPS co-ordinates for their target.

"OK, we're pretty much here," he said in a whisper. "We take the packs a bit further but the trucks stay here. Standard formation. When we get to the objective, take your lead from me. Initially we're there to observe and then pull back. If necessary I may need to send Dodger with his team around to check a different side, so be prepared and we'll react to what we find. Any questions?"

Louis received curt nods in reply, but double and triple checking was understood and part of their business; it was why they had the professional reputation they had. The Special Forces were a breed apart from the norm. They were capable of extreme violence when called for but a huge part of their life and work required absolute patience. There were times when they would lie in cramped and uncomfortable conditions for weeks or isolated in hostile terrain, gathering intelligence on individuals or targets in support of major operations such as the Iraq war. Conversely, they could be deployed deep into the heart of metropolitan society, having to blend into the surroundings and populace before carrying out operations that would stun the locals if they knew what was happening around them. It was a rare individual that could cope with everything the Corps had to engage in; it was why the selection was so difficult and so many failed. It wasn't purely physical, a huge part was mental. But when the tests had been completed and missions begun, each man knew that he was the best and those around him were the best too. Louis looked at his men and knew they understood. They moved out.

Chris took his place behind Louis in the centre of a formation that had Jon on point followed by Stan, the experienced sergeant, then Louis in line. The rest followed with Bobby covering their rear. The terrain had changed to low dunes and softer sand and as they started forward, their senses peaked at the highest of levels, every one of them straining to see signs of movement, to hear any sound or even to smell anything that may have been carried to them over the night breezes.

The situation was highly dangerous, even for men as highly trained as them. They were going into unfamiliar territory towards a target they had not seen before when they had almost certainly been compromised. Every few hundred paces, primarily dictated by Jon at point, they stopped to assess their progress and to take stock. So far they had neither seen nor heard any signs of life, but that was to be expected; it was approaching ten p.m. Even worse, the dunes they were now climbing had got slightly larger and they no longer had sight beyond the one directly in front, effectively reducing the visible horizon to less than a hundred yards. Their direction of travel was across the ridges and so they were forced to creep to the top of each one in turn, which produced a succession of rises and falls in adrenalin levels each time. When the GPS told them that they were with three hundred yards, Louis stopped them again and went to join Jon at point.

After the penultimate ridge they changed formation so that there were two lines of four abreast for the final dune. After dropping their packs, Chris took his place alongside Louis in the first line, with his weapon held forward and made ready. He moved up the face of the dune flanked by Dodger to the left and Jon to the right, with the second four some ten yards behind. This was it, the final approach to what Chris had been dreaming of for a decade. As they lay there, about to put their heads over the top he felt that cold dispassionate zoning take over his mind and steel him for whatever lay ahead, ready to engage as required. Once again at a sign from Louis, they moved the remaining inches. Chris could see the top of the dune come closer to his eye level. Another few inches and he was almost there. Finally he put his head over the top and froze, staring ahead, not believing what he was seeing. His blood stopped moving through his veins, his breath caught.

Nothing! Fucking nothing! No tents, no vehicles, no men, only the bitter emptiness of a slightly wider space before the next dunes started again a couple of hundred metres away. He fell backwards and rolled over onto his back, staring at the inky blackness of the desert sky and the thousands of stars that festooned it. How could this be? The disappointment of a litany of previous missions came crashing down upon him and he started to seethe. For fucks sake not again, not now after so long and having had such high hopes. He lay there while the others on the ridge made a further inspection from their position, then they too slid back down. When they had reached the others, Louis made his first comments, no emotion, the professional as always.

"Dodger, take your team and go south for two hundred yards. I'll go north for the same. We'll cross the dune, assuming it is safe and sweep the area from each end."

Louis, Chris, Bobby and Peanut headed north and when they had travelled the distance, edged up to the top of the dune again. This time however, they didn't stop but first Peanut then the others slipped over with Chris third in line. When they had reached the floor Louis sent Bobby over to the next ridge at a run to gain the top, check that it was clear and that they weren't about to be caught in an ambush. He got the all clear and when Bobby returned they started their sweeping inspection, line abreast, with Dodger and the remaining three doing the same from the south.

Pretty soon it was clear to Chris that they had come to the right place, just that within the last few hours, certainly within the last day, what had been a camp of some sort had been lifted. He could see the tyre tracks of light vehicles on the sand around him and the imprint of activity clearly visible. Frustration and deep seated anger wrapped its arms around him.

After a thorough recce the teams met in the centre of the area. Louis ordered the packs retrieved then took the squad off to the north, opposite to the obvious direction taken by the evacuating men and therefore the least likely threat direction. There was no conversation and virtually no sign of emotion; this wasn't the time, they were in a very vulnerable position. They adopted their standard patrolling formation and moved as a team away from the area. Twenty minutes later and a mile from the abandoned camp they stopped again. Chris had been feeling pretty black and wasn't sure what they were about to do. They now had no target, no information and were in hostile territory with no support. They had definitely been compromised and therefore there was the highest risk of ambush. The only crumb of comfort was that they had yet to be fully engaged and so their exact position might be unknown. This gave them the slimmest of chances to regroup and to find a way out of the mess. Louis finally motioned for them to halt in the dip between two small dunes, sending Peanut and Jon up on either side to act as lookouts. The rest came together and centred upon him, a silence dripping with disappointment held motionless between them.

"Looks like we've been fucked again boys," was the elegant summary from Louis

CHAPTER 7

The plane touched down and Mustafa relaxed. Although he was happy to be abroad and was confident in his ability to move between countries almost uninhibited, being this close to an operation and with all the pieces now in play, he would prefer to reduce the risk by being secure and with his men. By his calculations, he should be about four days ahead of the Special Forces as they made their way from Fujairah on the submarine, supposedly clandestine and with the advantage back on their side. He was still angry that the raid on the hotel had been so ineffectual. It seemed to him that unless he, or a very limited amount of his planning cell, were either in direct control of, or intimately involved in the planning of any operation, it just didn't work. In this regard he was jealous of the enemy. The West had a discipline within the entire team that he could only dream of. He knew that, personally, he could match any of them in planning, from the strategic overview to the intimate details of an operation, but when it came to execution there was always an element of risk that he could never entirely eliminate. Whether it was the fundamental nature of his men, which he couldn't countenance, or just that the training the foreign agencies had was peerless compared with his guerrilla warriors, he didn't know. Subconsciously he suspected it was a combination of the two but his pride couldn't admit that on a conscious level.

When in Dubai on the last leg of his journey from St Lucia, he had changed from the expensive business suit he used when in the West to his traditional Arab robes, in which he felt more comfortable. The meeting with his benefactor had gone well in the end and it was the last time that he would have to explain his actions or plans before putting them into place.

Now he was ultimately in charge, without the encumbrance of interference, just the way he liked it. This was his time now and he hadn't risen to become the head of operations for Al-Qaeda by falling short of the mark.

The next move had to be to pit what strength he could against the coming of the Special Forces. He didn't know exactly where they would arrive, but he was hoping to get an update soon from Colonel Taylor about when. Just by looking at a map with his military planner's vision, Mustafa would be able to work out the most strategically beneficial place to land the Marines for insertion towards his training camp. If he made a couple of small but reasonable assumptions, he should be able to put into place cover along the coast, probably small teams of six to eight men who would intercept them as they made their way inland. It would be ideal if he could catch them at their most vulnerable on the beaches, but the chances of that were slim given the amount of men available to him and the length of coast. It would be better to stand just back from the shore with highly mobile units that could respond to the positional updates he hoped to get from Colonel Taylor's man on the inside. That way it was less likely that the Marines would be able to slip past, gain position and therefore the advantage.

He knew there was risk. There was no guarantee that his men would be able to take out the opposing team, even though he had massive weight of numbers and firepower in his favour; he had ultimate respect for the men that were coming his way. If it hadn't been for the informant, both he himself and a large proportion of the Al-Qaeda leadership would probably have been killed in past operations, especially in Afghanistan before they had been forced to relocate.

His master strategist's mind always had a fallback option, however, and in this case he was ready to move his training camp at a moment's notice. If he could he would have finished training now and sent his teams into position around their respective targets but there was still work to be done. He was waiting for a consignment of particularly nasty fragment grenades to be delivered from his Russian arms supplier, a delivery that should have arrived a week before but had been held up through the borders of several of the countries through which it had to cross. They had used the Afghanistan drug smuggling routes to the southern Pakistani port of Pasni, from where they had left ten days previously on a freighter bound for Cape Town in South Africa. It was never going to get there. Under his instruction, the ship had been intercepted by one of the pirate gangs operating further to the north and was being brought into the coast. For weapons smugglers it was perfect subterfuge and to the eyes of the West was just another pirated vessel. To Al-Qaeda and associated groups however, like so many ships before, it was a way to import huge quantities of weapons into Africa with almost no possibility of being challenged once they had left their port of embarkation. On top of that, it was a very valuable source of income, making it attractive to all concerned.

The grenades should make landfall tomorrow evening and get to him a day later, leaving his teams time to incorporate them into their plans. He never underestimated the benefits of training and would ensure they were so familiar with their weapons that they could use all of them blindfolded before going into battle.

That constant desire for perfection now left him vulnerable though. By his calculations he had time to complete what he needed in the desert, just, but his contingency was down to a couple of days. If his deployed men were unable to intercept the Special Force team by the morning after their arrival, he would have to move from the current camp. He would be ready; he had an alternative sight planned, some fifteen miles further south and west from the original, but he didn't want to use it yet. The sooner he relocated, the more chance he would give the western security forces to latch on to his new position and therefore give them the chance to vector in their men. It had to be as late as possible, which was inherently risky, but could work in his favour. If he moved late, the old position could act as a honey pot to the enemy that he could exploit, regaining the tactical advantage.

It was this strategic and tactical game that, if he were brutally honest, had always excited him. He knew that before he could deliver the blow he and his cause so desperately wanted, he would have to outwit the best the West could send at him on the ground. However they had tried before and they would try again but his tactical choices had never failed. It was even possible that this operation would secure him an even higher position within the organisation, not that self promotion was his driving force, but it would allow him more opportunity to use his talents for the cause.

He switched on his mobile phone and waited for the signal to kick in. One thing about Somalia was that they may have little government and warring factions on every street corner but you could get phone signals throughout the majority of the country; the irony wasn't wasted on him - western technology liberated his world. Within moments he joined the local network and received a message from his men saying that they were outside. He made his way through the sieve that was nominally called security in Mogadishu and out to the waiting Land Cruisers. He felt totally safe here, despite the lack of government. Everyone important enough to matter knew who and what he was or at least knew what people to let through unchecked and un-harassed, especially when travelling in a highly armed convoy in two new 4x4s. He had protection in the highest of circles and he made sure that it would stay that way by liberally spreading cash in the right places.

It was late afternoon and, as he was making his way out of the city on the five hour drive that would bring him eventually to his camp, the message alert on his phone sounded. He picked it up and opened the text. It was from a number that he recognised as the Colonel's back in the UK and was simply two words: 'three days'. This was the message he had been waiting for. The men would be inserted into the country three days from now, one day earlier than he had thought. That was fine; he would adjust his plans accordingly. The next stage of the game had begun. He relished the challenge.

The following two days passed relatively slowly for Mustafa. He reached the training camp without incident and settled down to assess his men. They were ahead of schedule and as soon as the grenades arrived, he thought they would be ready within the week he had set aside. This was all well and good but it wouldn't be quite quick enough to be able to side step the British operation that had been mounted against him. While it was annoyingly inconvenient, nothing had fundamentally changed.

He had arrived late at night, when the camp was in darkness, and it wasn't until the next day that he was able to start making plans to counter the Special Forces, due in another two days. What he came up with was good, if not foolproof and involved squads of militia dispersed throughout the area. It would take a certain amount of luck, but war always did and the old adage that a plan never survived first contact with the enemy usually held true. In this case his risk was that the opposing team was small and he had no way of knowing their exact location. They could always slip through the net or be missed entirely as they walked a few hundred yards away from one of his teams in the dead of night. He would have to impress upon his men the need to be extra vigilant, and this was where his greatest fear lay. He could plan in detail and tactically deploy his men brilliantly, but if they lost their discipline and were less than alert, the plan might fail.

Late on the following day he got the next piece of good news; the ship carrying the grenades had been pirated and driven past the network of international warships sitting off the coast, then brought into the Somali anchorages. It was remarkable that the pirates had managed to get away with this for so long, but it seemed that the so called international 'powers' were nothing of the sort. It was a win, win situation for the pirates. If they were at sea in international waters, even if they were in boats that could be nothing but a pirate skiff and were armed to the teeth, unless they were physically engaged in an act of piracy, they couldn't be touched. Even if they were caught in the act, they would merely be taken on board by the warships, their boats destroyed and returned to Somalia ready to get straight back into another vessel and out to sea again. If they waited until there were no warships around and then took a vessel, as long as they had the crew hostage, which could be achieved within a couple of hours at the most, and threatened to kill them, then the warships would just stand off and effectively escort them to shore. It was incredible to Mustafa that those old powers that paraded themselves as strong were so ineffectually weak, hamstrung in all their military glory by blustering politicians afraid to raise their heads above the parapet and take the decision to engage. But such was the way of the decaying West, the old strength of imperialism sapped by the parasitic smothering of democracy.

The following morning, the day of the Special Forces insertion, Mustafa gathered the fifty or so militia men that were going to be his deployed teams and gave them the brief. He stressed the importance of what they were doing and the reasons, but when he looked at them, he couldn't help feeling that his plan was slightly weaker than he had originally hoped. These men weren't the zealots of his own volunteers, inspired by his and their own ideological cause; they were part of the local population, hired in for the occasion. Somehow, he doubted if without close supervision they would provide him with the protection that he desired and required. If there had been enough of his own people he could have manned the position with them and would have been more confident; as it was, he started to feel the first pangs of unease.

At the camp for the rest of the day, the men continued to train, getting to know their new weapons, how they felt to carry and how they were best employed. He insisted upon repetitive use, the only way that anything became second nature. Mustafa wanted his men to be so familiar with their equipment that within a fraction of a second, they could be reaching and deploying the weapon of choice, whether that be the small sub machine guns they would be carrying, the hand guns or the grenades. Mustafa himself had started to become nervy. He was well aware that only a few miles to the east, a submarine carrying a Special Forces insertion team was probably already sitting off the coast, observing the layout of the beach and watching for any signs of life. It reminded him of Afghanistan, when Al-Qaeda had been based in the Tora Bora mountain caves. Everyone there knew there were countless American and multi-national Special Forces teams scouring the country looking for them. At any point they expected either an attack or an air strike called in by an observing team. The same sense of nervous expectation filled him now, although this time, he knew, he had the advantage. What he had to do was to resist the urge to get nearer the action. It was far more important that he retain the strategic overview. He was the target. They were coming for him but at the end of the day, his strike teams were of most value. He had to get them ready and he had to keep them safe. He couldn't do that if he were involved at the front.

Frustratingly, in the vacuum of information that followed, hours started to drag, then minutes seemed like hours as the evening fell. Mustafa ate alone in his tent. Until he started to get information from his teams he was tactically blind, merely reacting. It was this loss of direct control that fed his anxiety, as was always going to happen in a situation such as this. He was aware of his almost control freak tendencies but that didn't make it any easier. He wasn't completely at the mercy of chance though; regardless of how his militia men performed, his trump card was still Colonel Taylor's man on the team. He must trust that in the worst case scenario, that last line of defence would suffice.

Mustafa sat in his tent with his copy of the de-code map in front of him and his mobile phone on the table. The remains of his dinner lay relatively untouched on the side. Every once in a while his phone vibrated and sounded the alert he was waiting for, but each time it was nothing important. Time crept on: eleven, midnight, one o'clock. Then finally, after there had been silence for a couple of hours and he had started to doze, he was brought swiftly back to full alertness. He received a text of only one word from the number he knew was the Colonel. 'Down'. It was the word that told him that the first signal had been received, that the Marines were ashore and that he was awaiting the first position, which should come in within the first three to four hours. Despite Taylor being kept out of the loop at Head Quarters, the resourcefulness of the man did him nothing but credit. Now it was up to the militia in the field to carry out their actions and get Mustafa the prize he wanted. The capture of the Special Forces team and the mileage that could be gained from it would be the gold standard, but failing that, anything that removed the threat would be excellent and even better, if he could take out the thorn from his side that was the man Edwards, he would consider it a complete tactical success. How much of that he would achieve would be decided over the next forty-eight hours.

He called his deputy to him and gave instructions to contact the men deployed in the field, telling them that the enemy had landed. The next few hours would be crucial, he knew, and he was well aware that it was approaching two a.m. Like all good military commanders before him, he knew that sleep was one of the most powerful weapons of all and that he needed some. Now that he knew that the Special Force team were ashore and feet dry, he felt a calming of the nerves; the expectation had subsided and he felt the fatigue that over anxiety brought with it. He lay down on his bed and tried to clear his mind, which was easier said than done. The possibilities of the next few days kept playing over until he fell into an uneasy slumber, troubled by dreams of conflict. Every hour or so he awoke and looked at his watch, trying to gauge how far he had come through this most important of nights. Each time he was disappointed that he hadn't been woken with reports of an engagement and preferably a capture or killing.

At six when he could lie in bed no longer he got dressed and went outside into the burgeoning heat of the early morning. His squads had foregone training, which they had normally started by this time and when he emerged, he found his deputy waiting for him.

"Have you heard nothing, Omar?" he asked.

"Nothing yet," Omar replied.

"Pull them back," Mustafa continued. "The British teams were inserted last night and if our men haven't picked them up yet, they may well be passed. They know that moving during the day is suicide so they'll be holed up somewhere until dark. Get our men back to the fallback positions and strike camp; we leave as soon as possible for the alternative."

Omar turned on his heel and made for the communications tent, an incongruous affair that had several aerials at different positions surrounding it which linked Mustafa into various satellite and computer systems throughout the world. On the way he barked some orders at various squad leaders and the rest of the camp sprung into action. Each of the strike teams made towards their target mock up areas, one of Lakeside shopping centre in the UK, one of Notre Dame, the last of Munich Bahnhof and began to rapidly pull up the rope outlines, putting the materials into the backs of the ubiquitous Toyota pick-ups surrounding the camp.

Mustafa looked on, slightly annoyed that he was having to do this at all. It meant that his teams had failed to intercept the Special Forces at the first chance; he hoped it wouldn't be a foretaste of what was to come. However, he had taken this possibility into account and he would move to the fallback location.

At that point his phone buzzed and Mustafa's heart quickened slightly as he recognised the Colonel's number. Sure enough, it was a simple message giving a reference position. The man on the team had obviously managed to find time to send a positional update. He hurried back to his tent and the decode map lying on his table. Even given the vague accuracy of the message, the place it gave was only six miles to the east and roughly twelve miles from the coast. He needed to tell his militia they had been out manoeuvred and to give them some direction. Once again he called Omar to him.

"Omar," he started when the flap of his tent was swept aside. "They are roughly here," he said pointing to the relevant area on the map. "Have a team go to the area to investigate. If they find them, kill or capture. If there is nothing, we will ambush them here tonight."

Omar paused before reacting. "Mustafa, we are committing our forces most specifically here and with little fallback. How do you know where they are? We have heard nothing from our teams."

Mustafa looked back at him. Omar was his lieutenant and had been for several years. In Mustafa's absence, he had absolute responsibility for the camp and held the most intimate details of the plans. He was able to carry on the mission planning and organisation if for any reason Mustafa himself was incapacitated. He also knew about Colonel Taylor and the other sources of information but the exact extent of Mustafa's web of intelligence was his own and he guarded the specifics jealously. The only thing Omar knew about the Colonel was that he was a high value source in the military and the only other person who knew of the traitor on the British team was Mahmoud, his sponsor, currently somewhere between New York and St Lucia. Even now, Mustafa considered, it was no time to change.

"Omar," he replied. "You must trust me. I know what I am doing," he said gently.

"Of course, it shall be as you wish," and Omar turned from his place to give the orders.

Mustafa got up and started pacing. This game of chess was being played out in real time now. The enemy had moved its men and his counter had failed to intercept. This was his next move and he could only hope that it would be more successful. It should be; he had the crucial advantage that he knew where they would be in about sixteen hours. As long as he allowed them to get into the position he wanted, he could close the trap. Timing was the variable factor he couldn't completely control and the one that might allow his foe to get closer than he wanted, but timing was usually his forte.

Another half an hour and the last trucks were ready to go. He climbed on board his own Land Cruiser and they headed off to the south along the line of the dunes. It was relatively slow progress as driving through sandy desert usually was, but he wasn't unduly worried. He knew that his opponents wouldn't travel through the day so he had the time to operate at his own pace, to dictate rather than react.

He made the alternative position within two hours and was pleased to see his men were already setting up the training areas. The landscape here was different, although only about fifteen miles from the last position. The camp was no longer situated on a flat area between sand dunes; they had started to reduce in size almost immediately and then about five miles ago had become little more than ridges. The ground here was now harder and flatter, offering less protection but probably more warning of approaching forces; what Mustafa had given up on one hand, he had gained on the other. It wasn't perfect, but it should be quite adequate, and military operations were all about the best of a compromise. Its position would also be protected by teams he had relocated just to the north.

His priority was the communications tent; a General unable to communicate with his troops was impotent and without information from the front, he was unable to reorganise his men optimally. While it was being erected and the equipment set to work, he spent nervous minutes waiting. As soon as it was up, about half an hour later when it was approaching eleven, he demanded that Omar get in contact with the militia teams to find out where they were. As he had feared, they had yet to reach their new positions and he cursed them, now starting to get angry. Why could he not find soldiers that understood the concept of discipline? He needed them there now and had made it perfectly plain those were his orders. He had lost the initiative over the first night. He needed to get it back while the Special Forces rested and this was his way of doing it. Why did they not understand?

Angrily he stormed back to his tent, attracting fearful glances from the men around him. He called Omar to him once again.

"What is the minimum time for the attack force to be prepared?" he asked.

"'We need another two days before they will be absolutely ready to carry out the mission." Omar replied. "It is not so much the weapons, they will be ready with those in another day, it's the logistics of travelling to the different countries, reaching the safe houses and the details of getting into the attack positions. If they get pulled up on crossing the borders and fall down on their cover stories, the whole mission is at risk. You yourself have said that successful planning is all about detail. Without knowing every part of the arrangement, we are at risk, and it is a risk you have said we can minimise through this training."

"Unfortunately my friend, the situation has changed," Mustafa replied. "In an ideal world, we would do exactly that. At the moment however, we have a team sent by the British a few miles away and we must have a contingency option. This is a fallback position to complete the ground training only; we don't need to be here for the final instruction. We will stay here for another day, by which time our men should have intercepted the enemy at the old camp tonight. If that goes well, we will stay where we are. They won't know where the new camp is so we still have room for manoeuvre. If it goes badly, however, we will move by midday tomorrow and withdraw our men to the city to finish off. We cannot risk their exposure any more when it is fundamentally unnecessary to do so. Make sure that the men know the intentions and in the name of Allah, make the militia understand what is required of them. I will not be thwarted by lack of performance from those incompetents."

Omar slipped out of the tent and Mustafa was left alone, brooding. His risks were increasing and he didn't like it. He was within a hairs breadth of being ready for the mission and twenty-four hours would complete the field preparations. But he had to ask himself, given the failure of his other men to intercept the opposition, was he taking an unnecessary risk by keeping his strike teams so close to the enemy when he knew they were intent on engaging him? He started the process of justifying his decisions once again. Whichever way he thought about it though and despite the current risks, he kept coming back to the same fact; he needed the extra time. Moving the camp fifteen miles south had bought him that time.

His biggest advantage was the potential ambush of the Special Forces as they closed on his abandoned position. No – at this point he could do no more and he should be safe. He would accept the risks and react to the next throw of the dice as required.

Mustafa sat waiting for another hour, taking lunch more as habit than through want. By just gone twelve his patience had stretched far enough and he went in search of the confirmation he wanted; that his pieces were indeed in the places he needed them to be. He moved out into the furnace that was the heat of the midday sun and crossed the few yards to the communications tent. Omar had seen him emerge and had broken from supervising the strike team's afternoon training session to come in moments behind him.

"Is there something you need Mustafa?" he asked.

"Get in contact with the teams and find out where they are," he barked. "I want to know they aren't going to let me down again."

Omar got onto the VHF transmitter to get a progress report. It was more powerful than the normal hand held equipment and had better reception capabilities. One by one he called the teams. One by one he was answered.

Several miles to the east and out at sea, *HMS Talisman* was at periscope depth.

"Captain, Wireless Office," came the shout over the control net from the watch keeper in the communications shack.

"Captain," replied Commander Mike Saggers from his position in his cabin.

"Sir, we're getting that VHF traffic again from inland. The translator seems to think it may be the training camp. The signal is coming in loud and strong, Sir, which means it's probably a large transmitter as opposed to a hand held set."

"Got it," replied the Captain. "On my way."

He left his cabin and travelled down the two decks to the

communications room, a very small compartment that had far more equipment crammed into it than would have seemed possible but which nevertheless served the purpose required. There he found two watch keepers, the Radio Supervisor, RS by title, and a translator who had joined them for their missions east of the Suez canal.

"What have you got RS?" he asked the senior man.

"Sir, we're picking up one side of a conversation on VHF, in the clear and on standard frequencies. It seems to be from a stationary position and is communicating to what sounds like a number of different teams. We aren't hearing any replies as the signal is too weak, which in itself means that this might be some sort of Command Centre using a more powerful transmitter. It also seems to be the same transmitter that we heard earlier this morning. We managed to get a line of bearing from before but the translator wasn't in the shack so we don't know if it was the same man or what he was talking about. This is a much longer discussion so we've got a lot more from it. I've just passed the updated line of bearing to the navigational plot and, given the time between the two intercepts, we might be able to get a decent cross fix."

"What are they saying?" Saggers asked the translator.

"It's a series of the same question to five or six different groups, asking them if they are in position. There's no follow up so I can only presume he's getting the answer he wants. It looks like they're repositioning."

"OK, tell me if you get anything good and I'll see if we've come up with anything from that line of bearing. Good work."

The Captain made his way up to the control room, the operational centre of the submarine. "Officer of the Watch, have you managed to plot that VHF intercept yet?" he asked when he got there a minute later.

The current Officer of the Watch, the senior man of the two who were responsible for the at sea running of the submarine twenty-four hours a day, got out of the Captain's seat as soon as he heard him enter the control room.

"We're plotting it now, Sir," and together they moved to the navigational plot where there was a map of the Somali coast and where the junior officers were marking on the latest bearing of the transmissions. Something didn't seem quite right to Mike as he stared at the chart. The cross position he was looking at from the two bearings was too near the coast. As far as he had understood it from the closed door sessions he had had with Chris and Louis on the transit down, the insertion point had been almost due east of the position of the camp, leaving them about an eighteen mile hike to complete. He distinctly remembered marking the position mentally when they had been deciding where to land. This bearing was entirely wrong for that position and looking at the chart, could only mean that the camp had moved south, and if they had come no closer to the coast, his command trained eye calculated they must have moved a good ten miles south, if not more. While he had been thinking this through the Executive Officer, his second in Command and a fellow 'Perisher' submarine command qualified officer had joined him at the plotting table.

"I've been listening in on the net, Sir. Is this the cross fix position?"

"XO, come to my cabin for a minute."

When the curtain had closed behind them, the Captain started to voice his concerns.

"I think our team are going to the wrong place. Those transmissions indicate a transmitter that can only be associated with the command centre and it has the same patterns as the one we had this morning. When we talked about the plan with Chris and Louis on the way down we landed them in position to make the shortest route to the training camp, give or take a couple of yards. The position we've fixed out there is just plain wrong."

"Could they have got the original position wrong, Sir?"

"As far as I know, the position that they had been working to had been confirmed by satellite imagery over flights and all sorts of communications intercepts, mainly by American assets. The only conclusion I can make is that the bastards have moved the whole bloody camp. Given the time frame and the sequence of events, it looks as though they moved on the same day that the team were meant to reach them. You've got to ask yourself why."

The almost inevitable conclusion hung in the silence between them for a few moments, heavy and unpalatable. Then the Captain continued.

"To my mind, that leaves one of two possibilities. The first is that they have been discovered on the ground, which seems a little unlikely as they would almost certainly have been engaged and we would have been called for an extraction. On top of that, if they had been fought off, Mustafa wouldn't need to move camp. The second, and this is the frightening one, is that they have always known about the insertion and have been keeping tabs on the position of our teams with such accuracy that they know they are near and about to engage. But how could that be possible? The only people who know the position of the teams, even roughly, are this crew, and nothing has left this submarine, one or two back at Head Quarters in Poole, and the team themselves."

Again there was silence while the Captain and Executive Officer tried to refute the logic of the facts.

"Sir," started the XO. "Am I right in saying that this has been kept to absolutely trusted people at HQ?"

"You were in on the discussions after we left Fujairah; that's the impression I got."

"It seems highly unlikely but it looks to me then that they've got someone inside the team who's sending real time information. If you agree, HQ have got to know. Even if it's nothing, at least they can try and task some assets to take a picture of the area and find out if the camp really has moved. If it has, they can get the new position out and more importantly, let them know they may have a mole with them. We may even be able to save some lives if we're quick."

The Captain picked up the internal phone and contacted the communications office.

"RS, this is the Captain. Get me Special Forces Head Quarters on secure voice network. I want to speak to the Director himself; he should be available. Ensure that it is the Director and don't get fobbed off with anyone else. I'm on the way down."

"Yes Sir."

Moments later the Captain arrived in the 'shack' and the Radio Supervisor reported that he had the Director standing by. Mike told the watch keepers to leave them and reported his views to the General, who seemed to take it remarkably calmly, but this seemed to be the way of the man. After the conversation was over, Mike sat back and turned the situation over in his mind. His mate was out there and as far as he could see, there was a distinct possibility he was about to be ambushed. He could only pray for some sort of salvation and that he'd been quick enough. It was half past two local time.

The Director in Poole put down the handset and looked at the operations officer, Major Shaw. Only a few minutes before he had been speaking with the deployed team. The conversation with the Captain of *HMS Talisman* had been fractionally too late to help his men.

"Get in touch with the Americans. We need satellite imagery of the camp about as fast as they can do it. I want to know if it has moved. If it has, our men are stepping into a much riskier situation than we knew and we need to tell them."

The General went back to the corner of the operations room and waited for the reply to come back from the Americans. He knew that the leak hadn't come from his Head Quarters as he was firmly locked down and therefore it could only have come from the team on the ground. This was a shocking revelation. There had to be two traitors - the Deputy Director Taylor he was sure was one, but someone deployed as well? The names of the team members played over in his mind but he couldn't single any of them out as viable candidates.

He looked at his watch; half eleven UK time. Even if the US had an asset available, the earliest they could get imagery and useful information back would be about twenty-one hundred UK time or midnight local, at about the time his men would be looking to investigate the camp. Even if the Major should get in touch again, which he wasn't planning to do, should he warn him or trust to his team on the ground? He potentially had information that they needed but they were currently on a limited communications routine, only contacting base when absolutely necessary and that could be any time overnight.

This was a horrendous dilemma and one for which no answer seemed right. If he told the Major of a possible second traitor and the suspicions weren't true, it could sow highly damaging seeds of mistrust among the team, something that would ruin their cohesion and probably prove fatal. If he said nothing however, there was indeed a second traitor and people died through his decision, he would never be able to forgive himself.

General Holbrook sat in his corner, staring into the semi-darkness, considering the options and assessing the risk; it was what he did. Each way led to potential disaster but he had to make a decision. He decided to say nothing. He refused to psychologically burden his men with an as yet unproven allegation. God help them he thought, and God forgive me if it goes wrong.

The operations officer came back to him within twenty minutes.

"Sir, the US can support but they won't have a bird overhead until nineteen hundred our time, twenty-two hundred local."

"Thank you, son," the General replied in that soft way that belied the furious rage that was being contained within him. "Make it happen," he ordered. If his men died because of these two traitors, particularly Colonel Taylor, whom he had known and operated with for decades, a man who had held his closest trust and confidences, he would kill him himself. As for the other man, whoever it was, he hoped the operation would claim at least one life. Until Louis got in contact again, like Mustafa, he could only sit and wait.

Mustafa walked a small distance from the camp. It was now approaching four pm and he wanted another update. He found Omar in the communications tent.

"Have you heard anything more?" he asked.

"Nothing yet," Omar replied. "The teams have been checking in periodically, all apart from the rock outcrop. The last time we heard from them they had got into position and had seen nothing. That was just after twelve."

"Get in contact again," Mustafa ordered. "I want positive control here, not assumptions."

Omar gave the requisite instructions to the radio operators and stood back for the reply. The first transmission got no response. Neither did the second. By the third, Mustafa could feel the rage rising in him. After the fourth, the cold dread of failure crept along his spine. There could only be a couple of explanations for this. Either there was something wrong with the radio, but only a fool would accept that as a possibility, or they had been taken out.

He had to assume he was one team down. In the name of Allah what was going on? He realised he had made a tactical error by splitting his men down to an individual team and now he had paid the price. It was time to repair the damage as fast as he could. He could only hope that he could plug the gap.

"Omar. Get in touch with the teams. I want at least two teams together at all times."

Mustafa strode back to his tent and threw the entrance flap aside furiously. He couldn't believe he had miscalculated so badly and cost himself so dearly. He didn't care about the local idiots, now presumably dead somewhere, it was the tactical mistake that angered him and bruised his pride so badly. An hour of contemplation later and with his composure regained, he was able to reassess logically. An hour after that and he was able to see that except for the loss of the men, the plan had fundamentally not changed. He now knew where the Marines had been and therefore obviously where they were going and with his men redistributed he would still be able to cover the ambush. He decided he needed some air.

The oncoming sunset was turning the sky a burning orange in the west and a dark blue in the east, a foretaste of the night that was so near. Despite the setbacks, he was still in control. The trap would still be sprung and with his overwhelming numbers, he should prevail. In a few hours it would be all over. If he could take prisoners it would be fantastic for the political gains but he was getting sick of the enemy's presence. He decided he just wanted to take the enemy out.

The eve of battle was upon him. What position would he be in come morning? The imponderables kept attacking him in a whirl of unquantifiable possibilities. The sun was setting. What would the future bring when it rose again?

He turned back to the camp. The heat had left the day and already he could feel the evening breeze start as the heat from the land rose into the cloudless sky. He looked to the heavens and intoned, "Allah is great. Bless me this night."

CHAPTER 8

Louis, Chris and the others were gathered together between two small sand dunes a mile north of the original camp site with Peanut and Jon placed high on either side to warn of any approaching enemy troops. It was almost two a.m. and the certainty that they were being played for fools had crept up on them like a sledgehammer! The only good thing was they had yet to be ambushed, so could hope they still had the immediate tactical advantage. It was time for Louis to step up to the mark. Chris didn't envy his position and wondered what he was about to say.

"OK lads," Louis started. "Looks like we're in a pretty vulnerable position. The camp has been struck sometime within the last day, most likely in the daytime. They obviously know what we've been doing, where and when. How the fuck that's happened I'm not sure but anyway we've got to work out whether the risk of going on is worth the gain."

"We've got to phone this in. There's no way that Head Quarters won't want to know what's going on. They may even make the decision for us but before I make the call, we need to understand what the chances of completing the mission are. Can we still achieve our goal? If we can, I think we need to go on, even though the circumstances of the operation have changed. If we can't, then we withdraw to the coast and get Chris's buddies to extract us. I want input – Chris?"

"Louis, even after all this we're still on our own and that's a huge advantage; we can operate to our own agenda. As soon as they start dictating the plan, then it's time to bug out. Can we still carry out the mission? It all depends upon where they've gone. If they're still in the near vicinity then there's no reason why we shouldn't be able to get into contact and disrupt at least, destroy if we can and certainly have a stab at Mustafa. As long as they don't have us cornered and we have freedom of manoeuvre, then we should go on. If they are out of the area entirely, then we should be too."

"Dodger, what have you got?"

"We should carry on. The risks are self evident but it's our job to minimise them as much as possible, not get frightened off. As Chris said, they still haven't deliberately engaged us yet and at the end of the day, somewhere not too far away from here, I suspect, there are a bunch of bastards making ready to launch something big at our home countries. If I bottled out now without trying to at least disrupt what they're doing and in two months' time hundreds of people died in London, I couldn't live with myself. I reckon there's only one thing we can do, and that's to go on until we're forced to retreat. Now is not the time; we should carry on."

"OK, has anyone got any violent disagreements with anything that's been said?" The question was met with a few shakes of the head. "I'll call it in and see what they say. This all depends of course on where this camp has gone. If it's fucked off completely, we're out of business. Pat," Louis called to the Canadian. "Get me the DIrector."

Within moments, Louis had the Director on the radio and was letting him know the bad news. The Director let him speak first and then started talking himself, going into some detail about what the submarine had picked up, the possibility they had come up with and the over flight that they had asked the Americans for that evening.

"We got the imagery about two hours ago and had the analysts on it straight away," the Director spoke without displaying the emotion that was within him; his men didn't need that. "They moved sometime today, but only about fifteen miles away to the south. We've got pictures of the same main tents as before, so we can presume it is the same set up. How are you set there?"

"We're fucked off that someone's selling us out but overall good to go, Sir," replied Louis, a direct answer to a direct question. "As far as we are concerned, we want to go on if there's the slightest chance we can get through."

"I agree, Major. We're still in the game at the moment. First off, get yourself to the new camp and try to establish what they're doing. If you can, identify the men in charge and report. It may be that we can take out the camp with a strike from *HMS Talisman* using Tomahawk missiles. The agreement from the Navy and the PM should be in at any time but the decision to fire will have to be backed up by the intelligence from other agencies and your intelligence from the ground. We'll have to work fast though so get onto it. Get back in touch when you have something concrete. I'll be standing by. Remember though Major, you have Mission Command. Take the decisions you have to before coming back to me. I'll back your judgement whatever. Good luck."

Louis ended the call and turned back to his men, relaying the instructions.

"We're on, boys. First thing is to get to the new camp, which is about fifteen miles to the south. With the trucks we can be there before daybreak and be in position to observe what they're up to. If we can confirm that it's a terrorist camp and even better, if Mustafa is there, then we call it in and see if we can get Chris's mate to send in some Tomahawks about dawn. We'll skirt about a mile west of this ridge and then head south. We need the trucks so we head back east first, standard formation. All understood? Right, let's go."

Louis indicated the direction he wanted to take, which was towards where Jon had set himself as look out a hundred yards away and after calling Peanut back from the west side of the dunes they took the same formation they had used on the approach. They walked with purpose now. They knew that their quarry was aware that they were in area and wanted to keep in front of whatever he put in the way. That meant that time was absolutely critical and the quicker they got there, the better. They also had to race the dawn.

Mustafa sat in his command tent, his own second in command, Omar, next to him. It was approaching two a.m. and he had to presume that the Special Forces had reached, or were very close to the original camp. It was time to close the trap. He nodded to Omar and they both left the tent for the communications area a few yards away.

Omar gave the orders for the men to close. One by one he got acknowledgements from the remaining teams and Mustafa could imagine them swinging into action, mounting into the rear of their pick-up trucks, checking their weapons and making their approach. Two teams were three miles north of the original camp, the other three, five miles to the south. They had to get there at the same time or near as damn it. As always, a plan was only as good as its execution and with the help of Allah he needed the execution of this to be right. If it was, he was sitting pretty.

Onboard the submarine, the comms shack fairly screamed over the net. "Captain, Sir, Wireless Office. We've got VHF transmissions from the same direction. The order has just gone out to move. Five transmissions repeating the orders. It sounds like they're carrying out operations, Sir."

Commander Mike Saggers virtually ran down the three flights and saw the translations for himself. "Get me HQ in Poole – Now."

The Director was sitting in the same corner of the ops room as before when the Operations Officer came out from his own communications office. "Sir, it's the submarine. They've got indications that the enemy are starting an operation. Our boys have only just signed off and we can't raise them. They're on their own."

The General looked calmly back at the man. "Then God help them, son - because we can't."

Jon's position on top of the easterly dune wasn't far but before they reached him Jon motioned vigorously for them to stop. Immediately they all dropped into defensive stances, covering all angles in the way they had done so many times over the last thirty-six hours. Louis gave it fifteen seconds to assess any immediate threat then scurried to the top of the ridge when beckoned forward.

"What have you got, Jon?" he asked in a low voice when he got there.

"I think we've got company to the north," Jon whispered. "Look over there," he said, pointing into the distance. He offered the night vision goggles to Louis who stared intently in the direction indicated. 'I think I can make out the outline of two trucks like those we saw at the rocks and then go left about fifteen degrees and there are two more' he continued. "If it's the same as before, that could be about sixteen men. What do you think?"

After a few seconds, Louis answered, "I think you're right. And by the look of it they've just started to come our way."

As he looked, Louis could see movement around the vehicles about two miles away. There were no lights showing but one by one the trucks started to move. They had been in a half circle. Now they had taken positions in line abreast, four vehicles in total, two pairs separated by about a hundred yards.

"First mistake," said Louis. "They've split their forces." He scrambled down the face of the dune the few feet to the rest of his men and considered his options. The dunes ran pretty much north-south and in the position they were at the moment, it was a natural gully. The desert ridges weren't huge here and they had narrowed somewhat from the area of the first training camp so that there was about one hundred and fifty yards of flat-ish ground between them. If you were caught in the middle of the gap and attacked from above, then you were pretty much a sitting duck, able to go forward or back, but nowhere else. By the look of it, the trucks were coming straight down the middle, albeit spaced slightly apart. This played absolutely in to their hands. With the enemy forces divided, it evened up the odds, although the plan Louis had would divide his men as well.

"Lads, we're well and truly busted. If what we saw before was a team, it looks like we've got two more coming down from the north now. They're about two miles away coming very slowly towards us. I reckon we've got about twelve minutes before they get to our position. We're going to have to fight our way out of this one and see where it leads."

"Dodger, stay here on the east ridge with your men and get behind it. I'll take my four to the west ridge and do the same. On my order, two of you take a truck each and mow them down. Make sure you get the drivers first so they can't get away. Basically, we need to take them all out. Use saturation firepower and shoot to kill. Got it? Go."

They still had their packs with them but Chris followed Louis, Peanut and Bobby over to the top of the west ridge at a flat run. The briefing had taken a couple of minutes, which meant that within about ten more, if nothing else changed, they were about to engage sixteen men who were highly armed and mobile. The element of surprise would help but you could never tell the outcome of any engagement after the first shot had been fired.

They spread out along the top of the dune and readied their weapons. The stillness of the night was claustrophobic, especially now, and Chris strained to catch the slightest hint of noise from the approaching vehicles. The only people with their heads over the parapet were Peanut, the first in line and Louis. On the other side, it was just Dodger. The rest of them kept their heads below the sightline, hoping not to show any profile that might give them away.

At first, Chris could hear nothing but the pounding of his heart. He held his weapon close to his chest as he lay with his back to the dune, almost caressing it. At that point it was the most important thing in his world. If it jammed at the wrong time, it could mean his death or one of his comrades. If it served him well, it would be the instrument of death for one or more of the approaching militia. They meant to kill them all.

Another few minutes of stillness and then the faintest sound of engines at low revs came through the air. Louis could obviously see the approaching men quite plainly because he let Peanut drop below the skyline and lowered himself even further, so that only the very top of his head was exposed. Chris listened as the sound of the engines got slightly louder and imagined their position. They couldn't be more than two hundred yards away now. He couldn't help wondering if the men inside the trucks were equally poised, perhaps frightened at what was in store, expecting some sort of interaction or whether the first thing they would sense would be the sudden noise of eight automatic fire rifles firing in the night or even the slamming of a bullet into their faces as they were mown down.

He could hear the vehicles approaching parallel with their own position, moving slowly forward. On the throat mikes Louis told them to take up firing positions and Chris turned over. With the other three men, he inched upwards and as his head cleared the top, he could see the battle ground in front of him. It was as Louis had predicted. The nearest pick-ups were only a matter of forty yards away and slightly below their position. They had also staggered slightly so that there was a lead vehicle and one following, mirrored by the remaining two on the other side of the gully. This was a perfect ambush and the excitement flared as the adrenalin of the moment filled Chris's body. His senses were driving fast up to overload and he needed the release of battle to calm his nerves. Fifty or so yards more and the trucks would be level. Louis motioned to Chris and Bobby to take the lead truck, Peanut and Louis would take the second. He waited what seemed to be an excruciating amount of time, then the moment was there. Louis started counting down on the throat mikes and Chris listened as three turned into two, into one.

At three, Chris released his safety catch, at two he took aim. By one, he had the lead sight on the cab of the truck and at zero he squeezed the trigger, a flood of emotion leaving him at the same time as the bullets sped from the muzzle of his carbine. There was nothing wrong with his aim. The first rounds slammed into the near side of the cab, only a few yards away. He watched the head of the man sitting there disintegrate and he knew it was time to engage the men in the rear. He knew Bobby was doing the same as within seconds, the truck had slewed off track, the driver having been taken out in similar fashion.

It was obvious that battle had been commenced at the same time on both sides. The stillness of the night had been ripped apart from Dodger's side as well and within a few seconds, the teams below had been decimated. But they hadn't been completely subdued. To their credit they returned fire almost immediately, wildly at first, then more aimed. The drivers had all been killed as a priority, which immobilised the transport, but those of the men that survived the initial assault and had been in the flatbeds were soon using the vehicle hulks as shielding and returning aimed shots.

Chris felt his blood roar as he aimed at his next target, a man behind the cover of the nearest truck only forty or so yards below him. Every few seconds he would raise his head and shoot towards their position and Chris would either hear the whine of the round as it flew overhead, or occasionally feel the hard thud as the rounds slammed into the sand below them. He managed another burst before Chris got the measure of him. He paused, knowing where the man would appear, took careful aim and waited. The world around him dropped out of his perception. There was only one thing now, the man below. He waited and then the target appeared for a fraction of a second, but a fraction was all Chris needed. He squeezed his trigger once again and saw a head explode in his sights, the high velocity round smashing through the forehead and ripping the top of the man's head off.

The engagement was over within two minutes and as quickly as it had begun, the silence crashed down on them as if resentful of its temporary displacement. At the end, sixteen men lay on the ground or in the front of their trucks, broken, bloodied and dead. After a moment, Louis stepped over the ridge and the rest followed, bar one each side who stayed to act as lookouts. The walk for Chris was a long one. This was only the second engagement since arriving and the brutal violence of it had shocked him, as it always had done in truth. He surveyed the scene and took no pleasure in it. He had just killed two men. There was never any pleasure in that.

Mustafa checked his watch. It had been ten minutes since the order went out. At ten miles an hour the southern four teams would be at the first camp in another twenty minutes, the northern teams in another ten. Each minute was excruciating. Over the years and through the many operations he had run, he had never managed to master the adrenalin surges that inevitably came upon him in waves as the action developed. Not hearing anything was the worst, even worse than being directly involved. You were left with a cold feeling of dread at the negative possibilities before you got the next piece of good news, when your adrenaline surged again. This time, he wasn't expecting to hear from the teams until after they had engaged. There had been an unexpected burst of static for a few seconds a couple of minutes previous that had broken the tense silence inside the communications tent but it returned to normal almost immediately. No – not knowing was the worst.

Chris and the others approached the battle scene in silence, their senses still operating at hyper levels. It was just as risky now as before. They had no idea if their opponents were fully taken out or if some were alive, waiting to score a hit; they would have to check all the bodies thoroughly, although by the look of them, there wasn't much doubt. There was also the noise that the engagement had made and the threat of attracting others in the area - they would have to make a very sharp retreat. While they could hold their own in limited actions, they were designed to carry out surveillance and clinical strikes, not major engagements.

Standing over and checking the bodies, Chris could feel the violence of the last couple of minutes still lingering in the air. Whether it was the smell of cordite or the imposition of silence after the huge disturbance, the air seemed to crackle with electricity. As he walked across the slightly sloping lower part of the dune towards his first victim in the front of the lead vehicle, he felt the strange flatness that he remembered, the cold dispassion after the zenith of the fire fight. His weapon was readied again and levelled at the cab, but nothing moved, indeed, nothing was going to move there again. The man's body was virtually headless, the majority of the skull having been removed by the bullets that had smashed their way into it in the fractions of seconds at the start of the engagement. He looked across at the driver, who had fared little better, his hands still gripping the wheel ahead of him but with no chance of making any more journeys.

Bobby was with him, watching his back and checking the other side of the truck. There they found two more bodies, the rest of the occupants, including the one that Chris had waited for and taken out so clinically. This was no time for reflection though. Once satisfied that their targets were history, they watched the others as, one by one, Louis got the thumbs up from each team. It had been as effective as they had wanted, sixteen men down and no casualties. Louis called them together. There was little preamble; everyone realised that what had just happened was their job, no more, however well executed.

"The game has changed again, boys," he started. "They know exactly where we are right now and I don't know how many people they've got looking for us but I'll bet this bunch weren't all of them, even with that first lot yesterday. However we've now got some pretty strong information about who's after us. This lot are local militia and are no more than hired hands. The fact that they knew where we were means that whoever moved this camp knows of us and has taken steps to take us out. That's a pretty well organised and funded operation, not just a local warlord or pissy little group of pirates; this can only be Al-Qaeda. The only question now is if Al Said is with them at the new camp.

"We've obviously lost the element of surprise," Louis continued. "But we've still got the tactical advantage and we've reduced the numbers of forces ranged against us. I know they're expecting us but as long as we can get some eyeball on the camp, we can call in a strike from the sub. Given the advantage that the vehicles give us, we could get to the camp from an oblique direction, pinpoint the position, feed it in to HQ and get a strike delivered within two hours. By my reckoning that's just about fast enough to throw Mustafa off guard. He's obviously confident of his boys taking us out or he would have moved his camp further away. I don't know where he gets his bollocks from or his information for that matter, but we can use it against him. I say we grab a truck, get off the expected track to the west, bypass whatever forces are waiting for us on the way and call in the strike. Anyone disagree?"

There was no dissent from the rest, still high from the fight and with adrenalin levels pumping.

"Bobby, Stan, find me two vehicles that still work. I want to be mobile and out of here in ten minutes. Peanut, Jon," he spoke to the two lookouts still at the top of the dunes. "You got anything?"

Chris saw the shake of the heads, signifying that despite what had taken place here over the last few minutes, the Marines were still on their own and had got away with the engagement. He looked over at Louis and watched him walk away with Dodger. He had been given no task so he walked towards the nearest vehicle to see if it was still operational. In those few yards between, his mind had the time to analyse what had just happened and he started to feel the crash after the adrenalin high. He had a lot of experience so was surprised at his reaction. He felt deep shock at the core of his body, as if he had been stunned, and then, as he approached the cab of the truck and started to see the bodies and dismembered heads of the men he had only a few minutes ago slaughtered, he was overwhelmed by revulsion. He had seen it so many times before, but it made him remember the looks on the faces of each new recruit after their own first engagements; the raw exposure to the fact of killing - the blood, the stench, the primeval bloodlust of the warrior soldier struggling with the higher consciousness that civilised society had taught them to value so highly – the value of life itself. He understood that look all over again.

After pulling the body of the driver out of the way, releasing his dead hands from the wheel in the process, he grabbed a piece of rag and wiped the surfaces clean. The keys were still in the ignition and he turned them. The engine sprung into life as if nothing had happened and idled there. He checked the tank, which was half full and then went round the other side to remove the second man kicking out the shattered windscreen when he got there. They were in luck, here at least. This was one of the vehicles they needed. He signalled to Louis and drove it round to the centre of the group. Peanut was doing the same with another; they had the two.

The two lookouts came scampering down from the top of the dunes to join the rest as they mounted up and headed out towards the west, their packs retrieved and slung in the back. Chris got into the cab of his vehicle with Louis beside him.

They found a low point in the dunes and crossed, then ran south for a few hundred more metres and crossed again. They kept on doing this until they had gone for about a mile, then Louis stopped the trucks and got out.

"Pat," he called back to the Canadian in the back of the second vehicle. "Get in touch with Head Quarters again."

Within a few minutes, Pat had made contact with Poole, the Director on the other end of the line as always. "Sir, we've had contact, sixteen locals taken down, no casualties." Louis explained the circumstances surrounding the engagement.

"What's your plan, Major?" asked the General.

"Sir, these men are just locals but the technology behind this is pure Al-Qaeda. I think we can safely say we've found our man, we just need some final confirmation. We've taken two of the pick-ups and are due west of the original camp. I want to get south to camp two as soon as we can and if we can make some sort of visual ID, I want to phone it in and get the sub to take it out with Tomahawk. Is that possible? We have the initiative here; I think we should use it. They certainly won't be expecting us to turn up on their doorsteps in the next hour. If we're lucky and it is our man, this mission can be over before dawn."

"I'm way ahead of you there Major Armstrong," replied the General. "We discussed the possibility of using Tomahawk with Captain Absolom at Fleet Operations earlier on today. The planners are sending out the missile instructions to the boat as we speak. If you can get there, they'll be ready. Your plan is approved. Get to camp two, get visual ID and call the strike in. The missiles will be on target twenty-five minutes after your call. After the strike, get some Battle Damage Assessment. I want to know who and what is gone. You have Mission Command Major but are you clear on your parameters and my intentions?"

"Got it, Sir."

"Good luck, son. We'll be here when you need us."

Louis turned to the rest. "We're on." Chris saw the relief on their faces, a couple even broke into smiles. They got back into the trucks and started to make slow progress to the south, this time along the lines of the small dunes. It was a lot easier going and they could have covered the ground more quickly but the name of the game was stealth; they had no idea what was out against them. They had just been intercepted by sixteen men in four vehicles. Lord only knew what else was out there.

Mustafa paced his communications tent. It was half an hour since he had given the orders to move and he was getting nervous. His teams should be getting to the first camp and engaging the Special Forces by now, if they were there. It was always the same when directing operations, whichever side you were on. Another five minutes and he would tell Omar to get in contact with the leader of each detachment for a progress report. He hadn't had an update from the Colonel on the position of his man for some time, which could be a good or bad thing. Either he was lying dead somewhere, which would be preferable, he was busy, which would be bearable, or the worst possibility was that the British were roaming free and closing in on him but he hadn't had the opportunity to send an update.

The range of options kept playing through his mind, each generating a plan that he could put into action if required. He decided that in the worst case and he had no idea where the Special Forces were by dawn, then he would abandon the camp and take his fighters elsewhere, into the safety of any one of the series of Mogadishu safe houses that Al-Qaeda had set up after the collapse of their bases in Afghanistan and Pakistan. They might be a day short of the training they needed to get fully up to speed but without knowledge of the enemy position, the risk of staying was too great. He reasoned that there was no real way that they could know where he was yet, having left it so late to move from camp number one and so he was still safe. He had his troops arranged to provide him a protective barrier to the North and he still had the tactical advantage. Clear in his mind about the way ahead, he felt a little calmer.

"Omar," he called to his deputy on the other side of the tent. "Get in touch with the teams. I want a progress report."

Omar turned to the radio operator and gave the requisite orders. The set was readied and he was handed the microphone.

"Team three, this is Base," he started to call the team leader of the larger and more southerly group. When there was no reply he tried again, then again, with nothing heard in reply.

Mustafa's fears grew large in a very small amount of time. Nothing? NOTHING? Surely this couldn't be. Why the hell weren't they answering. Surely they couldn't have been engaged; there were thirty-two men against a small force of eight. Such a group would run from those odds or would be wiped out in seconds, even if they were the Special Forces. He started to take the few steps to get to the radio set himself but as he was about to grab the microphone, a laconic voice came over the airwaves.

"Base, this is team three."

Mustafa stopped in his tracks and let Omar continue.

"What is your status?" he asked.

Again there was a slight pause but the answer came quicker this time. It wasn't what Mustafa wanted to hear.

"We are at number one camp and there is no-one here. We can't see any signs of movement or that anyone has been around."

"What about the other teams?" Omar continued.

"No sign," was the answer.

Omar looked round at Mustafa, who showed his puzzlement with a slight tilt of the head. That's not right, he thought. The southern teams were much further away from the base camp when the order to move was given. The northern group should have been there at least ten minutes or so before and should have flushed the Marines towards the much greater force, ready for an overwhelming engagement. Surely they must have moved when they had been told; he had been quite specific. This definitely wasn't right and his mind started to race. His plans couldn't have failed again, they couldn't have done. What was his contingency option? The last thing he wanted to do was to send his entire force further north. That would leave him horribly exposed where he was.

"Tell them to stay where they are then try to raise the northern teams."

Omar repeated the order to team three then made the call again, this time to team six, the lead team to the north. Nothing. Again the call was made, again nothing heard in reply. He tried a third time then turned again to face Mustafa, whose face had frozen.

This can't be. There had been sixteen men in those two teams. That should have been enough to force a retreat from the Marines and even if they did engage, there were enough militia to put up a fight, even to win if they were lucky and if they weren't, to retreat and call in the contact or wait for re-enforcements. What the hell was he going to do now? Mustafa lacked information and as always it was the unknown that he couldn't factor in. He was on the verge of pulling out of the camp he was in now but he had to try and get some facts to inform his decision. It was still an hour or so until dawn and he made up his mind.

"Tell them to send one truck north until they make contact with the northern teams, then call in with details. The rest of them, make their way back here and watch out for the enemy on their way; they could be anywhere."

"How long until dawn?" Chris asked Louis as they made their turn to the east and supposedly back towards the site of the second camp.

"About an hour now," replied Louis. "We'll take the vehicles another half a mile then we'll do the rest on foot. I'll only take six men with me in case I need to call for the trucks to come and extract us. We should be able to get eyes on in about half an hour, just enough time to call in the strike before the sun gets in the way."

Chris looked towards the east and saw a faint lightening of the inky black night sky that symbolised the coming of the new day. A few minutes later the trucks came to a halt and they dismounted. Leaving Jon and Peanut behind, the rest left their packs in the back of the vehicles and moved as silently as they could forward in formation, Stan in the lead with Louis and Chris following close behind, Pat with the communications, Dodger, then Bobby bringing up the rear. No-one spoke. They all knew what they were supposed to do.

Stan signalled a halt as he reached a ridge top and they dropped to the ground, again covering every angle. He motioned Louis and Chris forward.

As he reached the ridge, Louis very carefully raised his head above the sand and Chris did the same. There in front of him were a collection of tents, two larger than the others and slightly set aside. The ten or so others seemed to be ranged around camp fires that had burned low overnight. A couple of men were sitting there, with what looked like Kalashnikovs in front of them. These men weren't the same as before, these were most definitely of Arab descent, whereas the team at the rocks and north of camp one had been black African and obviously local.

Chris's heart started to race. Had he finally made it? Had he finally caught up with Mustafa? There, only five hundred yards in front of him, was what looked like the answer to his and a nation's prayers.

Mustafa was getting more and more agitated. Where the hell were his militia? The truck that had been despatched to investigate the northern teams had reported finding the site of an engagement and the bodies of all sixteen of his men. He had ordered a quick withdrawal back to camp two and was waiting for their arrival before quitting the area completely. As his frustration grew so did his discomfort and his tent felt too constraining; he needed space. With a couple of strides he swept the entrance covering aside and took his increasingly hot anger into the coolness of the pre dawn desert.

Chris gave a sharp intake of breath and jammed the binoculars closer to his face, if that was possible.

"That's him," he whispered, his whole body tensing in anticipation. "Coming out of the tent."

"How sure?" returned Louis.

"One hundred per cent," Chris replied immediately.

Louis looked at his watch then at Dodger. "Get Pat to call in the strike."

Dodger almost threw himself down the slope leaving just Stan, Chris and Louis. Chris saw him talking swiftly to Pat, who had the communications ready and within seconds was calling into Head Quarters.

Several thousand miles away, General Holbrook only moved a fraction when the report came in. "Make the call," he said in his quiet tone and the Operations Officer nodded to his own radio man. The request was made to Fleet Headquarters in Northwood, Middlesex, and quietly, a button was pushed on the computer that sent the order to fire to Mike Saggers onboard *HMS Talisman* off the coast.

"Order to fire message being received from Fleet Head Quarters, Sir."

Mike looked to his left to his weapons team. "Weapons Officer report."

"Mission loaded, parameters met, in the launch bracket."

"Standby to fire," came the preparatory order.

"Weapon system ready for Tomahawk launch."

"Fire."

There was a fractional delay while the weapon system went into automatic then a moment later, the boat shuddered as the first missile was rammed out of the forward facing tube and into the early morning half light.

"Captain Sir, Weapons Officer. First missile away."

A few seconds later and the boat shuddered again, then again as the next two missiles were launched in automatic sequence.

"Sir, all missiles away."

"Secure the weapon system."

"Aye aye, Sir," was the formal response.

The control room of the submarine was eerily quiet, as it almost always was in high action. Everyone knew their jobs; there was no need to talk. Barely five minutes had elapsed since the call from the desert.

Chris watched in fascination as the man who had dominated his thoughts for so long paced around the tent five hundred yards away. He watched as the man faced away from him towards the dawn and stood still, ironically facing the direction from which his impending death was fast approaching. He saw him turn and go back into the tent and again all was still. He lay back below the top of the dune and looked towards the men at the base of the slope. He could see Pat and the others crouching in position with Dodger over slightly to one side. They were waiting for confirmation to come to them that the weapons were inbound. When they did, they would probably have no more than ten minutes until the weapons hit the position and they would be ideally placed to carry out immediate battle damage assessment. Louis motioned for them to leave the top of the dune and join the others. As they moved down the slope, Chris could see Dodger with his back to the rest. He turned when he heard the others approach, putting some piece of equipment into his jacket pocket.

"When we get confirmation all but Chris and I fall back to the next dune." Louis spoke with calm assurance. The rest looked expectantly at Pat. A few seconds later he held the radio to the side of his head and looked up at his Commanding Officer.

"Inbound," he said simply.

Chris and Louis made their way slowly back to the vantage point and looked down upon the still scene as the others retreated to a safe distance.

This was finally it, Chris thought.

Mustafa walked back into the tent. He could see Omar talking into the set. Was this the report he was waiting for? Omar turned swiftly.

"The teams are two miles away and will be here in minutes," Omar replied.

"Wake the men and get ready to move. We're getting out of here."

Mustafa stalked from the tent once again, furious that his plans were being thwarted and afraid that he had now completely lost the initiative. He still couldn't understand what had happened to his men? They should not have been lost. They should not have been engaged. And now he had no idea where the enemy was. They were mobile and therefore could be anywhere. He had to get his men out to preserve the mission. Enough cat and mouse, it was time for the final contingency option; withdrawal. He saw Omar leave the tent behind him and walk towards the sleeping quarters. He almost snarled to himself. Despite all his planning, he had run out of time.

Chris stared hard as he once again saw his nemesis appear in front of him. He looked at his watch. He was expecting the missiles in a little over three minutes. He saw a second man exit the tent and start walking towards the cluster of what looked like the sleeping area. There was something about this man's face as well. His mind raced then within a few seconds he had it, Omar, Mustafa's right hand man and only slightly lower on the wanted list. This would be a glorious take down if they could get the two of them.

Mustafa felt the phone buzz in the pocket of his robe. He took it out and flipped it open. He read the text and his eyes widened. It was simply three words – 'Get out now'.

He spun around and looked towards the horizons. Nothing. He looked at the number on the phone; it was the Colonel. He must have heard from his man. Shit.

"Omar," he shouted to his deputy. "Get out now… NOW!" he repeated, and started to run to his vehicle parked at the side of his tent. Omar looked round and froze, startled by his leader's shout, then burst into action as he saw Mustafa sprint towards his 4x4. He ran to the tents and shouted a warning, raising the alarm to the best of his abilities.

Chris stared at the scene unfolding in front of him. Mustafa had pulled a phone from his pocket, then shouted something to his deputy. Chris watched as he started running towards the other tent. Fucking hell! NO, NO, NO! This must not be happening – not again – how could it? He looked at his watch. There was less than a minute left before the strike. It could be any time now. They could still get him. Mustafa diverted briefly into his tent and came out with a fist full of papers but little else. Thirty seconds. He made it to the car and jumped inside, gunning it instantly and Chris saw the spurt of sand as the spinning wheels found traction. Fifteen seconds. The car lurched forward and headed away. Omar had been partially successful and groups of groggy looking men were starting to emerge at speed from the tents. Ten seconds. Chris could see Omar running to where the rest of the vehicles were parked, fifty yards away. Five seconds. Chris held his breath.

With little more than a sudden rise in wind like the onset of a squall at sea, the scene in front of him erupted and time slowed to a crawl. The first of the missiles slammed into the centre of the sleeping tents. The shock wave from the explosion zipped over his head, but only for a second. He watched as bodies were thrown everywhere, scattered in a wide arc. He saw everything at half speed. Omar hadn't got far enough. Chris looked on with relish as he saw him flung forward off his feet and almost heard the snap as his head and neck preceded him to the bonnet of the nearest vehicle. He lay still after slumping to the floor.

Five seconds later and the second missile struck, this time what Chris thought must be the operational headquarters. The structure was gone within moments as the fireball engulfed the canvas. The men that had tried to escape were torn to shreds in front of Chris's eyes. But where was Mustafa?

Chris looked beyond the final tent and saw the 4x4 speeding away. Rage welled up inside him. Not this time! The mantra kept coming back to him as the third missile slammed into the second larger tent and the place that Mustafa had come out of only twenty seconds before. He temporarily lost sight of the escaping vehicle through the explosion and the black smoke cloud that followed, but stared in disbelief as the vista cleared and he saw the 4x4 continue to grow smaller. It turned as he watched and made towards the north.

"Louis," he roared. "That bastard's getting away again. We've got to intercept."

Louis called back to Dodger at the base of the dune to get the trucks fast and within moments, they flew in from the west. Both groups mounted up and they headed north east to try and intercept Mustafa's vehicle. As they passed the charred remains of what had only moments before been a training camp, Chris could see a number of bodies still moving, but even more lying still. He dragged his head round to the front and desperately tried to catch sight of the fleeing truck Mustafa was in. All they could discern was the plume of sand kicked up by the big tyres, but that was enough; that was a trail. They followed as fast as they could, ready to engage, not wanting their quarry to get away.

It seemed like they were losing ground, then the cause of the dust cloud seemed to stop. Perhaps there had been an accident. Please God, thought Chris, let us get him this time. They careered on, Chris's heart and mind both racing at equal pace. They were closing fast. This would be it. He readied his weapon. They approached the cloud still hanging in front of them, then like a veil of preternatural mist, it cleared and his eyes widened in horror. Ranged only seventy-five yards in front of them were six pick-up trucks, their crews protected by their structure, weapons ready to fire and levelled at the approaching troops. Again time slowed almost to a standstill. Chris remembered shouting and the driver, Stan, slamming on the brakes and turning the wheel. He saw the other truck do the same and both vehicles swung to the left. This only left a broadside to the ambush and with painful clarity he saw Mustafa standing behind his men on the running board of his 4x4 as the muzzles of the weapons they carried flashed a deadly volley. He could feel the huge sound as bullets ripped into the metal around him and another lurch to the left. He felt the truck go out of control and start to tip, all in slow motion. As it did so, he was thrown from the flat bed. The last thing he remembered was hitting the sand. 'Not like this' his final thought before losing consciousness, 'not like this'.

CHAPTER 9

Mustafa was consumed with blind rage. He had got out merely seconds before the missiles struck and had felt the jolt of the blast on the back of his vehicle. The last thing Omar said to him was that his militia were two miles to the north and he realised, when he came out of his initial panic, that his only hope was to seek refuge with them. His men, his glorious men, had been in the middle of the camp and would have stood almost no chance. His dreams of retribution were engulfed in the carnage of the camp's remains.

He turned north after a few hundred yards and hoped that the Special Forces weren't between him and them. He had seen nothing before the strike and still had no idea where they were. Unbelievably, he had once again been saved by the information from the Colonel - but this had been the closest yet; this time he had almost lost everything, including his own life. He gunned the car as hard as he dared and drove fast towards safety. He realised he was leaving a trail of dust to be followed but he didn't care; he needed sanctuary, he was too vulnerable alone with a pack of hunting wolves behind him. Then the General in him came to the fore once again and in the seconds that passed he realised that he could strike back. 'Come to me you bastards,' he thought. 'Follow my trail and I will obliterate you.'

Ahead of him, he could see his men's trucks stopped, the drivers frozen by the fear of the explosions that had ripped the dawn only a mile distant. He drove even harder, praying they wouldn't assume he was the enemy and engage as he approached. He pulled up short with as much disturbance as possible, throwing up more sand into the already heavily laden air.

"Spread the vehicles out in a line and get behind them, NOW!" he shouted to the leader of the group. "They will be on us in moments."

He didn't wait for an answer but accelerated hard again around the front of his men, turning about on himself at speed and eventually putting another wall of sand and dust into the immediate surround. With a final pass, he negotiated the end of the trucks and got behind them, ready for what he hoped would be a Pyrrhic victory. He stood on the door sill and craned towards the south. Come for me now, he thought again, and he wasn't disappointed. Only a few seconds later, through the 'fog' he could hear the sound of what he thought were two racing engines being pushed hard.

"Ready yourselves!" he shouted above the noise.

He could hear them coming closer, then, flashing towards him only some one hundred yards away, he saw the enemy, and saw the immediate comprehension as they realised that they were about to be slaughtered. Yes! The lead vehicle slewed to the left hard, the wheels slipping over the sand, but this only gave his men a greater target.

"Fire," he shouted over the din, his voice given power by the adrenalin of the moment. The first bullets spat forth and he saw at least some hit home. The first truck started to bounce on the slightly ridged ground, pushed too far by the crazy manoeuvre the driver had tried. One ridge too many and he watched as it tipped further and further, then reached the point of no return. He saw the two men in the back thrown clear and onto the ground, only just missed by the side of the pick-up. He would deal with them later. He looked beyond the first and watched the second a few yards behind. This one fared slightly better and managed to stay upright, but only just. This time the cab bounced round with the two men in the back being tossed like rag dolls. He heard the driver rev up again and saw him pick up speed.

"Get the second truck," he screamed at his men and the shots rang out. He saw one man go down and fall out of the back of the vehicle but watched bitterly as it disappeared the way it had come, protected by the very dust that had led it into the trap. He thought about sending some of his men after it, but very quickly came to the conclusion that to split his forces again would be wrong. To send an overwhelming force would spread his men too thinly themselves, and he had seen what happened when he did that. No – he had half of the Special Forces in front of him and under his control. That was a massive boon and he would consider how best to use it.

The noise of the engagement subsided and he surveyed the scene. The overturned pick-up was only forty yards in front of him, wheels spinning. He could see the two men that had been thrown clear lying still on the ground. The cab was facing away from him but he could see no movement from within.

"See if anyone is left alive and take them prisoner," he said to his new right hand man. "And bring them to me. Approach carefully; they may still strike back."

He remained at the side of his vehicle as twelve of his twenty-four remaining men walked forward in a line. He saw them check the two on the ground but they were obviously dead or out cold and didn't move. Four men brought the bodies back while the rest approached the cab, slowly. He watched them edge round from either side then relax. They signalled back that one man was dead and started dragging another from the wreckage before bringing him back to join the others. Another couple checked the body that had fallen from the second truck but also signalled back that he was dead. Three captives and possibly three on the loose; it wouldn't make up for the loss of his teams but it was some sort of revenge. The next step was to get them somewhere safe, somewhere that he could keep them away from the influences of the outside world. That ruled out the cities – but the pirate camps – now that was an option. The nearest camp that he had links to was near the coast to the north about thirty-five miles away. He would take them there before deciding what to do.

He gave the orders and dispatched three of the trucks with a man on each. The rest of his own men he took with him to check the remains of the camp and see if there were any survivors from the missile attack. There had to be something to salvage and he wanted to see if his beloved lieutenant, Omar, had escaped. They had both been at the forefront of planning for a decade. They had been the best team Al Qaeda ever had. If he was gone, he vowed revenge on a massive scale.

Chris came round slowly as the painful smacking of his head against the floor of a flatbed truck broke not so gently into his consciousness. He realised he was alive but kept his eyes shut to preserve the illusion of his incapacity. He could hear voices around him, the guttural tones of the local dialect. It was fair to assume he was in the back of one of the militia vehicles, but that was all he could glean. For the moment, he thanked God he was alive. But what state he was in he didn't know.

By the feel of the truck they were travelling at a slow pace over hard packed sand; rocks would have produced a harder jolt. He listened to the men around him and picked out two voices from either side. These had to be guards riding shot gun. He tentatively and very slowly tried to move his feet to gauge injury to his lower body. At the first pressure he felt a shooting pain in his right upper thigh, but that seemed to be more muscular than anything else. It was also the side he had landed on when thrown from the truck. In any case, he had movement therefore his spine was intact and he could count on mobility. Next, still with his eyes clamped shut, he tried the same thing with his arms. Again, the same stiffness and shooting pains but again there was movement; he thanked heaven for small mercies.

After the internal checks were complete, Chris started to replay the strike in his mind to work out how it had gone wrong; it had seemed perfect. How had Mustafa known to run? Immediately before, he had come out of the tent completely unaware of the impending doom. It wasn't until he looked at his phone. Chris remembered him taking a phone out of his pocket and then he panicked. So he had been warned – but by whom? Who could have sent him a message at the exact time that the strike was about to take place? Surely it could only have been the traitor back at HQ, but the Director had told them that he wasn't directly involved in this mission and certainly wasn't involved in the real time that would have been needed to get his warning through so precisely.

The answer was obvious and came crashing down on Chris like a tidal wave; he couldn't. There was no way that whoever was warning Mustafa in the UK could have known exactly when the strike was going to take place. The only people who knew that vital information were the men on the ground, the men in the ops room at Head Quarters at the time they called in the strike and the men on the submarine. The traitor had to be in one of those three places. It obviously wasn't the submarine because once dived, no communications could get off the boat without it being a formally ordered transmission, which left two. The ops room was a possibility - but that was supposed to be secure. It would be unlikely that anyone could have communicated from there while this was going on; the whole place would have been in lock down. Which left one option and Chris felt his insides churn again. There had to be a man on the team. His mind raced and took that intuitive mental leap towards the answer: Dodger. As Chris had come away from the top of the dune, he had seen Dodger slightly apart from the rest and putting something back into his pocket. Dodger? Surely not. This man had worked tirelessly against the very organisation they were up against now and had been decorated for it. He was a rising star in the Special Boat Service and tipped to head the branch. How could he be involved in this?

The frightening conclusions were brought to a sharp stop as the truck he was travelling in was brought up short. Chris could hear that they weren't alone. There were engine noises to both sides, so there must be at least three vehicles in total. That would mean about twelve men if it was still four men per team – not good odds. There seemed to be some discussion out ahead and some raised voices before the pick-ups moved forward, this time more slowly. He thought he would risk a glance and opened his eyes a fraction, all he could see though were the feet of a man who was sitting on the side of the flat bed. He shut them again to preserve his status. A few seconds later and he could hear more voices, at a slightly lower level than before, and again the pick-ups stopped. This time however, the tailgates were opened and he was pulled to the end by his feet and forced into a sitting position.

He was dealt a sharp slap to the face that brought tears to behind his closed eyes. He kept them shut but again he was slapped hard. It was obvious they weren't going to stop until he came round, so he opened them and looked about.

It seemed as though they were on the outskirts of some sort of village. He was on the back of one of three trucks that had pulled up outside a couple of rough buildings made of breeze block and corrugated iron. He managed to glance to his right and could see Louis being hauled from the back of the next pick-up, stumbling to his feet as he hit the floor. He looked in as bad a way as Chris felt, with blood on his face and stains on the top of his uniform. Chris saw his face contort in pain as his feet hit the ground; he must have been battered in the crash as well, he thought, but at least he was alive. Before he had time to look to his left his focus was brought sharply round by another slap to the head from the man directly in front, a Somali by the look of him, who was staring deep into his eyes with a look of intense hostility. Chris stared back with a similar look but did nothing. If they wanted to manhandle him, they could get on with it without his help. The man barked a few commands and two others dragged him to his feet. He winced as the pain burned through his muscles, but as he had already gathered, he could still walk. They pushed him hard towards and through a door into the nearest building, jabbing him with the muzzles of their Kalashnikovs to help him on his way.

He found himself in a dark and roughly square room. It was stifling in what he thought must be the late morning heat. Louis had been thrown into the far corner and was turning to rest his back against the wall. Chris felt himself being pushed into the other corner and stumbled forward, just avoiding cracking his head on the breeze block. He hit his shoulder hard as he turned and his knees gave way, leaving him sprawled on the floor. He felt the pain shoot through his own limbs and winced as his nerves screamed. He looked up at Louis who looked blankly at him then nodded in recognition. Their captors had stood back towards the door, levelling their weapons. A few seconds later and another figure was thrown inside – Bobby, then the door was shut and he heard a bolt slam home. He watched as the crumpled form of the normally jovial Geordie unfolded itself into a semi sitting position.

"Haway man, what's gannin on here like! That was like a bloody Saturday night out in Middlesborough. Have you two checked if this joint's got Room Service. I could murder a cheese sandwich and a beer."

Despite their state, both Chris and Louis smiled. It was the sort of comment they would have expected.

"Where's Stan?" asked Chris.

"He didn't make it out of the crash," Louis replied, and all thought of humour left Chris in an instant. Stan Baxter had been Chris's friend when he had first joined the Corps. He had operated with him many times and together they had faced many dangers. Somehow, when you had survived so much, you started to think that your friends would always be there. Not anymore.

"Peanut's gone as well," he continued. "I saw them bring his body over before we left. It looked like a gunshot to me. They must have got him in the back of the other truck."

No-one spoke. The loss of a comrade was something that they all expected at some point, but it was never easy to take or absorb.

"Anything on the others?" Chris asked.

"I didn't see any sign of them," Louis replied. "Perhaps they got away," he offered and again there was silence.

"Any idea where we are?" asked Chris eventually.

"Not a clue. It looks like it's about midday as well so I can't tell which way we've been heading." Louis continued, "I don't think we are anywhere big - it looks like a bit of a shanty town to me so my best guess is that Mustafa has taken us to a militia stronghold or village of some sort, out of the public eye. This area is littered with all sorts of encampments. There are tribal gangs, drug traffickers, pirates, and sometimes even just locals around here. We could be anywhere. By the rough time it took to get here and guessing the speed we were travelling though, I would think that we are about thirty miles from the training camp, what's left of it. At least we've got the benefit of knowing that we took that out, and the bastards in it, even if we didn't get Mustafa. God knows how he got away this time. That can't have been luck."

"It wasn't." Chris remembered the awful truth and immediately felt the bile of anger rise inside him. "It was Dodger." There was a slight pause.

"What do you mean?" Chris could hear an immediate hardness in Louis' voice.

"When we came off the dune, just before the strike, I saw Dodger apart from the rest putting something inside his jacket pocket. It didn't register at the time but I've been asking myself the same question. How could Mustafa have got away? There are only three possibilities: someone from the submarine, someone at HQ or one of us told him about the strike or to get out or whatever. No-one else knew. The sub is isolated and the HQ was locked down. Louis, it had to be one of us and he was the only one that was apart from the rest. No-one else could have sent a message. There is no-one else."

The enormity of the conclusion stunned Louis into silence.

"I hadn't even considered that," he said quietly. "And before I believe it I'll need more proof. I've been with that man for years. I trusted him."

"I guess we've all trusted people we shouldn't have done," Chris continued. "But it would explain some things. If he were part of a team, operating with the man back home, it would explain how we've been busted so many times. First, they told us that the man at HQ was being kept out of the loop but still they seemed to know when and where we were going to be. They met us at the hotel, even knew where my room was so they knew my name. Then they followed us to Fujairah and when we left there, we could have been going anywhere but by some coincidence, we were met by reception committees - and not just the one of them. Then we manage to get past the first, but as soon as we do, they come straight to us again. Let's face it Louis, they've had has from the start and have been playing us for fools all the way through. It's amazing we've got this far."

But Louis was stopped from replying as the door bolt was thrown back and a team of locals came in. Chris could tell from their eyes and their movements that they had violence on their minds and he was right. The beatings began.

They had been allocated three men apiece. It wasn't very sophisticated. Chris's shoulders were grabbed by a man on either side and he was hauled to his feet. The third stood in front of him with a cosh and looked at his face, paused for a moment then hit him hard in the stomach. Chris could feel all the air driven from him and he doubled over in extreme pain. A blow followed to the back of the neck and he hit the floor, this time a blinding pain shooting up into his skull. Boots followed into his stomach, back, shoulders and thighs. No area seemed to be spared. All he could do was try to protect his head and let them do their worst. It was only physical pain and it would stop eventually. Either he would be dead or they would have their fill. It was only a matter of time.

And time did eventually come to an end. There was a brief respite and he looked up, only to see a boot come careering into his head. For the second time that day, everything went black.

Mustafa watched the three trucks with the prisoners draw away into the distance with hatred in his heart. His plan was left in shreds. It would have been a glorious way to avenge the death of Bin Laden. It was how they would prove that nothing had changed, that the war continued; and now it lay in ruins. He got back into his 4x4 and called his troops to spread out ahead of him. The remaining Marines were still out there somewhere but he would deal with them later. First he would check for survivors among his men, then he would assess the nature of the prize he had captured and therefore what he could get from them.

They crossed the short distance back to what was left of the camp in a few minutes and from quite early on it was obvious that there was precious little remaining from the attack. As far as he could remember, three missiles had slammed into the small area; there was little chance of anything surviving. They stopped slightly short and walked the final few yards, some of his troops spread out around him checking the bodies, the rest securing the perimeters. One or two were still alive but their wounds were severe. They wouldn't fight again. He grew more and more bitter.

"Allah, how could you have let this happen?" he implored. "We are your servants." But as always there was no reply.

His thoughts turned to the enemy. He had three in custody being taken to the pirate village to the north-east but three had got away. There was no sign of them now but he could take no comfort from that. He would have to try and flush them out or they would continue to dog him he was sure; it would be unusual for the Special Forces to leave some of their own without at least marking their position. He would sweep the area in an attempt to either clear them out or push them away. Then later on, probably under the cover of darkness he would head over to the pirate village and deal with the captives. He had told the militia to soften them up and he wanted to give them time to carry out his orders. They might not have covered themselves in glory so far but he could at least trust them to beat up helpless men fairly efficiently.

He walked around the camp one more time. There was nothing left. His tent with most of the plans for the attacks had been completely destroyed, as had the communications tents. The last thing he had seen of Omar was him running towards the accommodation area. He followed in what he presumed would have been his footsteps, pausing by the occasional body. He stopped a few steps from where the tents had been. On the ground were the charred remains of a badly burnt body, but he could tell the form immediately. His deputy lay at his feet, his body still smoking, grotesquely arranged by the force of the blast. He felt an intolerable sadness. This was not what Omar deserved. He had been a faithful servant for his entire life, dedicating himself to the glory of Allah and the protection of the Muslim race. He should have survived.

Mustafa turned away, a mixture of sadness and anger boiling within him. He would rebuild. This was not over. His revenge would be even more extreme. Allah is great!

The second truck had driven for half an hour at some speed to clear the engagement zone when Dodger called a stop. They were in a bad way. There were only three left: Dodger, who as the second in command was obviously now in charge, Pat Mulhoon, luckily still with the communications kit in working order and Jon, who had been driving and had managed to keep the truck upright as they watched the lead turn over. They needed time to think. Dodger needed time to think. He was in an uncomfortable position. He had risked exposing himself to get the message out to Mustafa and now had no idea if his cover was blown or not. The lads in the truck with him obviously knew nothing; they had been absolutely normal. What he didn't know was whether Louis or maybe even Chris had cottoned on and managed to put the pieces together. He had no idea where they were, even if they were alive, what they knew or what the best move to maintain his anonymity would be. There was generally one rule with the Special Forces though – never leave your own. It would be extremely unusual if he was seen to abandon the others without some idea of their fate. The other two with him would expect some sort of recce or rescue mission to be mounted, so that would have to be done. When and if they found the others, he would have to play it by ear. There was no safe option here, no easy place to turn. In reality, he had to go on playing the part of the loyal man and deny any allegations if they arose. Even if there were suspicions about him, there must still be sufficient doubt to get him through this next throw of the dice. He made a decision.

"Pat," he started. "Get in touch with Head Quarters."

The radio operator at Special Forces HQ back in Poole started into life and virtually shouted across the ops room at the General, who was still sitting on the opposite side, in semi darkness but his eyes burning with keenness and intensity.

"Sir, I've got Captain Long on sat comm."

"Well talk to him, son, and put it on speaker," came the cool and measured reply, immediately calming the situation in the way that good Commanders always could. He made his way to where the operator was sitting and listened in as Dodger relayed the ostensibly fairly dire position and the fact that Mustafa had got away. For a moment, anger that the quarry had escaped the trap flared within him but an outsider wouldn't have known; he had a face that no-one could read if and when he needed to keep his thoughts private, and this was one of those moments. He took the mike and spoke directly.

"Stay where you are for the time being, Captain. We have a satellite overhead doing some battle damage assessment of the strike and I'll see if we can get some live feed; we might be able to get some idea of where they have gone. Keep smart son. We'll get you out of there and if they're alive, we'll get the others out too."

General Holbrook turned to the operations officer and told him to request the required overhead satellite feed. "Make it fast Major. I want to know if there are any survivors and if there are, where they're being taken. We stand half a chance if we get onto it in the next few minutes."

He retired to the other half of the room to be alone with his thoughts and to give the team time to put his instructions into practice; there was nothing more intimidating than having a General on your shoulder watching your actions. He now went through the same thought processes that Chris had gone through earlier. How had Mustafa been able to get away? It was inconceivable that he had just been lucky when the rest of the camp had been obliterated. Someone must have told him, but Colonel Taylor had been kept away from everything. Even if they had been wrong about him and the traitor was someone else, someone now on the inside and privy to the operation in real time, there were no mobile phones allowed in here and the ops room had been locked down. No-one had entered or left in hours, including him. The Royal Navy were completely removed from the picture so it couldn't be them.

Fairly quickly he began to think the unthinkable, that the possibility raised by Commander Saggers on *HMS Talisman* of a traitor on the team was true. But if so, who? Which one of his men, all of whom had proved themselves countless times, could be in on this, and if they were, were they operating alone or in cohorts with the Colonel?

The inevitable truth was that he had been betrayed by two people rather than one, but other than that, he had nothing to go on. What he did know, however, was that he had possibly four of his men either captive or dead and if alive, he needed to get them out. His assets were limited, three men in pretty bad order, any one of which could be allied with the enemy, but they were all he had; he would have to use them.

Within a few minutes, the ops officer came over to report. "Sir, the satellite on task reports that the force has split. Three trucks are now back around the camp and three are heading north east."

"Any idea where they're headed, Major?"

"Not really Sir, although if you take a line from where they were originally, there might be some sort of small village about thirty-five miles away."

"So why would Mustafa split his forces now and so soon after the engagement then?" The General played different scenarios over in his head before answering his own question. "They've got prisoners, son." A faint glimmer of hope started to rise within him and a plan began to formulate. "How long have we got the satellite for?" he asked the ops officer.

"Another twelve hours if we need it, Sir," was the reply.

"Get Captain Long on the line," he ordered. Almost immediately

Dodger was ready to receive orders.

"Captain, get yourself away from the area, out towards the east. We have eyes on a convoy of three trucks heading north east towards a shanty village some thirty-five miles away, which I wager has got our men in it. We'll watch their progress and steer you in. You just keep clear for now and await details. When you do get there, I want to know who is still alive and what I need to do to get them out. You now have Mission Command Captain. Do you understand your orders?"

Dodger turned away from the equipment and turned to the rest. "You heard what the man said. Let's get going."

They got back into the truck and headed east, away from the action, towards the coast and hopefully out of immediate danger, not stopping until they had covered a good ten miles. The distance passed in near silence, all three of them deep in shock and consumed by their own thoughts. They had definitely lost Peanut from the back of the truck; they had seen him shot. What had happened to the rest they couldn't know, although it was a fair bet that at least some were alive. Whatever their state, the team had suffered a catastrophic blow and they were all extremely shaken. It was their sheer toughness that kept them going now, their bodies running on the conditioning of many years, their minds alert to the vulnerability of their situation. This was not the end, this was just another phase. They would not leave their comrades in the field. The mission continued.

Captain Dodger Long had other ideas running around in his head. This was now even higher risk. Any rescue attempt would be fraught with personal danger. If Louis and Chris suspected him, then he would be walking into a trap that he couldn't get out of. If they knew nothing, he may survive and be able to resume his life; but which was it? He was now in charge and anything other than full adherence to the new orders would almost certainly give the game away. As far as the prisoners were concerned, his erstwhile comrades, he wasn't in the game of sacrificing his colleagues. His betrayal was simply a money thing; he had still worked with them in life and death situations over many years and he wouldn't deliberately let them down any more than he had already. The loss of Peanut had also hit him hard; he had been directly responsible for the loss of his friend.

Shortly after one o'clock local time, Pat got the signal to get in touch with Headquarters and Dodger was speaking with the General within seconds.

"We've got a location, Captain. They've reached the village we talked about earlier and are outside a couple of buildings within a fenced compound on the south west edge. You know the vehicles to look for so start heading north as soon as you can. You should be about thirty-five miles south of the position so it will take you about three hours to get there if you are being careful. Get into position, find the shack and get eyes on. Find our boys, Captain, and we'll work it out from there. The Major will give you the co-ordinates."

The General passed him onto the ops officer and they copied down the position from the satellite image. Dodger considered their situation. They probably had the entire Somali nation on the lookout for them and it would be foolish beyond measure to drive straight to the village in the open during daylight. He knew that time was of the essence but it was essential to get this right. Blundering in would serve no purpose other than to sacrifice their own lives, and if nothing else, Dodger looked after himself. He decided to wait until sunset.

The area around them had flattened out considerably, a feature of the landscape nearer the coast. There were a number of isolated and ragged looking trees and bushes and it was under one of these that he decided to shelter. He was as confident as he could be that they would be undiscovered; it was approaching the middle of the afternoon and few if any travelled in that part of the day. There were about six hours before they could start to think about moving and so he forced his men to rest, taking the first watch himself. The continued adrenalin of the last day would be taking its toll and they needed to de-stress slightly. Even given the experience of losing their friends, they were asleep in moments, exhaustion rushing up to engulf them. Dodger sat looking out at the horizon. Perhaps he shouldn't have bothered this time and should have let the bastard Mustafa die. It would have been much simpler and it would have avoided all this. His mind churned and he started to bitterly regret that he had let himself be blackmailed into the whole thing by Taylor. Now there was no way out. He continued to think until the sun started going down, letting the others get as much sleep as he could. There was no sleep for the wicked he thought bitterly to himself.

Mustafa was drawing close to the village by sunset. He had made the militia collect the bodies of his men and had given them as much of a proper burial as possible, ensuring that those that had been so willing to give their lives were washed, covered as much as possible by a white cloth and laid facing to the East; it was the least he could do. He had not been in contact with those holding the prisoners but he was sure that they would have been sufficiently worked over by now. He would have a look at them first then decide what to do with them overnight. He needed them to feel vulnerable and alone; the mind games were just as important before the interrogation as within it.

He passed the first barrier, a loose collection of barrels and wire across the nominal track with a nod to the militia there. They knew him and more importantly who he represented. Because of it he had privileged status. The trucks drew up outside the group of buildings alongside the other vehicles. His force was back together and he felt relatively safe again. He got a brief from the leader and heard that finally they had done something right. All three of the prisoners had been beaten senseless and would be out cold for several hours. That was as it should be and gave him at least a modicum of satisfaction.

He motioned for the door to be opened and he entered the small room where the Marines were being kept. Three figures lay prone in front of him. Blood was splattered over the walls and floor. He approached the first, a man in his thirties by the look of it. His face was swelling nicely. They wore no rank on their uniforms so he had no idea what position he held. It was the same with the other two, although they looked slightly older. Given the mission he was surprised that at least a couple of them weren't younger. Or perhaps they were older because they were more senior. Could he have managed to get the leaders? He supposed that it was a fifty-fifty chance and these had been from the lead vehicle. His hopes and mood rose. If they were, he would delight in making them scream tomorrow.

For now, he needed sleep himself. Tomorrow he would interrogate and consider his next move. He still had the other group to consider of course. He had set people to watch for signs of being followed but there had been nothing so far, so it was fairly safe to assume that he had made it here undetected. Somewhere out there three men must be feeling pretty low and alone. That was good as well.

'Somewhere out there' was thirty-five miles to the south and it was time to move. Dodger had woken the rest to protestations about having let them sleep but he waved them aside. He had been thinking. He had a part to play here and he was uncomfortable with the amount of risk that he was carrying. If he hadn't given himself away fully, then there would be suspicions when full mission analysis took place. He had a choice to make. He had to find a way to protect himself as much as possible. That started with obeying orders.

They got onboard the truck and headed north. The twilight was setting in fast. In a few minutes it would be dark and their progress would be slower but as long as they took it steadily, they should be invisible to anyone observing. It should take about 3 hours to get into position around the village, which would take them to somewhere approaching midnight. That was fine by him. Midnight onwards was the easiest time to infiltrate, the time when guards were at their most lax, especially in places such as this.

He still had his GPS set and they were able to make an almost direct approach to the shanty town. About five miles out, they altered slightly to the west so that they could approach towards the supposed site of the captives. Two miles short and they slowed to a crawl, one mile and they stopped.

It was pitch black and the air was still as Dodger, Jon and Pat got out of the pick-up. They could hear nothing at present, which added to their tenseness. Now being only three, there was no option to leave anyone with the vehicle; they had to keep together. The mission was to locate, to observe and to work out a way of getting the others out, then call it in if no opportunity presented itself. In a slightly staggered line, offering each other as much protection as possible, they walked forward to cover the last distance by foot.

They took it slowly, pausing every few hundred yards or whenever anything caught the eye of the point man, Jon. Dodger was expecting there to be sentries. Mustafa knew that they were out there and must consider that they may make an approach. They weren't disappointed. Jon stopped them half a mile later with a raised fist. They immediately dropped to the ground. Without a word, Jon signalled a direction and the fact that there were two men. Dodger came forward slowly and looked ahead. He could see the vague outline of two men by the cover of a tree, but instead of looking towards the Marines, towards the threat direction, he could see them with their backs resting against the trunk. There was no sound but as he watched, there was the glow of a cigarette end as one of the men took a drag. How often had he localised a target by that one simple act, he wondered, fleetingly?

He motioned for Pat to stay where he was and offer them cover, then motioned for Jon to take the man on the left. Given the lack of background noise, silence was the key here and the two of them inched forward in a crouch, watching each footfall closely. They made it to six feet, each step now a torturous process; they were still too far away, however, to get to the men at a rush and be sure of the advantage. Dodger paused and Jon reacted to his lead. It was time for the final steps and they carried their knives drawn and ready. Dodger nodded and they started to move again, this time concentrating on the men ahead, not the ground. And it was the second step that gave them away as a loose stone was moved by Dodger's right boot.

Still four feet away, the nearest man obviously heard the noise and started to spin round. At the first movement, Dodger jumped forward, closely followed by Jon to close the remaining distance. They were on them in an instant, too quick for them to shout out as hands closed on their mouths. Dodger took the head of his man in the crook of his arm and used the momentum of his turning body to fling him over face down towards the ground. At the last moment however, he pulled back sharply on the neck, twisting with all his strength at the same time and felt the body go limp as the bones in the man's neck snapped and his life was instantly torn from him. Dodger paused in position then let the body drop. He checked Jon and saw him removing his knife from the man's left side ribcage. Two down.

Dodger called Pat forward. They propped the two men back against the tree and resumed their approach to the village. This time they started to hear faint domestic noises, the hum of a generator, the closing of a door. They had found the village, but had they found the right place? They crested a small rise and stopped. Now only a few hundred yards away from the edge of the nearest shack, they could see outlines, and it looked as if the intelligence had been bang on. They had come slightly too far west but off to their right they could see a number of pick-up trucks similar to their own outside a couple of rough looking lean-tos.

Dodger lay prone and stared intently towards where he assumed the survivors must be. He started to pick up small movements as his eyes got accustomed to the scene and he made out a couple of men moving around the vehicles. As he looked closer, he could see another outline, slightly different from the pick-ups and realised that Mustafa's 4x4 was also there. The pieces of his plan were coming together. He decided that if it was at all possible, he would have to attempt a rescue and it would have to be tonight, before the bodies of the outer guards were discovered. First task though was to locate the prisoners and work out a way of getting to them.

Half an hour later and there still seemed to be just the two men outside. There had been no other comings and goings and Dodger decided it was time to try and get closer. The three of them edged round to the right, staying behind the top of the ridge all the way. Another twenty minutes and they had made it to a point directly opposite, less than a hundred yards from the nearest guards. They stopped and Dodger assessed his options. How to get past the guards and to steal a look inside the building? There was precious little cover except that the vehicles interrupted the line of sight. He would have to use them.

He motioned for the other two to cover his advance then waited for his moment. It wasn't long before he got it when one of the men by the door asked the other for a cigarette. With their attention diverted inwards, he crept over the top of the ridge and made to the right and the side of the building. He covered the ground silently yard by yard in a low running crouch, at any moment expecting to go down in a hail of bullets as the guards spotted his movement and brought their weapons to bear. Nothing happened and he made the rear of the nearest truck. He could feel his heart pumping, the adrenalin of the moment kicking in but he stopped where he was, assessing his next move.

There were now several of the trucks between him and the sentries, which he used as cover as he edged further round to the right. He looked more closely at the building and could see the front door was bolted from the outside with a crude bar. It shouldn't be too difficult to get through that. Next, he looked along the side of the building and could see an opening. He needed to look inside and again waited for his moment. The guards were talking in a local dialect only ten yards from him. As long as they kept talking he was all right, they hadn't seen him. Unfortunately, one was almost facing him and would certainly see him move across the divide. He stayed completely still, waiting for his moment, but it didn't come. Instead, he lost his chance. His senses were in overdrive now but directed to the men by the door. He almost missed the sound of footsteps coming from the other side of the building. Just in time he registered the danger, dropped to the floor and managed to roll under the truck he was using for cover. Fractions of a second later, two men came round the corner and turned directly towards his position. He froze, praying hard that they had missed the movement and that the first guards had seen nothing.

The new men gave no indication of having seen anything and kept coming at a steady pace to the corner of the building. The first guards had turned so maybe they had heard a noise, but as the reliefs came round the corner, not ten yards from where Dodger was lying, they relaxed, if anything putting the noise down to the approach. Dodger, however, was as tense as a steel bar, every fibre in his body ready to fight, but the conversation continued, now including the newcomers. There followed an horrendous few minutes as the handover took place but eventually, a life time later to Dodger, he saw from under the front of the truck the boots of two men turn and start to walk towards him. He watched as they turned the corner and walked away, then his body kicked into immediate action as he saw the other two move slightly away from the building in the opposite direction.

This was his chance and he rolled immediately out and back into the low crouch. One look around the bonnet confirmed that the new two had moved slightly further away and he had his window. He took it and headed across the divide as fast as he dared, gaining the side of the structure unnoticed. He pressed himself as flat as he could against the wall and listened. There was nothing, but he was now at his most vulnerable. He had to get the insight he needed and get back out to relative safety.

He could hear nothing around him so he shifted to the opening and looked inside. His eyes took in the scene in an instant; three crumpled forms lay on the floor, roughly in the centre. A low light illuminated the room, allowing him to see the blood and the bruising. They had been given a proper work over. To his dismay, he saw at least two more guards within. That was something that he hadn't counted on. They would have to be factored in, but at least he had confirmed that three men were inside and, he assumed, alive.

Dodger moved back to the corner of the building. He paused and then allowed the smallest part of his head to look round it. He could see the two guards but they were no longer turned away, now they had turned back and were starting to come towards him. He had nowhere to go and for a moment he had no answers. He drew his knife and looked over to where Jon and Pat were lying, ready to cover him if required. He thought he could see them watching and knew that they would be with him in a flash if he needed it. All he could do was pull himself back into the shadows and press himself as hard as he could against the wall, ready to attack. He waited for the first shade to appear, his body tensing more with every passing second. He could hear the voices of the men as they approached and knew that he would have to hit hard and quickly but at the same time that if he did, the rescue would be over before it had begun after the inevitable raising of the alarm; he could take down one without being noticed, there was no way he could take down two.

The voices got closer and as he looked along the wall he saw figures in the darkness, but it wasn't the guards, it was Pat in a half crouch running across the open ground towards the back of the trucks. They had seen the danger and were taking steps to support him, as risky as that was. A second figure followed Pat and they both skirted towards him and the nearest vehicle. At least the odds were better now. He sank further back trying to find an even darker spot. Then the figures rounded the corner and turned towards him. They were still talking in low voices and initially carried on then stopped abruptly as they faced him, struggling to accept what they were seeing. It was that slight pause that saved Dodger, for in that time when all their attention was focussed forward into the shadows, they missed the soft padding of footsteps behind them. Dodger watched as two hands appeared across their mouths and knives from around their bodies. Their eyes widened in surprise and then in pain as first shock, then imminent death coursed through their consciousness. Again the bodies slumped but before they dropped, they were dragged back to the trucks and thrown under a flat bed. Four down.

That was it now; the die was cast. They had taken down the first two and still had breathing space. The absence of the second two would be noticed in short order; they had to move and move fast.

"See if there are any keys in the trucks," Dodger spoke in hushed tones to Pat and Jon. "Find one then knife the tyres of the others; we're going to need a quick getaway."

They hurried off while Dodger invented a plan. There were at least two more men to deal with. They would have to get in, take them out and then evacuate within seconds. Contrary to popular belief and the movies, they would not crash in to the shack, that would only alert the men inside and possibly more guards outside, depending on how close they were and the noise created. They would open the door as if it were the men outside and then get through it at speed. At the range they were talking about, it would be handguns and silencers, then react to what they saw.

He watched as the other two found a suitable truck then started knifing the wheels of the others. He could see each one settle on one side with a muffled hiss as the knives went in and hoped that the noise would go unnoticed. So far so good he thought as they all returned to the front of the building.

Dodger stood directly in front of the door with Jon and Pat to left and right. The door would swing in, which would help them again and he counted down on his fingers; five, four, three, two...

Pat pulled back the securing bolt with an easy motion, it grated rusty metal on rusty metal; now they would be alert inside to someone entering. With a nod of the head, Dodger levelled his silenced pistol and nodded. Jon pushed the door at a normal pace and Dodger stepped quickly forward, followed closely by Jon. As soon as his feet had crossed the threshold he saw the first man, sat lazily on a chair facing slightly away from him. He was looking over his right shoulder at the door and so was in the worst possible position to bring his weapon to bear. All that happened was that his eyes widened slightly before the first round entered his right eyeball and the back of his head exploded onto the opposite wall.

It was now time to rush. While Dodger was taking out the first man, Jon had moved around the door and spotted the second. He was in a much better position to react and although sitting in a chair, he was facing the action and was bringing his weapon up to a firing position. Jon quickly swung his own pistol and loosed off a shot, although he fired a fraction too early and it missed just wide of the mark. This allowed the guard too much time and his face contorted in triumph as he realised he was still alive. His Kalashnikov was powerful enough to take out all those in front of him and he thought he had his chance. For everyone in the room, time slowed to a fraction of normal speed. The guard looked at the scene in front of him and tightened his grip. His weapon was only at waist height but it was pointed at those in front of him and he could feel the pressure as the index finger on his right hand pressed the cold sharp edged metal of the trigger.

Dodger was in the process of spinning round following the take down of the first man. He could see the walls of the building in a blur as his head turned to the right towards the second, taking in the missed first shot from Jon, seeing the automatic rifle come up ready to cut them in half, swinging his own pistol round but knowing that it would be too late.

Jon was the man in the frame though. He had felt the soft jerk as the first bullet left his barrel and sped over the left side of his target's head. He couldn't believe that he had missed. He saw the eyes of his man focus on his own, then saw them narrow from disbelief to action and he knew he had fucked up. Jon's own weapon was still in motion though, still arcing towards the target. He had a fraction of a second before they would all pay for his error, but that was still a fraction of a second. This time he 'felt' the shot and he knew it was right. His pistol spat a second time and this time there was no mistake. He could almost see the round as it flew across the room and smashed into the guard's left shoulder, spinning him round and off his chair. Unfortunately though, the man was in the process of firing and that action continued. Before he was thrown off completely, his finger had closed enough on the trigger to loose off two rounds. They slammed into the back of the door, missing Dodger by a fraction, but it was the noise inside the confines of the shack that was deafening and it stunned them all into immobility. Jon recovered first though and quickly sent three more rounds into the now prone body of the guard.

"Get the others into the back of the truck," Dodger ordered, all hopes of further secrecy shattered. "We've got about twenty seconds."

CHAPTER 10

Chris was brought from deep slumber to instant wakefulness by the sudden boom of an automatic rifle at close range. His eyes shot open and he couldn't believe what he was seeing. There was Dodger, the supposed traitor, standing over him with Pat and Jon in close attendance. He could see two guards lying on the floor, covered in blood, but before he had time to take anything else in, Dodgers hands grabbed him and pulled him upright. His legs faltered, the pain of the crash and the battering he had taken shooting through his body. His head felt as though it was about to explode but somehow the pain and the reality of the situation made him come alive and focus.

Pat and Jon grabbed a man each and headed fast towards the door. A brief glance outside and they headed straight for one of the trucks. They had barely reached it when the first shouts of pursuit were heard coming from behind them. Jon jumped straight for the driver's seat and gunned the engine into life with a roar. Louis, Bobby and Chris were thrown into the flat bed and Dodger and Pat jumped in behind, bringing their weapons up to face the inevitable back lash to their raid. The vehicle lurched forward just as men could be seen running from the nearest buildings. Suddenly there seemed to be an army boiling up from every corner, men appearing half naked but all with weapons ready to fire. The first shots were random but they were only forty yards away and still uncomfortably close. When they had focussed on their target the real fire fight began. Chris had no rifle so couldn't help. Louis and Bobby similarly had nothing to contribute which left Dodger and Pat to return fire. As the truck pulled ahead, they loosed off as many covering rounds as they could.

The emerging militiamen scattered as they realised they were being engaged but continued to throw a wall of lead in the Marines' direction. Inevitably they started to find the target and bullets started to fizz all around them. Pat, the big Canadian, lurched backwards as a round flew into his right shoulder, his weapon dropping down beside him. Chris was alert enough now to take his place. As the truck swung around to head towards the exit, he grabbed the rifle and brought himself to his knees. Now it was Dodger clinging on to the roll bar behind the cab and Chris hanging on to the side for stability trying to give them some modicum of protection. As he doggedly lay down more rounds at the militia, he saw Mustafa emerge from around the corner of the prison hut. He wasn't the only one. As Chris looked up, he saw Dodger notice Mustafa as well and, incredibly, saw a distinct hesitation in his firing. It seemed that the worst of his fears were being proved. Dodger was the traitor. Dodger was working for the man in front of him. Dodger was responsible for their plight and the deaths of Peanut and Stan Baxter. Dodger was responsible for the beatings and the failures here and God knew where else.

But this realisation wasn't going to stop him. He spun back around and fired towards the man, seeing Mustafa duck but seeing no sign of injury. The vehicle picked up speed and started bouncing over the rough ground. This made any sort of aimed shots almost impossible, but the idea was to suppress and they could do that by firing in the general direction. As the distance increased both the amount and proximity of enemy bullets started to lessen. Chris could see some of the men running towards their own trucks. The pursuit had begun.

Mustafa couldn't believe his eyes. In front of him a truck bearing his prisoners and what must be the remnants of the SF troop were escaping. "Get in the trucks," he yelled at his men, and several sprinted forward. He grabbed a weapon from the body of one of his men on the ground by his side and let a flurry of bullets go in the direction of the retreating vehicle. Seemingly aiming wide of the mark, he ran to his own 4x4 and wrenched the ignition key round. It roared into life and he slammed it into gear, but the moment he moved forward he felt the unevenness in ride that told him all he needed to know; they had slashed the tyres. He looked to the others and saw the same looks. He jumped out, even more infuriated. "Get more vehicles," he screamed.

Chris looked back with a certain amount of satisfaction and stopped firing. It seemed as though the rescuers had disabled the other vehicles; none of them were in pursuit but it had bought them a few seconds, forty-five, fifty at the most, before more trucks would be found. Still, it might be enough. He looked around to see Louis standing up holding on to the roll bar and issuing directions to Jon. They needed to face the next threat, which was the barrier at the border of the village. This was bound to be manned and they would have to pass it to have any hope of getting free.

Jon steered them onto the rough road leading out then stopped sharply. Chris looked ahead and saw the barrier in place, manned by three armed men. Louis took two seconds to take in the scene then bellowed, "Go left."

Jon gunned the engine and the wheels spun as the power kicked in. He swung the steering wheel hard to take them along the continuance of the slight rise behind which Dodger had crawled and hidden on his approach to the shanty town. This took them to the rear of a number of similar buildings from which people were emerging, some with rifles themselves. They were becoming highly outnumbered and they had to get out. It was only the speed of the vehicle that saved them from being engaged from every quarter. By the time that the inhabitants realised who they were, they were past and clear, but inevitably Chris knew their luck would run out and one of the occasional random rounds fired at the rear of the truck would hit home. Jon kept going, doing a fantastic job of keeping the truck under control and they were flung around the back as he negotiated tight spaces and turns, all at a speed Chris wouldn't have thought possible.

Then they saw their chance, a gap to the right leading out into the desert. They took it again at speed, the rear of the truck sliding dangerously to the left as the back wheels lost their grip but Jon used it to swing the cab round, applying power again at just the right moment to steady them up on a new course out and away.

This was scrub desert though, ridged and uncomfortable. There was no time to take stock or even pause for thought. They were in the middle of an evasion but Chris knew they had been lucky so far and had the feeling worse was yet to come. He looked round and saw Bobby and Dodger looking after Pat, who was lying where he had fallen after being hit in the shoulder. Dodger looked up at Louis, who was still standing up on the roll bar, trying to work out the best options for getting them out of there. Their eyes met and Chris saw unvoiced suspicion in Louis' eyes.

"He's OK, the bullet passed right through."

Louis merely nodded. As far as he could see they had a problem. They were about to be chased through the desert by locals who knew the ground and they had nowhere to go. He turned back to Dodger.

"Where's the comms gear?"

"We had to leave it in our truck. It's about a mile south west of the village," replied Dodger.

"Jon," Louis had to shout above the roar of the engine. "Head for your truck. We've got to get in touch with the sub to get us out of here."

Jon drove on straight for another couple of hundred yards then swung the truck right. Normally they would have gone straight out into the wilderness, but they were in real trouble if they couldn't get in touch with their means of evacuation. They were another man down, who would only become more of a liability the longer they were in theatre. To back track across the line of the village was incredibly risky, effectively giving the militia time to pick up the scent, but Louis evidently judged it a risk worth taking.

Mustafa's eyes gleamed cold and hard. Word had reached him that they had been turned back at the road block and were inside the ridge that marked the boundary of the village. They wouldn't be able to cross that for some time, if at all, so he still had them within his grasp. His first priority was to get mobile; he had to get more vehicles or the game would be up. There was more and more shouting from around him as the crowd grew but he was oblivious to it. His mind was racing. What had happened? It was obvious that the last remaining men had come to rescue the others. That surprised him. He would have thought that the odds were far too overwhelming to attempt such a foolhardy mission – but at the end of the day, he hated to admit, they had got away with it so far – probably because he had underestimated them – something they had factored in and used against him. But they weren't free yet. He still had a huge advantage; they were on his patch and he wasn't going to let them get away. Just by coming back they were playing him for a fool. His anger raised another notch. How dare they treat him with such disdain.

In fairly short order, three vehicles raced into sight from the centre of the village and he climbed in beside the driver of one of them, all of them loading up with militia. He ordered them forward and raced out to the road; while the Marines were trapped inside, he would skirt outside. They would have to try to escape at some point and he would be waiting to cut them off. He saw more vehicles arriving as he screamed towards the barrier, now lifted high to let him pass and watched as they followed the route the SF had taken inside the village wall. He himself continued out into the naked scrub and turned left, the same direction as the enemy, but faster he was sure. They had about a minute on him but that would soon be eaten up. He must have them now.

'Shit this is risky,' thought Chris. They hammered over the sand, effectively back the way they had come at about fifty miles an hour. They were far enough away from the village to avoid direct fire from there, but still close enough so that their movements could be tracked. He could see a couple of trucks racing along the path they had just taken inside the boundary; their lead was just a few seconds he was sure. The only chance they had was to try and lose them in the darkness and get away. First they had to get to the communications, then they had to evade.

Suddenly Chris's senses peaked again, but this time he was alerted by noises from immediately ahead, maybe slightly to the right. There was no moon so there was very little to see by but he could hear, and what he could hear filled him with dread. It sounded like more vehicles approaching fast; their plan had failed and it seemed as if they had run straight into the path of another group of pursuers; he hoped that speed would be enough to keep them safe.

Mustafa stared ahead. They must be gaining on them. And then he saw them, just to the right, looming very fast out of the night from only about a hundred yards away. At this speed it would be like a medieval joust and over in seconds, but he had three trucks and they were one. Mustafa's truck was now the second in line. This could only end one way — with the enemy finally wiped out.

Time slowed once again for Chris. He saw three trucks coming fast towards them, the backs crowded with men, all with weapons pointing their way. There was nothing else to do; they were too close not to engage. They would have to pass and try to inflict as much damage as possible, hopefully taking a few out and not suffering too much themselves. He reloaded his weapon and brought it to bear, as did Dodger, once again up by the railing. The others all hunkered down, even Jon the driver, trying to protect themselves from the barrage that was about to come their way. Chris hoped the structure of the vehicle would provide some protection but wasn't too hopeful.

The yards closed one by one to his super fast functioning mind. There were only fifty yards to go. He started to fire, as did Dodger and the barrel kicked. He was aiming directly at the cab of the nearest pick-up, hoping to take out the driver to prevent pursuit. Thirty yards and he saw his bullets hit home, smashing the windshield, but the truck kept on coming. He could see a couple of the militia go down as Dodger fired at the same vehicle. He felt the heat and noise of very close bullets and gritted his teeth. If this was it, he was going to take some of the bastards with him.

The first vehicle suddenly slewed to the left, out of their path and into the path of the third, missing the second by inches in doing so. In a moment it had reared onto two wheels then tumbled over, spinning fast as if it had been rolled by an invisible hand and presenting the sight of several bodies crushed beneath the metal structure. The third managed to steer left and out of the way, but not before it had been thrown off course. The immediate action continued with somehow the odds evened.

Chris couldn't believe what he was seeing. They had obviously hit the first truck and taken out the driver, but they had nearly taken all three at the same time. The second kept on coming, however, and in the hyper slow motion he was now experiencing the few yards left between them crawled past. He could see the men in the back firing his way and both Dodger and he brought their guns to bear on this new target. The rounds flew from both sides, impossible to aim accurately, flung wildly into the arena in the hope that something would find the mark.

It was impossible that all that lead wouldn't yield some result and as Chris continued to fire, crouched in the back of the truck, mostly hidden by the metal of the flat bed, he saw Dodger suddenly jerk back. His right shoulder was flung away and he saw a look of shock pass over his face. As Dodger's head was brought round, their eyes met for a brief moment and they stared at each other, the instant captured indelibly on Chris's memory like a snapshot photograph. But that wasn't the lasting image. As he stared at the man who had most likely given them away, a follow up shot careered towards them. He saw it fly into the side of Dodger's head and exit the other side in an explosion of blood and brain matter. Chris saw the lights go out instantly in those guilty eyes and watched the body crumple.

The loss of Dodger was the final act in the joust. The pick-ups flashed past each other at a combined speed of about a hundred miles an hour and at that rate, the Marines were clear and had the slight advantage; they were going in the right direction and had momentum. Chris could hear Louis shout 'faster' to the driver Jon and the vehicle surged forward again. He clung on harder to the side of the truck with Pat and Bobby alongside him. Now they were five and one by one they were losing the team. He was starting to feel more vulnerable. They had to get back to the other truck while they had a lead and get the communications gear or their chances of escape would be minimal; they only had about twenty seconds or so while the pursuers regrouped. They had to make it count.

A few seconds later and they were swallowed by the darkness, the only give away now the screaming of the engine. The last thing Chris saw as he looked over the tailgate was the second vehicle rounding in their direction and the third coming back to join the other. The overturned truck lay on its roof, smoke issuing from the engine bay. As he watched, there was an explosion that engulfed it in an orange fireball as final destruction was confirmed.

They sped on, trying desperately to reach the other vehicle. The village came slightly closer on their right and they could see people on foot running around the perimeter. It was obvious that they had stirred an army into action. Their job was to stay a step ahead, a challenge that seemed almost beyond them to Chris, given the quarter step they currently enjoyed. He just couldn't see how they could turn hot pursuit into evasion and give themselves long enough to get in touch with the submarine, get their boats and get out. The only thing that gave him hope was they were still alive.

They crossed the road that led back into the camp and continued straight across. As yet, Chris couldn't see the men following, although he thought he could hear the engines above the din of their own. There must come a point when they had to slow down; maybe then the darkness would be their ally and cover their movements. Their direction jilted a couple of times as Jon got his bearings and adjusted his track. What seemed like an hour later, but could only have been a couple of minutes, the rescuers original truck loomed out of the dark. Jon slammed on the brakes and suddenly it was relatively quiet. Louis jumped out of the cab and sprinted to it, returning seconds later with the communications pack.

"Jon, give your rifle to Bobby, Chris, get ready with yours," ordered Louis. He himself took hold of Dodgers from under his body and jumped into the rear. They were now all there bar Jon who was driving. Listening behind them they could hear the militia but couldn't yet see them; somehow they still had the advantage.

"Go south Jon, slowly," Louis took charge again.

John pulled away without making too much noise and managed to get almost into the blanket of the night before they saw their hunters. Chris could hardly dare think they had got away with it.

Mustafa screamed at the top of his voice. "Stop!"

After the crazy joust when he had seen one of the Special Forces men blown apart from his position in the cab of the second truck, he had watched as the enemy sped off in the opposite direction. He waited a moment for the other remaining truck to join him and then drove off in pursuit; he couldn't afford to let them get ahead. Immediately they started to disappear into the night, which would make tracking much more difficult. He knew the general direction they were travelling and so would follow that. What he couldn't understand was what they were doing there in the first place. If it had been him, he would have headed straight out into the desert; that was where safety lay. But no, they had turned back on themselves, back towards an enemy that they knew must be giving chase. There was some reason for it, but he couldn't work out what it was.

Then, after some minutes of chasing, the answer became obvious with the appearance of another truck off to his left. His shout had startled the already pumped up driver into slamming on the brakes and the truck skidded fast to a halt over the sandy ground.

"Over there," he pointed and once again the truck jumped into life. He saw a movement in the distance, this time off to the south; it had to be them. They had to have come back to this truck to get something, although what had been worth the risk he had no idea. Now he had them again and the chase was back on. "Go," he shouted, and he felt the keenness of the hunter course through his veins.

Chris saw the militia career to a halt and assumed that they had been spotted. Louis assumed the same thing and barked 'drive fast' at Jon, who floored the accelerator. They had almost got away. Now they were back in the sights and with a sinking feeling, Chris wondered how long the chase would last. Louis turned to Pat, still conscious after his shoulder wound and using his spare arm to cling on in the back.

"Pat," he started, edging the comms gear towards him. "Raise HQ and have them stand by. We need the sub to be ready to take us any time in the next three to four hours."

"No probs Boss," came the reply and with one hand he started the job. It was a short message and a short message in reply. "They'll be ready," Pat said, moments later.

The vehicle continued to pound over the desert.

Back at Headquarters in Poole the operations room had sprung to life.

"We've got them Sir, three men down and five men being pursued wanting evacuation within the next three to four hours," the radio operator shouted to those gathered.

"Tell them we will support," was the simple response from General Holbrook. After he had done so, the General continued. "Get in touch with the sub. Tell them to get ready for an extraction. God help them," he added quietly to himself.

Onboard the submarine they received the message minutes later.

"Captain Sir, Wireless Office, flash traffic being received on the broadcast. The signal's on its way up." Cdr Mike Saggers threw the curtain back and within seconds a Wireless Operator appeared. He felt even more on edge than he had done just a few moments before. This was his long time friend doing something, in his opinion, that he shouldn't have been anywhere near. Furthermore, if it all went wrong, he felt that he would have to be the one to tell Elizabeth. What he found out when he read the signal filled him with dread. It was simple.

"Make ready for an emergency evacuation of five personnel within the next three to four hours."

Only five personnel! What the hell happened to the other three? The answer was obvious but who had they lost? His heart sank. Please don't let it be Chris.

Chris was hanging on for dear life in the back of the truck while Jon tried to keep ahead of the pursuing forces. He was driving like a maniac, but in the circumstances it seemed acceptable and was even getting some results. In the darkness they were managing to gain a slowly increasing lead, although all the dust they were pushing up into the atmosphere made it hard to get clear, even in the dark. Something had to change. This was full flight now and they had to get to the boat on the beach. They would need some limited time to get it rigged before launch, which meant that they had to slip their pursuers, even if it only gave them ten minutes or so. God knew how they were going to achieve that. Louis was obviously thinking the same thing.

"We've got to change the odds," he shouted. "We're only about three hours from daylight and if we don't get clear by then, we're fucked, which means we're going to have to take some of them out, or at least throw them off for a while. We're heading due south now but we need to head southeast to get to the boats, which I think are about eighteen miles away."

Chris looked back and could see the vague shapes of the hunters just on the edge of visibility.

Louis continued, "When we next lose sight of them and maybe get some sort of cover, I'm going to get Jon to pull hard over to the left. They'll close pretty quickly but we might be able to get just far enough off track to surprise them and get some rounds off before they realise. The priority will be to take out the vehicles. Without them, they can't follow unless they get replacements, which must be a few minutes behind at least. Get ready to lay down some fire."

Chris watched as the militia stuck doggedly to their tail, albeit some hundreds of yards behind. They kept this way for what seemed like an age, then the chance came, suddenly and in a particularly dense cloud of dust.

"Now Jon!" shouted Louis over the wind that was whipping around the truck cab and banged the cab roof. The vehicle swung hard over to the left and Jon gunned the engine even harder, leaving a fresh cloud of sand behind them as the oversized tyres bit into the surface, adding to the already confused picture. At first they could see nothing happening; the path they had just left revealed no pursuit. Then, when they were one hundred and fifty yards off track, they saw the lead of the two vehicles giving chase. A fraction of a second later it was obvious that they had been spotted as well, as both the first and the second chasing vehicle seemed to slam on their brakes and slow rapidly. This was what they were waiting for and ironically, it was exactly the same way Mustafa had trapped them after the Tomahawk strike at camp two.

"Now!" screamed Louis, and the Special Forces brought their three remaining weapons to bear on the slow moving targets behind them. It was never likely that they would have much success, they were moving away at speed across uneven ground, but it seemed to be the only chance they had at present. Chris watched as the rounds flew, feeling the kick of the weapon into his shoulder. He thought he had hit his target, the second truck, but he couldn't be sure. He thought he saw it lurch and drop at the front.

Mustafa had become increasingly frustrated that the men in front seemed to be keeping him at bay, just far enough to stop him engaging. His men standing behind the cab were letting off the odd round when they could see through the dust, but the Special Forces driver was skilled enough to handle the terrain at huge speed. Something would change however, he knew it. This sort of mad chase couldn't keep up indefinitely. He watched as the billowing dust clouds thickened and thinned, then became particularly thick, as if the hunted had gone through a heavier patch of sand instead of the scrub of the last few miles.

"Faster," he yelled at the driver, whose eyes were already wide in fear and knuckles pale as they gripped the wheel. He expected to catch sight of the men within seconds but this time, something was different. He felt momentary panic as he failed to see the back of them as he expected, then confusion. "What the…

"There," he shouted again, pointing over to the left. Out of the corner of his eye he had seen the Marines trying to make a break for it. He needed to get straight back into the trail but his shout only had the effect of stopping the vehicle, not redirecting it.

"Drive you fool, over there," he screamed this time, but he could see the tactical error as soon as they had slowed. The second truck had come to a complete stop behind them and while his vehicle leapt forward at his insistence, the second truck didn't have his direction to get them going again and was now just a large target, even at that range. He looked back as he heard shots ringing out and saw several hit home. The front tyre took one of the first hits and he saw the vehicle drop. One of the men in the back crumpled like a rag doll and he had to assume that he had lost another man to these foreigners. More importantly, that was the truck out of his force. He was now down to one, his own, with only four men in the load bay. The odds were no longer in his favour and he had to make a difficult decision. Did he carry on in the chase, or did he wait for reinforcements?

Damn them! He had no option but to wait. He knew that his supporting forces were coming up behind and that without superior numbers he would most likely be taken out himself. The enemy would be given a head start, a lead he could ill afford to allow, but thanks to Colonel Taylor's man on the team, he did know which way they had to be headed; it had to be the same place they came ashore. His forces were depleted and he no longer had the men in place behind the beaches to intercept, they had all been with him at the village, but he did have the advantage of more resources being imminently available. He could intercept when the advantage was again his and in the name of Allah he swore that they wouldn't get away. They still had to pay for the damage that they had inflicted on his plans. He would chase them to the ends of the earth to exact his revenge, one by one if necessary. He hadn't lost them yet.

Chris allowed himself a gritty shout of "Yes!" as he saw the scene behind him. He had indeed taken the second truck out as it had slowed Unlike the first, it had pretty much stopped completely and it hadn't started again. The first had initially turned towards them, looking like it was going to continue the chase but just before his vision was obscured totally by the sand and the darkness of the night, he saw it turn back; they had given up, at least for the present. Now was the time to press home the advantage and to get the fuck away. Louis swung over to issue fresh instructions to Jon driving.

"Go straight for another mile then take a sharp right to go south again. We need to start putting in some turns to confuse the trail before we head for the boats. If you see any landmarks we may be able to use, head for them. Pat, have you got your GPS?" All the personal kit of the three held prisoner had been taken during captivity.

Pat was looking increasingly pale as the shock of his shoulder wound was starting to take effect but he rallied slightly at the question.

"I'm afraid not Boss," he replied. "Dodger had one though."

Chris saw Louis look down at the body of his previous second in command, still lying at the tailgate of the truck flat bed, albeit with a large part of his head missing, and edged forward. He started to rifle the jacket and brought out a small black device from the breast pocket. Chris could see him stare at it, uncomprehendingly at first, then he saw his face harden and he looked Chris straight in the eye.

"It's a positional message transmitter," he said, anger making his lips tight and his voice thin. He held Chris's gaze a few seconds longer, then continued his search, eventually taking a hand held GPS set from the side of Dodger's trousers and retracing his steps to the roll bar behind the cab.

Nothing more was said. It didn't need to be. Louis entered the security code then waited for the GPS to lock into their position.

"Right, we're fifteen miles as the crow flies from the boats. I reckon sunrise will be in about two hours. That gives us about an hour and a half until nautical twilight. We need to get to the boats in an hour and get to sea. I hope your boys are ready for us Chris."

"They'll be there," Chris replied. Please God let them be there, he thought silently to himself. Jon continued to put in frequent turns but also slowed his pace to something that would reduce the noise they were creating and reduce the risk of a crash but still keep them moving away from the threat behind them. How much time they had gained overall no-one could know. Quite obviously their canoe was still fairly far up shit creek without much of a paddle. They were still in hostile territory and had to assume hostile intent at any moment and on every level. They had a break. Now to make best use of it.

Mustafa was standing by his truck, deranged with anger. It was five minutes after the engagement and every second was crucial. Luckily the engine on the second truck still worked and it was just a case of changing the wheel, but that wasn't a simple exercise on soft sand. He had been in radio contact with the rest of his teams and they were only about five minutes away. In short order, he would have six teams ready to be deployed. He would take his own and two others in pursuit of the fleeing special forces and send the other three straight towards the coast. He had a rough idea where they had come ashore. He may be behind now but he still had every chance of catching up and taking them out.

As he formulated the plan, he heard trucks pulling up to him out of the dark and shapes began to loom. His teams were there and he sent the first three straight off. Another couple of minutes and the tyre had been replaced. Mustafa looked at his watch and snarled. Ten minutes behind! Now the hunt would truly begin. He had to follow the track through the dark, no mean feat. He began in the direction he had last seen them as the other two trucks pulled in behind. As the ground began to roll under his feet, he remembered his youth in Yemen, where he had learnt the hunter's trade during the civil war, tracking through the night in conditions much like this, perhaps a bit rockier and more difficult. He could see the tracks the large tyres of the pick-up had made ten minutes before, illuminated in the vehicle headlights and had no problem seeing when they turned. He could follow at a reasonable pace. As he considered the disposition of his men, he knew that he was still in the game; the enemy hadn't got away yet. After all, they were still on his territory and he once again had the numerical advantage.

The Marines continued to travel over scrubland, making frequent turns to try and throw off pursuit and stopping occasionally to investigate noises they thought they had heard out in the desert. They also made fairly good ground and as the minute hand approached the hour mark, with only an hour to go until the light from the morning twilight would start to make them much more vulnerable, they got to within a mile of the boat position. Jon was driving at a crawl now; this was not the time to go steamrollering in. So far, they had avoided any signs of pursuit, but they couldn't assume that they were clear or that the boat site hadn't been compromised. Louis called a halt.

"We'll have to go on foot from here boys," he said, the weariness of the last few days finally seeming to catch up on him. As Chris looked round at his comrades' faces he could see them all suffering. Louis and Bobby had both been badly beaten in captivity and their faces were bloodied and swollen as a result; he realised that he must look the same. Jon was the only one who was relatively unscathed, but you could see the tiredness of the effort he had recently put in. Pat of course was in the worst condition, having taken a round to the shoulder. Chris knew exactly how he felt and he remembered the pain that had exploded in his body in Jamaica when he had sustained his own injury those many years before, the injury that had ended his Special Forces career. A closer look and he could see Pat was in a very bad way; loss of blood and traumatic shock had turned his face ashen. He would be a potentially devastating hindrance to their evacuation, especially if they came upon opposing forces, but there was never any question of leaving him behind; he was theirs and would stay with them, whatever the end state. Chris looked round at the body of Dodger lying in the back of the truck.

"What do we do about him?" he asked to no-one in particular.

Louis was the one that answered. "Leave him here; he could still kill us if we get caught trying to bring a body back. We can't afford the risk and I'm not prepared to take it for him. Leave all the kit except weapons. Let's get moving."

Bobby and Jon moved to each of Pat's sides. Louis took point and Chris fell in behind him. They got a direction from the GPS and started walking. Chris prayed that they would be unmolested. At the moment all was silent. How long that would last was anyone's guess.

Here by the sea they could smell the salt in the air even if they couldn't yet hear the waves. The sand had started to increase and they were walking over small dunes towards their boat. It was still night although Chris could sense a lightening of the sky towards the east. They had to hurry; the last thing they wanted was for their movements to be seen in the fast approaching daylight. They had to get into the water under the cover of night. Each dune they crossed just seemed to lead to another and it was painful progress. Not only were their muscles crying out from exhaustion and abuse, they had to carry Pat, who was barely able to stumble forward with them.

They walked for a few hundred yards then Louis called a stop to listen. They heard nothing and continued. Another few hundred and they reached the last of the remote dunes. From here they could hear the light crash of the waves upon the shore. Chris dared hope that they had made it, then his worst fears were reawakened; he heard the dull engine noise of an approaching vehicle. In the faintly growing light he could see the bushes where they had left the boat. He knew that they were no more than one minute's walk away but that seemed a huge distance over fairly flat sand with some sort of truck approaching. He wasn't naïve enough to think this was anything other than Mustafa or his gang. They waited, frozen to the spot. Time was running out and the light was getting perceptibly stronger, although they could still see little further than their immediate goal.

Chris could hear the engine growing louder; it was definitely coming their way but he couldn't tell yet if it was going to be between them and the boat or the boat and the sea. If it stayed like this for much longer, it was arbitrary; any movement would be spotted in the half light anyway. Then it got worse. From the other direction they heard another engine.

"Fucking hell, not two of them!" exploded Louis. "This is fucking ridiculous." The strain and frustration was showing on them all, but Chris was surprised to hear it from the normally controlled Louis. "Right, bugger this," he continued with some purpose in his voice. "Looks like they've released the dogs, boys, and we have to get into the water pretty quickly. If we start poncing around with a boat in the daylight they'll be on us in seconds and they'll just cut us down. We've got to have time to get from the tree to the water. We'll do it in two stages. First, Chris and I will get to the boat and dig one of them out of the sand; it's only shallow and we should be able to do that. The rest of you, stay here and cover us with the rifles we still have in case those arseholes spot us. When we're ready to go, you, Bobby and Jon will have to bring Pat to us and put him in the boat then help us haul it over the last bit to the water. If we can get there, we can get away. Got it?"

Again there was nothing but nods from what was left of the team; they were too tired to think any differently and took the lead from Louis, knowing that he was in command.

"Ok, wait for my sign boys and for God's sake cover my arse will you."

Chris passed his rifle across to Bobby and took out the personal weapon he had taken from Dodger; this was not a time to be unarmed. He could still hear the noise of the engines getting louder. Wherever they actually were, they were running slowly down the beach towards them and therefore would soon be a problem. Use the dark, he thought to himself, and they went over the top at a crouching run.

It was less than a minute but it seemed like an eternity before they made the bushes. At each second, Chris expected shots to ring out and to be cut down. They both threw themselves flat and listened; the trucks were closer still. What the hell were they doing out here? The reality of their position hit home to Chris and for the first time he questioned Louis' judgement. This was suicide. They had just brought themselves out of cover and put themselves right in the line of two approaching vehicles. What had Louis been thinking and furthermore, why hadn't Chris said something? He guessed he was just too tired to question the orders, but that was no good now. He looked to the north, to what seemed like the closer of the two vehicles and stared, praying for some minor miracle.

And then he saw it, the first of the trucks and it was as he had known it would be; the same type of pick up with at least four men in the back, all armed with the usual Kalashnikovs and all scanning the horizon. They were going to pass right in front of the tree, about twenty yards from Chris's position. They were horribly exposed. The distance between the forces reduced as the militia cruised slowly along the beach, looking inward. Chris and Louis had done what they could and in the moments that they had before the militia came too close, they had thrown sand over each other to try and blend in. All they could hope for was that their desert combats would be enough in the now semi-darkness to conceal them.

Chris stuck his head down as much as possible to try and hide the brown of his hair, and averted his face to avoid any shine from his white skin. He could hear the moving truck and as its bearing moved faster, knew they were closer still. They were obviously only yards away when his worst fears were realised as one of the men in the back let out a low shout. The vehicle increased in speed and he braced himself for the inevitable rain of bullets that would end his life, but they never came. He risked a look and a flood of relief rushed through his body; they had spotted the second truck, not Louis and himself lying twenty yards landward, and had gone to meet them.

The nightmare wasn't over, the two groups were now only fifty yards away to the south and right on the edge of visibility. Chris and Louis could do nothing while they were there, and the light continued to brighten in the eastern sky. He had never wanted there to be dark clouds more than now, but it was going to be another bloody glorious day; there was nowhere to hide.

Mustafa urged his driver on once again. He could smell the quarry not too far away. They had been following for an hour and were almost on the coast. This must be it, he thought. The tracks had led them here without any doubt… and then he saw it, the vehicle up ahead. One of his hands shot out to the dashboard and the driver stopped short. He had them now but where were they? Were they waiting for him, an ambush set to spring? He motioned for the other two vehicles to come abreast until all three were level. There weren't enough men left to overwhelm his force. He could afford to spring the trap and then rush the Marines if required. He sent the right hand pick-up forward slowly and it rolled gently over the intervening sand coming to a stop ten yards short. Nothing happened, not even when a couple of the men jumped from the back and moved closer. They scouted the area then beckoned him forward. As he approached he could see the kit the foreigners had carried left on the ground and a body of one of them in the back of the flat bed. They had obviously abandoned the site but he still didn't believe he was too late.

He looked around and then saw the tracks moving off eastwards towards the sea. He had men down there, he would still be in time. Looking at the sky and seeing the dawn approaching, he ordered his men to form a line and started to move forward. He had overwhelming numbers and could afford to waste a few. He would use them as beaters and flush out his game. They started at a fair pace following the still fresh tracks through the sand. His heartbeat quickened.

Chris lay frozen in place. What the hell were these men talking about? They had been in the same place for at least five minutes, time that would have been used by Mustafa to close in. They had to get away and fast. Another few precious moments and at last he saw some movement. The truck that had passed them started forward then turned to its left in an arc to retrace its steps. This was the miracle that Chris had prayed for. A turn to the right and it would have run straight over them. A turn to the left took them further away and they passed slowly, seventy yards away. One look at the other vehicle and he saw it do the same. This was their chance, possibly their only chance. Louis knew it as well and with a quick sideways look, they both sprang into life, diving for the shallow spot where they had buried the boats. It didn't take long before Chris felt the rubber of the side float and he heaved on the attached rope with all his might, as did Louis at his side. The boat came clear and they grabbed the bag that had shielded the engine from sand contamination. He prayed that it had worked or this could be a very short attempt at escape.

A look over his shoulder and Chris saw Louis beckon to the others. He saw them heave Pat from his prone position by the last mini dune. While they started to cover the distance, he started to heave the boat forward toward the shore. They had covered twenty yards this way before the others caught up with them and put Pat carefully onto the bottom. There was no sign of any counter-detection; the trucks had cleared and he could see and hear the waves lapping gently at the shore. They were going to make it.

Mustafa looked up. At the edge of his sight he was sure that he saw figures rise up and move forward, away from him. He quickened his pace and moved to the front of his men, bringing them with him, the anticipation of the kill surging through his veins. He would get closer, make sure of it. He dropped into a crouching run and brought his weapon up. Revenge would come soon now.

Chris looked to both sides. They each had a corner of the boat and were making better time, a halting run. They had to make the water's edge, now only a few yards away. They were vulnerable, not able to train their weapons, their backs exposed to anyone that cared to attack.

Mustafa got to the last ridge ahead of his men and looked out at the beach. They were there, only a hundred yards ahead with a boat slung between them. He stood tall and started to run at full pelt. With glee he saw that they were at the water but only just. They hadn't made it yet.

Chris was euphoric. They had made it! They put the boat into the surf and continued to push with all their collective might. A few seconds more and they would be away. But as quickly as his euphoria rose it was suddenly quashed by the scream that erupted behind him. He turned fast to see Mustafa only yards away running down the beach with what looked like a small army at his sides. And then the first bullets came and it was like a scene from *Saving Private Ryan*. The water on either side of them started popping as rounds fizzed into it, missing them by inches.

"Keep pulling," shouted Louis and he redoubled his efforts. "Bobby, Jon, engage them," and with that the two men that had supported Pat grabbed their weapons again and brought them round. Almost immediately Jon was hit in the left arm but that didn't stop him. They both opened fire with everything they could and for a moment checked the advance. And that was the time they needed. Louis and Chris were heaving the boat deeper and the sea bed fell away quickly. When the water had reached their waist they clambered into the boat, their two comrades still laying down rounds in defiance at their attackers. Chris dropped the outboard and turned the ignition switch. One press of the starter button was all it needed and Chris thanked God once again. The water churned into life as the propeller bit.

"Grab on," he screamed at the two men still in the water behind the boat and they launched themselves desperately at the grab ropes running down each side, letting their weapons drop into the water as they did. Louis threw himself to secure Jon's one armed hold with his own and as soon as Chris saw their hands tighten he opened the throttle fully, feeling the boat surge ahead and leaving the shooting match behind them. As they got further away, the rain of lead started to die and once more the euphoria returned. They'd fucking done it.

As soon as he dared, Chris shut the throttle and the boat died into the flat of the Indian Ocean. He spun to check on the men trailing behind and dived over to help Bobby. He was a dead weight and almost unconscious but the grip of his hands on the side rope was almost too hard to break. The strain on his arms of being dragged through the water had almost killed him itself. All he could do was look up and as Chris looked down he saw pleading in his eyes; 'for God's sake get me out' they said.

With a huge effort that was almost too much at this stage, Chris hauled on the heavy Geordie, made heavier by his saturated clothing and slowly he inched him up the side of the boat. Louis was having the same issues with Jon but they made it, collapsing into the bottom and clasping the sides for dear life. Chris grabbed the outboard again and the engine roared into life. Drive, he thought to himself. Anywhere. Just drive.

Mustafa let loose a howl of rage into the pre-dawn sky. He had to watch as the men in their little boat somehow made it through the barrage of bullets that had scythed the water around them. The blood was raging within him. How! This should not be! Another shout of anger did nothing to assuage him. He stared out to sea listening uncomprehendingly at the sound of the engine growing fainter. Then his hopes rose as the engine seemed to die. Had it failed? Were they stranded? Could he yet get out to them? A maelstrom of contingencies rushed him but suddenly they were all cruelly slain by the sound of the engine running again.

"No!" he shouted again. This was not the end. He wouldn't let it be. They could not come into his land and destroy everything that he had worked so long for. He would do the same to them and hunt them down in their own country, one by one and starting with Colonel Taylor who was now a severe liability. Next on the list though would be the man who had been chasing him all these years. Edwards. He would have his head... and the revenge would be sweet.

Chris drove at full throttle for what seemed like an age, straight out into the ocean. They had no radios, no way of contacting the submarine. All he could do was hope that they were there and were listening. He scanned the horizon. Please Mike, be there.

"New fast revving contact bearing three two zero." The shout from the sonar room brought Cdr Mike Saggers instantly back to full focus. He jumped from the Captain's chair.

"Raise attack periscope," he ordered, and the soft hydraulic hiss saw the gleaming tube rise through the submarine's hull. He followed it up from a crouch, getting his eyes immediately onto the eyepieces by the time it cleared the water.

"Mark that bearing." He could feel waves of relief course through him as the pent up frustration at not knowing found something to focus on. He watched as the small boat, still some two thousand yards away headed straight towards him.

"Standby to surface!" They were the words he had been longing to say and he had never felt better saying them.

Chris kept sweeping the horizon for some clue that they were not alone. Backwards and forwards his gaze panned the flat water, now illuminated by a pale dawn that had broken from the east. Nothing. Surely they must be here. And then he saw the most welcome sight he thought he had ever seen. From the depths, first a conning tower, then the bow of the most beautiful black submarine emerged ahead of them like some sinister and enormous monster from the deep. He looked down at the others, all of whom were sprawled at his feet, their exhaustion wracked bodies on the point of giving up completely. Pat and Jon had injuries that had to be attended to fast but the rest would survive pretty much intact.

He headed like an arrow to their demonic salvation, watching as it turned in a great slow arc towards them, and they were soon bumping the side of the vessel. A few seconds later and the main access hatch opened. Men started streaming onto the casing with jumping ladders, ropes and stretchers. Chris slumped back against the outboard engine, all his energy spent. He couldn't remember ever feeling like this. All he could do was stare up at those who were trying to help. As he looked, he saw a familiar head reach the hatch and then a body he knew well. His friend Mike stood above him and looked down, horror inscribed onto his features.

"You look like shit," he said without a trace of humour.

Chris smiled and he knew that he was safe.

CHAPTER 11

Mustafa sat in first class on the Turkish airlines flight to Istanbul for his connection to the UK, still seething from the ruin that had been rained upon him by the British and furious that he had been so close to avenging Osama Bin Laden's death and the other leaders lost over the previous years. It had been three days since he watched the men and the boat disappear into the early morning light and he had wasted no time in plotting his revenge. The first step had been back to the village where the captives had been held and an attempt to identify the foreigner's bodies that had been accounted for along the way. He knew they had originally been eight and he had killed three of them, one older and one younger man after the strike on the camp and the body of the man in the back of the abandoned truck. Unfortunately, none of them had been Edwards, which was something that choked him. That man had dogged him for the last fifteen years; it was time for him to be removed from the picture completely. Then there was Colonel Taylor. He had been incredibly useful and his information had saved Mustafa numerous times but he had been frozen out of the picture and was now compromised. That was a risk too high to live with; he too would have to go.

Twelve hours later he walked out of Heathrow to a waiting driver and was whisked away along the M4 motorway west and into Berkshire. As he passed Windsor he looked at the castle away to his left, the seat of monarchical power that had been supported through the centuries by this country's imperial and exploitative past. He looked around at the river of cars and people, bitterly reflecting on how lucky they had been and how close their cosy worlds had come to being dealt a shocking blow. He would have to start all the planning again but that was in the future. For the moment his destination was the New Forest. There he would meet his UK team in a cottage that Al-Qaeda owned and finalise his plans. He was within striking distance of the first target in Poole. Colonel Taylor was in his sights.

Chris and the remaining men were three days into their return trip on the submarine. They were about to rendezvous in the middle of the Indian Ocean with a Royal Fleet Auxiliary support ship that had helicopters with enough range to evacuate them within two days to Oman. They needed proper medical treatment and repatriation to the UK and this would get them home two days earlier than staying on the submarine all the way back to Fujairah. Pat and Jon had been patched up by the submarine doctor as best as he could, but a cramped bunk in an overcrowded tin can was no substitute for a hospital ward and a nice nurse to tuck you in at night. Louis, Bobby and Chris had spent most of the time sleeping. They had been utterly exhausted by the action and they knew they were lucky to be alive. The mission itself had been a success; they had disrupted the training camp, killed most of the operatives and prevented the wholesale slaughter of innocents back home, but it had come at a heavy price. They had lost three of their men, although one of those had almost definitely been a traitor.

Sgt Baxter, Stan to his friends, had served in the regiment for twenty years, was almost time done and due to leave very soon. He had served with Chris many times and they had saved each other's lives on numerous occasions. He left a family back home with two grown up children, a boy and a girl, both through university and making their own lives. His long suffering wife had put up with all the upheaval and fear that being married to the Special Forces involved and had been hugely thankful that Stan had made it through to the end of his career still alive. After everything else, all the worries, all the sacrifices, this was the last mission… 'just one more' she had said to herself as she saw him leave for the last time.

Peanut had been a passing acquaintance to Chris previously but they had become friends over the course of the mission. They had worked together in Afghanistan a couple of times, albeit in different troops, and though relatively young, he had been a respected team player. Peanut's life had been the Marines and he had no girlfriend or wife. In a way that made his death harder to take. This was a young man who should have had the rest of his life ahead of him. Not anymore. The corps would give him a military funeral, as long as the family wanted it, and Chris would be there.

Dodger was the only one that he hadn't known but that wasn't the reason he didn't lament his passing. Louis' report to Headquarters had voiced their suspicions, including the discovery of the manually keyed satellite transmitter. It had been fairly easy for MI5 to chase down information when they had been tasked and within a day, there emerged the existence of a separate bank account with enough funds in it to provide for a very nice retirement fund. The question was where those funds had come from, which was taking slightly longer to uncover. There seemed to be a link in the UK, but where, they didn't yet know. Another three or four days should do it.

For the moment, Chris had nothing to do but wait. Onboard, he was part of the Special Forces team, not the submarine crew, and although he knew some of them quite well, he kept away, not wanting to answer any awkward questions. The one exception to this was his friend the Captain, Mike Saggers. Chris spent several hours a day with him, talking through what had gone on and trying to work out where he went from here. He had been brought back to support a specialist mission but he was under no illusion that he was out of touch. It had been too long since he had been involved on a day to day level. He realised that being current was crucial if you wanted to live through one of these operations, and more importantly, not to be a liability to your comrades. In any case, he now had a new wife, a woman he adored and wanted to spend the rest of his life with. He wanted to make that as long as possible and what had happened over the last week wasn't conducive to old age.

Mustafa took his supper in the cottage with the six men that made up his ground team here in the UK. There were many other operatives, but in the nature of Al-Qaeda they were sleeping cells, minimally trained and only to be called upon when needed for possible martyrdom or a particular mission. The men he now had around him were highly trained individuals, brought in from the camps in Pakistan where they had been made into soldiers and hidden within the extensive Pakistani community in the North of England; it provided perfect cover for the men and he could be fairly sure they would remain undiscovered.

The next morning he carried out his prayers and sent the first of his teams after the Colonel. Their mission was to locate and trail. Mustafa needed to know his daily routine so that he could choose the best time to intercept. This was no suicide mission but the first stage of a multi phase operation that needed to be efficient and clinical; he needed his men to survive.

The inevitable wait for information, as ever, made him tetchy. He was once again in full planning mode, running through the possibilities, the options, courses of action, but this time he didn't have to wait long. Two hours later his team had picked up the Colonel on his way to work from his civilian address, a private cottage in a quiet village fifteen miles outside Poole. His journey had taken him to the Headquarters in approximately thirty minutes. Mustafa swapped the teams in the early afternoon and the second picked Taylor up as he left for his return journey. He used a different route, which may have caused a problem, but a look at a local map told Mustafa all he needed to know. As with most small villages in the South of England, there was only a single road in from the direction of the base and whichever way the Colonel tried to vary his journey, he would have to pass a single spot. That was his vulnerability and that was where Mustafa would take him.

The next day the pattern continued and reinforced Mustafa's decision to strike the following morning. He would catch Taylor as he left the village, one team tailing him, one blocking the route out. At that time there would be minimal traffic and maximum chance of closing the trap unobserved. Mustafa's operational juices were flowing once again and he could feel the excitement of the imminent take down building up.

The next morning Colonel Taylor woke early, which itself wasn't normal. He would generally sleep through until the alarm went at six. That night he had slept fitfully and at five decided that enough was enough. He was worried about the consequences of the mission. His 'employer' and his operation had been decimated. The Marines had taken casualties, including his man Dodger, but they had prevailed and were on their way back. There were two things that worried him most. First, he had never been let into this mission. That was unheard of and he was fairly sure that his cover must be blown. Secondly, he had heard nothing from Mustafa, which was even more disturbing. He would have expected to have been ordered to explain personally. Up to now the silence had been deafening. Could he hope that Mustafa had died in the attack?

As he sat in his cottage, drinking the first coffee of the day and waiting for the weak early summer sun to crest the horizon, his thoughts turned to Dodger. He had lost a valuable asset, one that he had invested a lot of time and money in and his absence left him even more vulnerable. The man had been tipped for the top and would have been the perfect replacement for Taylor himself. His mind drifted back to when he had first met him, a young man in Afghanistan and the son of an Army Lieutenant General, distinguishing himself in action and making a reputation as a strategic thinker as well. It was only by chance, five years before when getting off a train from Poole into London, that he spotted Dodger walking along the platform in front of him. He was about to say hello when Lieutenant Long got through the ticket turnstiles and greeted an obvious partner. What was most interesting, though, was that the partner was a relatively small and effeminate man and obviously gay.

While there were no regulations any more about being homosexual in the armed forces, there was, in some quarters, still considerable stigma attached. Certainly there had been no suggestion of homosexuality before and that meant that Dodger was leading a double life. This was a gift to Taylor. In the following few days he postponed his own plans and set about doing what the Special Forces do best, trailing the young Lieutenant round some of the more low key areas of the capital. More interesting still was the nature of some of the venues visited. There was a sub culture in the city that he hadn't been fully aware of before. As he trailed Dodger however, he found out just how many sadomasochistic clubs there were.

After a few weekends he had enough evidence to realise that there was a considerable 'dirty secret' to be exploited, something that if known in the Corps would probably mean expulsion, if nothing else on the grounds of being prone to blackmail, exactly what Taylor now planned to do. It would probably mean the end of his father's career as well, which meant extra pressure.

The approach had been gradual – small tasks first, making Dodger 'his man'. It became a working relationship and the young officer was pleased to have a man of Taylor's seniority as his sponsor. Over time, he was hooked in deeper and deeper until in the end, he was completely under Taylor's control. It had been easy.

The hands on the kitchen clock walked slowly round to half six and it was time for the Colonel to leave. He stepped out into the pale dawn light and got into his car, wisps of mist rising from the fields around the cottage. What would the day bring, he wondered?

Mustafa and his men were up long before dawn to set the ambush. The first vehicle with Mustafa in the passenger's seat made its way to the village and parked at one side of the quiet triangular green. He looked out at the peaceful scene, the duck pond, the village pub, the scattering of thatched cottages and it sickened him, so far removed from the harshness that he had endured as a child. They were so soft, these 'First World' powers. They didn't know what it was like to suffer, only how to inflict their morals and values onto others, morals born from a pandered existence with no possibility of having to make the stark choices that might determine if your family ate or starved, lived or died. They did know how to exploit and to strip people of their rightful wealth however, both economic and spiritual. They had raped everywhere they had been, both physically and economically, and stolen the innocence of sovereign people. They must pay one day and it was this thought that had kept Mustafa so absolutely dedicated to his cause over the years.

He watched with a rising sense of anticipation as the minutes passed, and then the Colonel's innocuous Ford Mondeo passed on the other side of the green. He could plainly see Taylor, his former employee, alone at the wheel and oblivious of his impending fate. With a word the driver moved slowly away from the curb. Mustafa radioed the second team that the target was approaching and then urged his own driver to close. They reduced the range to the Colonel to within one hundred yards, keeping him firmly in view. The man was driving slowly through the outskirts of the village. So much the better to allow the pieces to be put in place, thought Mustafa. They had seen no other traffic; it couldn't have been better.

At the end of the main street, the Colonel turned left, as Mustafa now knew he would, and the trap was set. Another half mile along the road was the Range Rover with his second team. Mustafa radioed them to start their approach as he himself turned behind the Colonel. There was no way out now. The high hedgerows marking the edges of the arable fields flanking the narrow road provided cover from the surrounding countryside and prevented any sideward's escape.

"Get closer," Mustafa urged, and his own vehicle sped up. He could see the back of the Colonel's car only a few yards away, then he saw the rear end dip as the front wheel drive kicked into action and it started to accelerate. They had been spotted.

The Mondeo sprinted ahead and seemed to be pulling away fast, but only for a few seconds. As he reached the next shallow corner, Mustafa saw the car slam on its brakes and come to a shuddering stop; he must have seen the other team. The reversing lights shone bright in the early morning air and Taylor started to come back towards them at full speed, closely followed by the bonnet of the second team's Range Rover.

"Block the road," Mustafa ordered, and his driver swung the wheel to the right, putting the large 4x4 across the path of the Mondeo. It stopped only twenty yards distant and for a moment, nothing happened. Then the door opened and the Colonel got out, looking directly at Mustafa. He was standing with the door open and his hands at his sides, no jacket on and with no evidence of a weapon. How foolish, thought Mustafa, picking up his own pistol and opening the door. His teams did the same, and the Colonel was surrounded by seven armed men. Taylor held Mustafa's gaze then scanned the teams coolly before turning back again, holding his gaze for a full ten seconds before speaking.

"What do you want?" He spoke dispassionately, as if he had no fear of what could be about to happen.

"I want you Colonel," Mustafa replied, equally calmly. "You have done your duty for me, but now that time is over. You have become too much of a risk. I can't let you jeopardise my plans. It is time."

The Colonel nodded. Mustafa couldn't tell what was going through this man's mind. He must know that his death was imminent but he stood there waiting, without panic or protest.

"Then make it clean," he said, plainly, and turned back to his car, placing his good hand above the driver's door with his back to his would-be killer; his prosthetic arm hung lifeless at his side.

Mustafa paused a few seconds more then walked forward, bringing his weapon up with his arm outstretched, levelling it at the back of the Colonel's head. The man just stood there, and Mustafa grudgingly gave him a measure of respect. This man was no coward. He may have been a traitor but he had served Mustafa well. He stood there now in dignity, waiting for the executioner's axe to fall. He would give him the honour of a clean death. Mustafa stopped a yard away.

"Thank you for your service Colonel," was all he said before pulling the trigger. The heavily silenced weapon kicked in his hand as the bullet left the barrel but the bullet flew true. The round entered the base of Taylor's skull and thudded into his brain, ending his life instantly and without pain. The body crumpled and hit the floor. Mustafa looked at it with a slight tinge of regret. This man had kept him alive many times. It would be difficult to find someone equally as useful.

He turned and strode back to the car, as did the rest of his men. He needed to clear the area before this was discovered and then get back to the cottage. Part one was complete; time for part two: Edwards.

Chris watched as the military airport at Thumrait in central Oman slipped away beneath him. They were in the back of an RAF Hercules on their way to the UK. It was the best way, given their physical state, the undoubted comment they would attract and the need to keep some sort of low profile while they were extracted. The two injured men had stabilised but they were accompanied by a full team of Royal Air Force doctors and medics for the flight and would be taken straight to Hedley Court, the Forces rehabilitation centre of excellence, when they landed. That left just Louis, Bobby and Chris to report directly to Poole on their return. It was an overnight flight and they would arrive early the next morning. It wasn't until the debrief was complete that Chris would be able to get home. He needed to; it was time for reflection.

Sleep was almost impossible in the antiquated aircraft; it was most definitely a military transport, no frills allowed and Bobby complained loudly about the quality of the trolly dollies to the RAF loadmaster but to no effect. The group had recovered somewhat over the last five days and the privation was of no consequence. The bruising, however, had blossomed and Chris had obtained colours on his body that he didn't know existed, but the pain had subsided and the aches had receded enough to allow some normal degree of movement and flexibility. This post operation period was always difficult, usually typified by mental numbness after the high octane intensity and violence of the preceding days. They didn't speak much, just small talk as each reflected on what had gone before and of course on the loss of such a large number of their comrades. This had been a different operation. They had engaged in full combat, mostly because they had been expected at every turn. The traitor at Headquarters and Dodger within the team had done a proper job, forcing them to fight all the way.

Chris dozed fitfully overnight and by the time he reached the RAF base at Brize Norton, he was dreading the day of debriefings that were inevitably ahead of him. If he were lucky, he would get out late in the day and get home tonight. If not, he might have to stay over and leave as soon as possible tomorrow.

As soon as they had landed and were walking across the tarmac to the waiting crew transport, Chris could see Louis switch on his mobile phone and went to do the same; it was good to be able to do the routine things that gave you reassurance of being secure and finally at home. He waited for his signal to lock in but was surprised to see Louis' phone ring straight away. Louis answered it and stopped in his tracks, Chris stopped with him. He could see a stunned look come over his friend's face and for once Louis seemed speechless. Having gone through so much over the last few days, Chris couldn't imagine what could have caused such a strange reaction. He waited.

Louis pulled the phone from his ear and stared back at Chris.

"That was the Director. The Colonel's dead, Taylor, this morning, assassinated outside his village on the way to work. He was tapped in the back of the head and left in the middle of the road."

It was shocking news. Bobby had also been on the periphery and had overheard the message. The three of them stood, motionless. Chris was the first to break the silence.

"Do they know anything else?" he asked, plainly.

"That's it," replied Louis. "We're to get straight back to Headquarters for a debrief. They'll give us more there if they have it but at the moment that's all they know. Chris… he was the traitor."

Like an enigma machine when the wheels aligned and the message became clear, it all clicked into place for Chris, although he could scarcely believe it. The Colonel was the traitor. For two decades Taylor had been either involved in or controlled almost every operation the Special Boat Service had put on, either deployed with his men as boots on the ground, as the operations officer at Headquarters or higher in various staff positions. He had been one of the most trusted men in the organisation. No-one would have questioned his loyalty, no-one. After the repeated shocks of the last few days, the numbness of post ops trauma came back to them. Chris wondered when it would all end.

The journey back to Poole was made in near silence. Two hours later and in the early afternoon they pulled up outside the familiar gates and were let through with the minimum of preamble. No-one they met seemed to want to talk and there was a subdued air throughout; the word had obviously got around. They were led up to the Director's office, where they were met by General Holbrook, the Operations Officer Major Shaw and a small number of men that had a vested interest in what had been happening.

"Come in chaps." The General's voice was as soft and controlled as ever. He invited them to sit in front of his desk.

"Can I say first that you have carried out an extraordinary operation, gentlemen," he continued. "As far as mission objectives are concerned, you have saved countless lives not only in this country but we think in Paris and also somewhere in Germany. These men are from MI5," he gestured around the room at those they didn't know, "and have been in contact with their counterparts abroad, who seem to agree. I can't say, however, that I am as happy as I could have been. Let me stress this is not your fault, Major Armstrong, indeed I think that your leadership and the decisions you made were first rate, but we have lost valuable men and a wealth of experience, people that we will be hard pressed to replace. My overriding feeling at the moment, however, is a sense of betrayal. We had guessed that there was one traitor among us, we had no idea that we had two. That, I'm afraid, is my failing, a failing that contributed as much as anything to the casualties.

"Leaving that aside for the moment, we were trying to root out the traitor here and were pretty sure that Colonel Taylor was the man. It would seem that we have been proved right. As you have no doubt heard, Taylor was assassinated this morning; his body was found outside his home village lying by his car with a bullet to the back of the head. I think we can say that confirms our suspicions. God forgive me but I have to say that I'm not displeased with that particular outcome. It removes the problem for us and has the benefit of saving the Corps the disgrace of negative publicity. It does beg the question of who committed the act, which is where MI5 come in. That will be their follow up.

"Lt Cdr Edwards, I can only extend my heartfelt thanks for your participation in the operation; your contribution has been invaluable. Did you find it easy to make the transition back to Corps life?"

"Sir, I feel as though I contributed very little in the grand scheme of things. I was brought in because of Mustafa and the bottom line is that we lost him. To that end I feel incredibly frustrated."

"No, son you're wrong," the General cut in. "Your mission was to save lives through the disruption of his plans. You achieved that in spades. The capture of Mustafa was a secondary consideration. You have been vital in this team throughout and have proved yourself fully capable. In any case, I have a feeling that the Mustafa story isn't over. I don't know what he'll be planning, but I do know he'll be planning something. What I need to know is whether you would be willing to help me again if it comes down to it? Take some time to think about that and be ready for the question if and when I need to ask it."

Before Chris knew it the words came tumbling out. It seemed that his subconscious had made the decision for him. "Sir, I'll be there like a shot whenever you want."

"Thank you. Right gentlemen, there are some things that I need to discuss with my visitors, so will you excuse us? Major Armstrong, I will expect a full debrief this afternoon, so back in here with Lt Cdr Edwards at fourteen hundred. Chris you will be released tonight. I've cleared it with Captain Absolom that you can have next week to recuperate."

They got up and left and although they had been praised for their actions, both Chris and Louis shared the sadness that seemed to exude from the General at the circumstances of their victory, a reflection of the personal betrayal and loss that surrounded the mission. They spent the rest of the time reviewing all the details, making sure they had the pertinent facts to hand. When it came to it, the Director went into some depth over the conduct of the operation, more than usual for a man of his rank, paying particular attention to the actions of Dodger throughout and the discovery of the transmitter. The explanation for each of their decisions was accepted and agreed and by the time that Chris left the building, it was approaching eight in the evening. After everything that had gone on, all he could think about was getting home, which was still a three hour drive away. He was tired and he had managed only a quick ten minute phone call to Elizabeth at the start of the day. He needed to forget, even for a short while, everything that had gone on and spend some time with his beautiful wife. As he drove away and saw the gates recede behind him, he felt a weight lift slightly.

It was dark as he pulled off the main road and started along the half mile farm track that led to his house. As always, with each passing yard his mood lifted, as if he were leaving the harsh outside world behind. He drove slowly, savouring the tension release that he loved so much, while watching the startled rabbits scurry out of the way of the headlights and looking out for the owls that patrolled the fields at this time of night. He covered the distance in a couple of minutes, feeling a rising sense of excitement at the thought of his wife waiting for him, as he knew she would be.

He switched off his headlights as he turned the final corner to see if he could surprise her and saw the barn in front of him, the final few yards of light coloured gravel laid out like a welcome mat. Strangely, he thought, all the lights were out in the front room. In the three years they had lived there, he couldn't think of another time when she had left them off after dark. He assumed she must be through in the kitchen at the back engrossed in something, probably preparing a special meal. He paused at this point as he often did and drank in the view, counting his blessings. After having gone through so much in such a short space of time, this was his haven, his castle and his refuge.

As he looked closer, however, and took in more details, something started to feel wrong. He stayed in the car but looked to the right through the window to where he should see the dull glow of light from the kitchen, if she were there. There was nothing. She wouldn't have gone out; her car was still there and she knew he was coming back. Perhaps, he smiled to himself hopefully, she was in the bedroom and he checked the first floor window. Again, it was dark. Something was definitely wrong and a feeling of dread started to engulf him, the hairs on the back of his neck rising. Not here, not his wife. He immediately and automatically switched into operational mode.

As quietly as he could he opened the door of his car, releasing the boot lid remotely as he did so. Taking his knife from his kit bag, the only weapon he had, he backed away around the high wall that enclosed the drive and dropped into a crouch, considering his options. No doubt if there were someone inside they would have seen him arrive and now be primed. They would expect him to come in from the front; it seemed the only way. What they might not know was that although the farmhouse and barns were surrounded by a moat, there was a narrow path along the back of his property along which he could gain access to the back of the house. He would try that way first.

His house was really four buildings in a square, set out like an old Roman villa with a garden in the middle. Apart from the very front, all the windows faced onto the courtyard; the outside walls were all weather boarded. The front, the side he was facing, was two storied and contained the living rooms and the bedrooms. The right side of the square was a long, low, single-storey kitchen that led onto some decking in the far corner. The far side, the part that backed onto the moat, had been made into a detached sports room. The final side, to the left, was a double garage. He didn't know what he would find at the back of his house but he knew it would be better than a full frontal assault.

He broke into a crouching run, keeping himself below the top of the wall and therefore unseen. He stopped at the left hand corner of his property and edged round. Everything looked normal but he took no chances. Massively aware of his vulnerability, he ran hard round the outside of the garage to the far corner and through a wicker gate that led to the back of the building and the edge of the moat. There was still no indication that he had been seen so he stopped again and paused for thought. The path along the side of the moat was only a few inches wide but he could navigate it with care. It was about twenty yards in length along the back of the sports room and would lead to the decking in the corner at the rear of his kitchen. From there he could try to gauge the enemy disposition, see if he could identify numbers and work out a plan of attack. His priority was Elizabeth. At all costs she must be kept safe, if it wasn't too late already, but in doing so he fully intended to kill every one of the bastards that may have dared to threaten her; he vowed they would not get away with this.

Silently, he inched along the narrow path, trying desperately to keep his balance, eventually making it to the gate at the end. The first quick look round the corner revealed no-one at the rear of the house and he pulled back the gate very, very, slowly, trusting that it wouldn't give him away. He edged his head round and took his first look into the back of the kitchen where he could see two figures partially hidden in the darkness, the first concrete indication that people were there. His resolve stiffened and anger rose within him, a cold clinical anger; he was going to take them down. He made to put his first foot through the gate and froze. The tiniest sound had come from around the corner, at the entrance to the sports room; whether it was the rasp of light breathing or a fractional movement he couldn't be sure, but he knew someone was within feet of him.

He checked his advance and every muscle in his body tightened, including the hand round the ridged grip of his knife. He was obviously undiscovered but now he didn't know where his closest enemy was or indeed how many. He looked into the kitchen and saw the backs of the men; they were facing away from him. If he made the wrong move now he was as good as dead, as was Elizabeth. But he couldn't just stay there, he had to move.

He started again, this time even slower than before, each fraction of an inch taking an age. Finally, he saw him. Only two feet away was the first of the intruders, obviously guarding the back of the building but looking the wrong way. He was leaning against the opposite side of the barn wall to Chris, sheltering underneath an open awning area and separated by only the thickness of the black weather boarding. He would have to be quick. Any sound and the game would be up at the outset. He had no option but to attack and go in hard.

With the pace and power of the killer that had been reawakened in him, Chris's left hand shot round the man's mouth, stifling any sound. At the same time, he brought his knife sharply up underneath the left side of the rib cage and pushed hard, straight through the ribs and into the heart. He could feel the blade grate against the bone as it sliced through the flesh and the quiver as the body reacted to the shock of imminent death. There was no sound and as the body started to fall, Chris got behind it, dropping it gently over to one side and out of immediate view of the back door of the kitchen. He stood up and flattened himself against the weather board wall. There was no alarm, no shouting. He had got away with it and he had got himself a second weapon, a low velocity pistol and even better, a silenced one. He checked the magazine and made sure it was ready to fire.

He still had no idea how many men there were in total but because he had taken control of the building's back corner, he could see along the length of the kitchen and could see the next two targets, now the subject of his entire focus. The next stage of the plan started to crystallise in Chris's mind. He must assume there were more inside the main body of the barn but the first hurdle was to knock down the odds. He checked the accesses and could see that on the inner side of the kitchen, overlooking the courtyard garden, there was a window open. The men were about ten feet inside the window and slightly in front of it, again their backs to him. He then looked across the central garden to what was the back of the main part of the barn and could see the window to the first floor master bedroom open as well, directly above the kitchen and accessible via its low roof.

There was always going to be a degree of assumption, but if he were holding a hostage, he would want them in the most difficult place to access, which would probably be in the master bedroom. Chris's priority was to secure Elizabeth and everything must be tailored to that aim. Beyond that, there would definitely be men in the front of the house. If he could divert or distract them, get them away from her, he could get onto the roof of the low kitchen and gain access to the bedroom through the open window to secure her safety. Then he could go after the rest.

He checked the weapon he was holding again, very gently releasing the clip and confirming there were rounds available. There were; he had twelve shots. He cocked the weapon, trying hard not to make any sound, and edged to the open window. The men hadn't moved and the night seemed to be as silent as the grave. The next action would be crucial; he was about to announce his presence, quite deliberately. He raised the barrel and took aim, centring on the back of the head of the man nearest. He only had time for one shot apiece. Anything more and the surprise would be gone. Without it, Chris would be dead.

He squeezed the trigger and a dull spat saw the first man drop. There was the merest of pauses while the second, taken completely by surprise, took half a second to register the noise and then the body collapsing beside him, and it was the half second that Chris needed to shift the aim of his weapon the few degrees required. This time he let off a double tap and saw the side of the head disintegrate, but there was no time to delay, he spun round and darted back to the corner decking, trying to reach the opposite side of the kitchen, the blind side that had no windows. As he ran past the back door however, the glass shattered behind him as a swathe of bullets from a silenced semi-automatic followed his movement; they had seen him.

Speed was crucial. He had to confuse them again. He ran hard along the outside path, this time away from the decking and towards the front corner where the single storey of the kitchen met the higher part of the front of the barn. After a scramble he made the low edge of the roof, but the weathered tiles weren't easy to get purchase on. He hung there, four feet off the ground trying desperately to get his feet onto the gabled roof, half knowing that at any second he would feel bullets slam into his side as they left the inside of the building and chased after him. This was his most vulnerable point, his weapon useless while his arms struggled to pull him up, but as the moments ticked by and his purchase grew stronger he started to think he might get away with it. They must have been unwilling to take the risk, not knowing where he was or how he was armed, because he made it onto the sloping and slightly slippery roof tiles without the dread of attack being realised.

If Chris was right, Elizabeth was now tantalisingly close, just above him. The open window beckoned and as soon as he could stand he moved towards it as fast as the insubstantial grip of his shoes would let him. Still they didn't come, although as he reached the lip of the window he heard the voice that had been the drive behind so many missions calling from the far end of the kitchen.

"Edwards," Mustafa called. "You can't win and we have her. Give yourself up or I promise you she will die at my hand."

This did nothing but spur Chris on. The next second he scanned the bedroom and saw nothing but a small figure curled up on the bed in the darkness; there was no-one else. He vaulted in through the opening and ran to his wife, who lay trussed hand and foot on the bed. As she saw the figure approach her eyes widened in shock, then realisation and relief. He took his knife out and cut the bonds with a swift flick, each moment making him more enraged. They would fucking pay for this with their lives.

She started crying and flung her arms around his neck, clinging desperately, furiously, but he had no time for this. He had the advantage again; they must have thought he was still outside at the back of the building trying to get in. He tore her arms away from him and saw the sheer panic register in her eyes. Before removing the gag that was preventing her from speaking, he motioned her to silence and whispered, "Stay here." She said nothing, just looked terrified, but they both knew he had to go; the threat was still there and very real.

He walked as softly as he could to the bedroom door and crouched behind it. He didn't know if there was anyone on the other side and again prayed that luck was with him. He lifted the iron latch and froze as the lock made a click. There was no reaction so he pushed the door as slowly as he dared. It opened a fraction and he looked down from a galleried landing onto the ground floor below and into the main body of the house.

His plan appeared to have worked as there was no-one to be seen; the men that had been there must have been drawn towards the back by his attack as he had hoped. It was time to make use of his slight advantage so he pushed the door open wide, allowing him full access to the landing and widening his field of fire to the whole of the central section of the ground floor. He moved stealthily across to the far end, which gave him a view down to the opposite corner of the room and through a double-sided brick fireplace that separated the central section from the corner sitting room, directly under the master bedroom.

Chris made his way noiselessly down the carpeted stairs and began to calculate; he had taken out three so far. He guessed there might be seven or eight in total. The odds were still hopelessly stacked against him so there was no option – he had to lower them.

As he got further down the stairs, Chris focussed on the corner room and started to see the outline of a man's back in the doorway that separated the two sections, his next victim; but how to take him out? If he could do it silently, he might get ahead of the game again. He reached the bottom of the stairs and started to creep forward. Each step, if heard, was a potential death knoll but each passed without noise. He saw the man now no more than six feet in front of him move forward slightly, out of his view and further towards the kitchen. At the first sign of movement Chris stopped but as the man changed position he saw his chance and moved more quickly. Gaining the now empty doorway he could check the enemy disposition. There was one man only feet away, looking down the length of the kitchen. Three more were in the kitchen itself. He had four more to kill in total.

He covered the distance to the next victim in two strides and this time took him with the knife again; the hand over the mouth, the thrust into the ribs and the instant limpness. He tried to drag the body out of sight unnoticed, but in reality that was never going to happen. The next nearest heard a noise and before Chris could get clear round the corner, there was a shout followed by bullets smacking into the brick and wood surrounding him. His face was showered with splinters and the body he was holding in front of him shuddered as it was hit again and again by lumps of lead but shielded as he was, he made it through the gap and let go of the body.

Pulling out his own pistol, he spun round to the other side of the fireplace, dropping to the floor and taking aim through the large gap in the brickwork that housed the wood burner, waiting for his pursuers to appear. Resting on one knee with his pistol raised, he saw the next man stepping into the now vacant corner room. As soon as Chris caught sight, he fired shots in rapid succession into his stomach and had the satisfaction of seeing him double up and blood spurt from an obviously severed artery, the noise of the man's shout changing from rage to pain with the frightening knowledge of his impending death. The man hit the floor and for a moment, Chris looked straight into his face and saw fear. This was no time for thought or forgiveness though - it was time for the man to die and Chris paused only a fraction before pulling the trigger. The face disappeared. One more down.

He could hear the remaining two running towards him from the kitchen, presumably Mustafa and one other. Then someone yelled, "STOP!" and it all went quiet.

Chris had no idea how many bullets he had left in his weapon, but he knew there were two men left to kill. There was a pause and the sudden silence was deafening. Chris was still kneeling on the other side of the fireplace, gun in hand. As the moments stretched on, he stayed there. He had actually run out of ideas. There was nowhere else left to go. The two men knew where he was and there was little chance of him being able to move from his current position without giving himself away, leaving Elizabeth unguarded or opening himself up to attack. At the same time, it would be incredibly difficult for Mustafa and the one remaining man to move either – stalemate. Chris's mind raced in desperate search for a strategy. A movement from above caught his eye and he looked up sharply to see Elizabeth at the door of the bedroom. Anger shot from his eyes as a warning and she backed away looking scared. His focus returned to the matter at hand but he still had no answers.

"It's been a long time coming Chris hasn't it?" The voice floated towards him, still and calm; it could only be Mustafa's. "How long have you been trying to get to me now? Fifteen years is it? Twenty?" The heavy accent filled Chris with revulsion. After everything that had gone on, his nemesis was only a few feet away, in his house, having threatened his wife. He said nothing.

"If it's any consolation, you came close, many times. If it hadn't been for Taylor, you would have had me. You should take credit for that."

Still Chris said nothing. He had no interest in talking to this man. There was only one agenda now and it involved Mustafa's death.

"I believe we find ourselves at an impasse. It's fitting really that after so long we should be unable to destroy each other at the last, don't you think?"

What the hell was he trying to do, Chris wondered? If he were a betting man, he would say he was playing for time, but for what. Chris's mind started to race. Could there be reinforcements? Was he playing a game? What did Chris need to do to regain the initiative? He decided to move back, to inject some small variable into the situation. Very slowly, trying to make no sound, he started to move back, keeping his weapon to the front. After the first step he straightened and then saw the reason for the delay. Ninety degrees to his left, previously shielded by a large sofa in front of double French doors leading out onto the central garden he saw the figure of the other remaining man standing with his semi-automatic rifle raised ready to fire. A surge of adrenalin kicked his senses into overdrive. The danger of the situation made itself pre-eminent and Chris saw his impending death in the barrel of the upraised weapon.

Chris started to throw himself back and down, anything but present a motionless target. As he did so he saw the glass of the French doors shatter as bullets ripped into and through them, all heading in his direction. He felt no ripping pain though and dared to think he had made it. Before he reached the relative safety of the floor however, his back hit the low coffee table that was behind him and he was pulled up short. Looking towards the threat, he saw his man stepping through the now shattered doorframes, bringing the barrel of his weapon down to point at Chris's head. At the same time, Chris brought his own weapon round and although he had no time to properly aim, his natural instincts took over. The bullets flew towards their target and into the neck of the man standing over him, the viscid spray of blood confirmation that his aim was true.

Unfortunately, at the same time, the man squeezed his own trigger and it was reciprocal action. As Chris saw his man drop, he felt the searing pain of at least one high velocity round enter his leg, another in the arm holding his pistol, spinning him off the table with the impact. His weapon was thrown away from him to land out of reach and as he hit the floor he saw Mustafa's legs through the fireplace edging towards him.

He had to get out, to move, get to safety. He tried to stand but as soon as he put his weight down the leg buckled. He knew that Mustafa was within feet of him in the next room. He had to move.

Using every ounce of strength left, Chris heaved himself back towards the far corner of the barn and the door leading to two lower bedrooms. As he made the opening he heard bullets smash into the wall next to him and with a gargantuan effort he threw himself back, shrieking with pain as the nerves in his leg fired excruciating impulses into his brain. He continued to crawl backwards into one of the bedrooms and heard Mustafa cry out in triumph.

Chris had no weapon left, he was defenceless and his nemesis was closing in. Was this how his life was going to end? Had he lost at the final hurdle? He felt the side of a bed behind his head and realised he could go no further. At the same time he saw Mustafa edge round the corner, leading with his pistol. All Chris could do was look up and feel defeat – and Mustafa could sense it. He came fully through the door frame and looked down upon his victim. There was no smile; it was going to be a Pyrrhic victory but a victory none the less.

"You have taken all my men Edwards," he started and stared straight into Chris's eyes. "You have proved yourself but as was only right, I will have the final word. You deserve to die, you, the Colonel, your friends, for the destruction you have brought to everything I had planned. I want you to know that they will be next. I will hunt down every one of them until I have my retribution."

Chris stared back at him with loathing. "Do what you want you shit. We will always send men like me to take you down and eventually one of us will get you. You've been lucky so far but your days are fucking numbered. You can kill me now but look over your shoulder, because my shadow will be there, somewhere, sometime, and eventually you'll fucking meet your God." Chris virtually spat the words, his pain-wracked mind drowning in vitriol.

Mustafa smiled for the first time. "And you make it sound like it's a curse. If I die fighting for my God, I will live in eternal glory, you fool. We are God's soldiers; we cannot lose. When we meet him it will be with open arms."

And then the world changed in front of Chris's eyes. He looked up at his tormentor and the barrel of the pistol pointing straight at his head. Mustafa's eyes hardened slightly, a look Chris had seen many times as the prelude to killing, and he saw the trigger finger clench. Chris shut his eyes and heard an almighty report as an un-silenced weapon was discharged just a few feet away, but instead of being engulfed in the blackness of death, he opened his eyes and watched as blood started to trickle from Mustafa's mouth. Chris didn't understand; his life should have been over. He watched as Mustafa's eyes looked down at his own chest, at the pool of blood that was now appearing on his shirt, then as he slowly looked back up towards Chris, incomprehension written all over his face, he dropped to his knees and Chris saw his salvation. Standing a few feet behind he saw Elizabeth, a look of horror contorting her features and a pistol held shaking in her hands.

Mustafa slumped forward onto his face and was dead before he hit the floor. It was to be his last movement. At the same time the weapon fell from Elizabeth's hands and she cried out in anguish at what she had done, running forward to throw herself into Chris's arms. There was nothing he could say. He knew what this felt like and all he could do was to be there to understand, to comfort. He knew that this would stay with her for the rest of her life.

He closed his eyes and let her tears flow. Amongst the devastation and horror that had violated their home over the last hour, he at last felt relief. This was the end of decades of frustration, of trial, of colleagues lost in the pursuit of this evil man. Mustafa al Said lay dead at his feet and for a while the world would be a safer place. Chris finally had closure and knew for him that this was the end.

CHAPTER 12

Chris stood on a white, sandy beach in the Maldives and looked over the crystal blue water towards the west. The sun was still a couple of hours away from setting and he watched as his wife swam up and down in front of him. She had taken it remarkably well, considering, but it had been a rough three months. He had been lucky with both his arm and leg; the bullets had torn the muscles badly but they were in the process of recovery. It would take a while yet but they should heal almost completely.

He had spent a lot of time thinking about what had happened in his life, from that moment so long ago when he had joined the Special Forces. It had been an incredible journey. He had been involved with the most punishing operations, with the most extraordinary objectives, the sort of thing the normal punter would only see in a book. A vast part of the journey had been chasing one man, Mustafa al Said. The final chapter in that particular story had now been written though, and with Mustafa gone it was time to draw a line under that part of his life.

The last few moments back in Essex had been pretty messy. Elizabeth had been barely capable of phoning for an ambulance but once she'd realised that he was in a pretty bad way, she snapped out of it and got help. The police had been on it straight away; it wasn't often that a provincial force had to cope with all out warfare in their back yard, but once Poole and MI5 got involved, it all went away and he was left to recuperate. It had been three months already and he had another month off before he had to return to his old job at Northwood and this holiday was a reward for both of them. They couldn't really afford it but given recent events, Chris believed they needed a bit of time to adjust to the shock of their recent experiences and for the ugliness of what they had witnessed to be washed away by the beauty of this tiny island.

Louis and the Director had come to visit while he was in hospital, of course, and they had taken time to talk through everything that had happened. He had explained in detail the events at the barn, living out each scene one by one in an horrific mental slide show, but it had been cathartic and he felt better able to handle the memories afterwards. They had left him well enough alone after that but Louis had promised to call round when Chris was back on his feet.

The other lads, those who came back, were doing OK as well but the wounds that Jon and Pat had suffered were more serious than Chris's. By the time Pat had got back to the UK, he was stable and out of danger but it would take another six months before he was ready to get back to work, and even then a fair amount of physiotherapy would be needed. Jon wasn't quite so bad but his wounds were reminiscent of the shoulder injury that had forced Chris out of the Corps all those years before. Geordie Bobby was his usual self and when he came round to visit the hospital he brought flowers, but not for the patient. He gave them to the prettiest nurse he could find, barely paying attention to the invalid. Nevertheless, his constant and irrepressible humour did Chris a huge amount of good.

Stan's widow was devastated, naturally. All the dreams of the last years, of his retirement and the life in front of them were in tatters. Chris went to see her as soon as he got out but there were never any words good enough. He stayed only as long as he thought he should.

Peanut had left the least behind him, only his folks. They say that no parent should have to bury their child and at the funeral Chris saw the reason why etched onto the faces by the grave.

The one that wasn't mourned at all was Dodger. He was given a military funeral in his absence and his involvement was covered up, but a select few knew. Monetary links had been established between him and Colonel Taylor – substantial, as it turned out. There were also indications of a double life in the more colourful communities of the London scene that no-one had any idea about. Chris didn't care. As far as he was concerned there were no excuses and the fact that he had sold his colleagues out for cash made him scum, whatever the reasons.

As Chris stood in the sun, he started to think about the rest of his life. Despite everything that had happened, he allowed himself a smile. He had decided that he had had enough of the Service and had submitted his notice. He would leave and find something else to do, something that would allow him some semblance of normality with his beautiful wife. The two of them had grown even closer now she understood some of what he had gone through and experienced firsthand the horror of it all. She had been fairly quiet in the weeks after the event but was coming out of it slowly. The haunted look had gone and the nightmares were less frequent. She was even engaging in more small talk as her mind struggled to reassert its own concept of normality on the situation. Her small frame sometimes detracted from the fact that she was tough underneath and mentally very strong. With his love and support she would be fine.

For now, Chris would cherish his time alone with her, here where no-one could get to them. He deserved it. They deserved it. This was the start of the rest of their lives without the shadow of Mustafa Al Said gnawing at his soul.

ABOUT THE AUTHOR

David was a serving officer and career submariner in the Royal Navy for 22 years. In that time he was involved in a huge variety of operations and missions at every level, both deployed and in Head Quarters. Drawing on that experience, using the current political climate and knowing the capabilities of the military world, he generated the storyline for 'Hostile Intent', a fictional action thriller.

'Writing this novel has been hugely rewarding and exciting. As the words flowed I 'saw' the action unfolding in front of me and the adrenalin that it produced swept me along with the characters. I hope it invoked the same reaction in you and that you felt as relieved as I did at the end when Chris survived. Thank you for sharing the adventure with me. The experience has inspired me to write again and the plots are already taking shape.'

David Bessell – June 2014

7283323R00116

Printed in Great Britain
by Amazon.co.uk, Ltd.,
Marston Gate.